# ORIENTAL
# ILLUSIONS

*In the mysterious orient, nothing and
no-one are as they seem...*

# James Keegan

SLEUTH HOUND BOOKS

**ORIENTAL ILLUSIONS**
ISBN: 978-0-6484856-5-0

## *A note from the author:*

No disrespect of any nation's ruling party, its politicians or associated government departments is intended in the telling of this 'story'.

Views expressed about religion and associated organizations are by fictional characters and are not those of the author.

Views expressed about politics and associated organizations are by fictional characters and are not those of the author.

Views expressed about Thai people and their culture are by fictional characters and are not those of the author. The same applies to views expressed by characters about persons of any other nationality or race who may appear in the 'story'.

The author knows that policing can be a dangerous, difficult and thankless task performed under constant scrutiny, and has the greatest respect for those professional Royal Thai Police officers he's dealt with over the past twenty-five years. There are rotten apples in every large organization, and in all walks of life, everywhere.

Corruption is a cancerous mole on the face of humanity. A crime-fiction novelist who pretends it doesn't exist might as well write fairy tales.

'Oriental Illusions' was written for entertainment purposes only. It is not a social commentary on Thailand or Asia. It is a work of fiction set in a real location and nothing more.

*For Natalee,*
*A heavenly angel on Earth*

# ONE

*Lisa's travel diary – Monday 17<sup>th</sup> September*

*This is so weird that it's freaking me out. It's close to lunch time and our bus has stopped at the checkpoint where we'll cross from Cambodia into Thailand. Tim just told me this place is called Poipet, or something like that, and we need to wait for immigration guys to get on and check our passports. What's weird is that I can see this guy out the window who looks so much like Mr Saysamone.*

*I think I've already written about Mr Saysamone. He's the creepy headmaster of the school I was volunteering at, the one who tried to grope and kiss me at our farewell staff party. And it wasn't the first time he tried to come onto me during the month I was there. He got in massive trouble with his boss and I've heard he might even lose his job.*

*The guy outside my window is moving away from our bus now, towards a row of food stalls. Crap, he even walks the same as Mr Saysamone. He's thin and short, just like him, but then again a lot of the local guys are. And I'm sure I've seen Mr Saysamone wearing that same blue cap and fake sunnies in the school playground. Surely it's not him? He wouldn't follow me to the border, for three-hours. Would he? Crap. Should I ask Tim to go and talk to the guy, to see if it is him? My god, I'm shaking as I write this.*

*The guy who looks like Mr Saysamone has gone now. He walked off towards a carpark, and that's such a relief for two reasons. One, I'm on my way to Bangkok and don't need any weirdos ruining the excitement. Two, I'm really busting for a wee and refuse to use the disgusting toilet on this bus. There are a few casinos over to our right that would have a clean toilet. Maybe I should get off and quickly go use one?*

*Over near the food stalls a little boy's selling umbrellas. The poor thing has no shirt or hat. And no shoes. He's skinny and dirty and just baking in this crazy heat. And watching him just now as he smiles at people walking past, his smile is so big and radiant that I can't help but smile too.*

*Far out, my mouth's really dry and I'm so thirsty but hanging for the loo at the same time. How long are we supposed to wait on here for these guys to check our passports?*

*That's it, I'm getting off the bus to buy some water for me and this boy, to give him some snacks, and hopefully use a toilet that doesn't have puddles of wee all over the seat and floor.*

# TWO

Dan Porter peered at glass panels on his right to watch the reflections of those watching him. The two men in grey suits had tailed him since he'd arrived on a flight from Sydney barely five minutes earlier. He stepped to the side of the crowded walkway then glanced back as he placed his briefcase on the floor.

The men in grey stopped abruptly, ten meters away. They spun to face the wall then faked interest in a mural with golden temples. Both were bald and wore dark sunglasses. Hip-holstered pistols bulged beneath tight jackets.

Porter sighed, because he wasn't crazy and paranoid. Guts churned as his heart beat faster. The men were definitely following him. But who were they?

He studied the airport terminal's lucent ceiling as late-afternoon sunshine caste a pink hue over the ginormous glasshouse. Sweat trickled down his forehead. Humidity threatened to suck all life from him. He took a bottle from the briefcase and drank. Luke-warm water cooled a parched throat.

When he swooped to return the bottle the men in grey suits removed sunglasses and shuffled closer. Both were Asian and as lean as a professional kickboxer. They met his gaze with stares. The cold, hard stares of men familiar with violence and death.

He realized the assassins planned to take him out on the walkway. A mixture of excitement and instinctive fear sent a shiver down his spine. He frowned, unsure who had hired them and why. Had his reputation made him a target? Did local authorities aim to prevent him from entering the country and becoming an inquisitive pain in their ass?

An overhead sign told him Passport Control was two-hundred meters ahead. He considered avoiding a fight with the men in grey and seeking help. But help from who? Were the assassins crooked immigration cops, the type he'd read about? Did their mates wait up ahead to detain him?

He reminded himself that he was an alien in a foreign land and decided to stick to the tactic that'd served him well. *Don't know who to trust? Trust no-one until you do...*

The assassins moved closer again and hovered. Waiting for the perfect time to rush forward and shoot him at close range? Nah, too many surveillance cameras watched from above. He suspected they wanted to stab him with stealth then disappear amongst the crowd.

Porter was strong as an ox, a brawny ex-rugby player who'd won more fist-fights than most. And whilst he usually welcomed confrontation because it provided answers, he needed to even the odds against the younger assailants. He couldn't choose when to rumble but he could choose the place.

He straightened to his full 6'3 height to peer over the crowd and grinned when he saw a men's restroom forty meters ahead. It was perfect, a confined space where the assassins' two on one advantage might be nullified. He grabbed his briefcase and started for it.

He got half-way there when buzzing chatter echoed throughout the terminal. Seconds later a red-shirted mass of passengers flooded the walkway behind him. An

Asian lady led the mob with a yellow flag held high above her head. A second lady strode alongside it and yapped like a drover's dog. The babbling tide of humanity surged towards the immigration queues and carried Porter with it. He glanced over his shoulder. The men in grey suits scowled from the rear, unable to get to him.

He scurried ahead of the mob and bypassed winding queues to join a short one for passengers with diplomatic visas. He turned to scan the area and saw no sign of the would-be assassins. When he reached the front of the queue an immigration cop in brown uniform beckoned him forward. He approached the booth and placed his passport on the counter.

The cop sighed to make it clear he didn't want to be there and snatched the passport up with one hand. He opened it in a huff and flicked through pages.

"What flight?" the cop said.

Porter rubbed a prickly chin. "QF23. Qantas." He pointed to the arrival card he'd filled out on the plane. "Did I forget to write it down?"

The cop didn't answer. He leaned forward to look him up and down then grunted as he sat. "You diplomat visa but not look like diplomat. You fly business class but not look like business man."

Porter studied the cop's brown face and waited for a smile that never came. Was he fair dinkum, or taking the piss? Why the smartass attitude? He studied his own outfit. He wore a long-sleeved business shirt, black trousers and black leather shoes. How did he look different to the average traveler going about his business?

"Everything okay?"

The cop ignored him, turned dials on a stamp then dropped it onto the desk. He stood, whistling as though bored and dawdled to a cordoned area behind the booth with passport in hand. He conversed with two others and showed them the passport. The other cops frowned then summonsed a fourth cop who appeared to be of higher rank.

Porter scratched behind an ear. Were these immigration officials crooked and working for the same mob as the blokes in grey suits? The four cops snarled at him then broke into laughter. So much for the warm and fuzzy welcome the in-flight tourism authority ads had promised...

The highest-ranking cop entered the booth and dropped the passport on the counter. He looked up at Porter. "My colleague asked me to check your passport," he said in near-perfect English. "He thinks it's fake."

Suffocating heat rose from Porter's chest to throat. He wanted to tell him that he too was a cop. A cop who'd got his hands dirty policing the scary outside world for fifteen years, not a pretend one who stamped passports in a protective bubble and feared paper cuts instead of stab wounds. But he bit his tongue, because his boss Steve Williams had advised a strictly 'need to know' policy regarding the true reason he'd traveled to Asia.

"What are you blokes on about?" Porter said. "I'm frickin' knackered and wanna get out of here, so can you just stam--."

"You have many scars, Mr Porter." The cop pointed at his face. "You look more like a boxer than a diplomat and if you intend to fight for money, or do any other type of work, you will require a valid permit."

Porter rubbed the scar running down the middle of his forehead and then a smaller one on his chin. "A boxer? Bloody hell, mate, I'm going on forty and way past that caper…" He frowned. "Contact the Australian embassy if you doubt my credentials."

The cop smiled with pursed lips and avoided eye contact. He stamped the passport then handed it back and waved him through.

Porter shook disbelief from his head. Had he been harassed or legitimately screened? He suspected the former as he hurried to the baggage carousel. His suitcase hadn't come out. He switched on the cell phone Interpol had provided, one already set up for international roaming. The phone beeped and a message appeared on the screen. 'I hope you arrived safe, Daniel. Waiting for you outside Exit 4.'

Porter spotted his suitcase and dragged it off the carousel. He read the numbers showing on the combination lock. '597'. Strange, because he'd left the lock on '000' when he'd checked it in. Had someone opened and searched his suitcase? He unlocked it, placed the briefcase inside then locked it again. He remembered he didn't have cash in the local currency and scanned the room for a money exchange office. He found one and headed for it. As he did, he spotted the men in grey suits. They stood shoulder to shoulder near the Customs exit, thirty meters to his left.

He considered the options. He could walk past them, leave the terminal and meet his contact outside. But curiosity, needing to know who the men were and why they'd followed him, overpowered any concern for his immediate safety. The blokes in grey had played a silly game and the time had come for him to end it.

He stopped at the money exchange office and gave the middle-aged woman behind the security glass his most charming smile. "I'll be back in a sec to change some money." He pointed to the suitcase. "Can you watch this while I go to the loo?"

The woman shrugged then smiled and giggled.

He gave her a thumbs up sign. "Thanks, sweet."

He swiveled left, saw restrooms in the far corner and strolled towards them. He came to a narrow corridor with 'Men' on the left and 'Ladies' to the right. He paused to glance at the Customs exit. The blokes in grey watched him enter the corridor.

He scurried into the men's restroom and ducked into the last cubicle in a row of five. The door-latch slid to the left. Locked. He rolled sleeves to elbows then waited. Questions needed answering.

He'd been in the cubicle for less than thirty seconds when someone entered the restroom. Light footsteps. Soles squeaked on freshly mopped tiles. Voices. Porter strained to hear. Two men whispered in a foreign language he didn't recognize. The men in grey suits? The footsteps got closer to his cubicle then stopped. He bent to look through the foot-high gap at the bottom of the door and saw four, shiny black toecaps.

Tap. Tap. Tap. The sound of metal on metal.

"You hear that, Porter?" a man on the other side of the door said in broken English.

Porter stepped back and slowed his breathing. Silent.

"It's my gun hitting this pathetic little door," the same thug said with an accent that confused him. German? Russian? Slavic? Why didn't the Asian bloke sound Asian? "This door is cheap metal and these rounds will go straight through it."

Porter cursed under his breath. Why trap himself in a cubicle while armed men waited outside? His plan had relied on an assassin opening the door. So much for that…He scanned the ceiling and three walls for a way out. Nothing. He would have to leave the way he'd entered.

Tap. Tap. Tap.

"I'm losing patience…Will you stay in there and die a coward? Or come out and face death like a man?"

Porter silently slid the latch to unlock the door. He rocked back against the rear wall and sucked a breath.

"Last chance, Porter. Out in five seconds or I fill your little hidey hole with death."

# THREE

*Lisa's diary – Monday 24<sup>th</sup> September (I think...)*

*I'm fairly sure I've been in this tiny room for about a week now. There are seven X's on the wall and I put an 'X' on it every time the old lady brings my dinner and wash bowl, and I don't think I forgot to do one. She puts a cloth sack over my head whenever she comes into the room so I only know she's old because her perfume smells like my nan's, and sometimes I brush her wrinkled hands when she passes me the plate. She never speaks. There's no hole or window in the door so I don't know where she goes when she leaves me.*

*As I wrote a few days ago, I still don't have any idea where I am. Am I still in Cambodia? Or am I in Bangkok? I wish I knew who was doing this to me and why. I got off that bus in Poipet and everything since is a blank. I woke up in this room without any idea how I got here and it's still a mystery.*

*I haven't been able to stop crying. Just haven't felt like doing anything. The old lady brought me some American magazines and a deck of cards. I haven't touched them. I just want my phone, and to call mum, and to go home.*

*From the second day onwards a guy has come into my room every morning. He makes me wear the cloth sack* too so I never see him. He smells like a guy who never washes. He speaks good English with a slight accent and sounds a bit like a Filipino school friend from back home. He injects me with a drug. He said it's heroin. I didn't even try to stop him the first time. I don't know why. Or maybe yes, I do.

Yesterday he threatened again to take this diary away from me but I pleaded and promised not to write anything bad about him. I need this because writing my thoughts down keeps me sane. As I can be.

# FOUR

Porter braced himself, ready to aim a front kick. He needed enough power to knock the cubicle door outwards and seize the advantage of surprise over the thug who'd threatened to shoot him.

"Three seconds, Porter," the thug outside the cubicle said. "I will kill you. Two seconds…"

Porter gritted teeth, stepped forward and grimaced as he balanced on a dodgy right leg. He raised his left foot then used all the strength his dehydrated body could muster to drive it against the metal door. A loud bang. The door buckled but didn't fly outwards as planned.

"One," the man shouted.

Porter dropped to haunches, flattened himself against the cubicle's side wall and waited for the spray of bullets he feared would end his life.

"Goodbye, Port--."

The thug behind the door made a wheezing noise. A pistol clattered on the floor. Bone shattered. A skull thudding against hard tiles?

Men shouted from further away, possibly near the restroom's entrance. Porter didn't recognize the language. The second man outside the cubicle shouted a reply, followed by the sound of heavy footsteps. A man yelped. A body slammed against the cubicle door then slumped to the floor. A body in a grey suit. Porter tried to pull the crumpled door open but the body got caught underneath it. He swore then kicked the door again. It didn't budge.

He listened as two or more men fought at close quarters on the other side of the door. Grunts and groans. Squeals of agony. Violent thuds of bone against flesh and bone against bone.

A bright-red rivulet ran under the door. Blood pooled near Porter's feet. The Asian bloke in the grey suit had been shot? By who? Nothing made sense.

Silence. The fighting had stopped. Then a woman screamed. A cleaner, maybe? A man moaned and Porter saw hands at the bottom of the door. The hands rolled the grey-suited body aside and cleared the doorway.

Porter heard a loud 'click'. A loose ammo mag being fed back into a pistol? A slide racked, which meant he had seconds to act and couldn't worry about who might be standing on the other side of the door. He kicked it hard. It broke from hinges and flew into the restroom.

A man shrieked as the door pulverized his nose. Shaking hands reached for it. A pistol dropped to the floor. Blood and snot poured onto his black suit.

Porter charged from the cubicle, slammed his right shoulder into the man's ribs and sent him reeling backwards. The man's head slammed into a tiled ledge above a wall-mounted urinal. His neck and skull cracked in unison.

Porter watched the blond-haired thug slump against the wall. Unconscious but not dead, he hoped. He swiveled to his right. A second blond thug in a black suit lay near the cubicle. He stood over him and guessed he was Eastern European of some sort. But he couldn't be certain, not with the golf ball-sized hole where an eye used to be.

He turned to the entrance and saw the two Asian men in grey suits, motionless on their backs. A shocked tourist nearly stumbled into them. Porter dismissed him then moved to examine the closest Asian. Mangled fists. Bloody pulp for a nose. He checked for a neck pulse then did the same with the other man. Both were alive but in no state to answer questions. He thought about taking one of the Glock pistols from the floor but decided against it. Too risky. Potentially incriminating...

He checked the man's jacket. No ID. No wallet. Nothing but a smashed pair of sunglasses. As he searched the second one, eyelids fluttered open.

Porter grinned at him. "Welcome back to the world... Now tell me, who the hell are you blokes?"

The man groaned and tried to sit. He was strong but light as a greyhound and Porter had no problem pushing him back down.

"Nah, mate, you're not going anywhere until I know why you've been following me."

The man shook his head. Veins at temples bulged.

Porter nodded. "No English, eh?"

The man yelled.

The language was slightly familiar but Porter didn't understand a word. He returned the angry stare. "Right, neither of us is in the mood to do this now. Until next time…" He punched him in the face. The man's head lolled as eyes closed. "Enjoy the kip. I'm jealous."

Porter cleaned himself at the washbasin. He finger-combed a dark-brown fringe to the side and straightened his tie. He glanced at the mirror then hurried from the restroom, repulsed by the jet-lagged ghoul that'd glanced back.

He returned to the exchange office to collect his suitcase. As he waited for the cashier to change money a dozen security guards ran towards the restrooms. Some blew whistles and yelled at no-one in particular. Within five minutes the airport would go into lock-down. A few minutes later they would pull his image from security footage and circulate it.

He thanked the cashier and rolled his suitcase towards the exit. He walked briskly past the lone Customs officer seated by an x-ray machine and into the Arrivals hall. He saw the sign for Exit 4 fifty-meters ahead and quickened pace. Halfway there he sensed he had unwanted company and glanced back as he walked. The two men in grey suits were thirty meters away and gaining. He grinned in admiration of their persistence.

He jogged the remaining distance to Exit 4, wary of drawing attention but needing to reach the meeting point before others started searching for him. He left the terminal via automatic doors. Intense heat whooshed against his face as though he'd walked into a giant blow-dryer. Grit tickled his throat and he coughed to clear heavy air from lungs.

He swiveled to search the covered walkway on both sides of the exit. Traffic wardens blew whistles, louder and longer than they needed to. Taxi drivers yelled at tourists. Tourists with young faces full of shock and wonder and confusion. Professional drivers stood docile next to luxury cars with arms folded across chests as though they'd been born to wait.

Where was his contact?

He noticed the men in grey suits reach the automatic doors. They stopped inside and watched him.

"Hey. Daniel Porter? Here."

Porter turned and peered across the three-lane road in the direction of the female voice. A woman in a cream-colored business suit stood on the opposite side and held a sign bearing his name. He heard automatic doors slide open behind him then grabbed the suitcase and hurried down the slope towards her.

He studied the woman as he crossed the road. Her suit hugged a figure as lithe as Lucy Lui's, his favorite of Charlie's angels. Her smile mesmerized him and for a second obscured all peripheral sights and sounds.

He didn't see or hear the pickup truck as it travelled towards him. Strong hands pushed him in the back and sent him sprawling forward. He landed on elbows and knees then rolled sideways to cushion the blow. His temple thudded against bitumen and it dazed him. He glanced to his right and saw a blurry, black pickup truck speed away. He lay on his back near the curb and rubbed his head.

The gorgeous face looking down on him came into focus. Chocolate almond eyes sparkled when she smiled. She helped Porter stand and led him off the road. "Hi, Daniel. I'm Nok, your partner here at Interpol," she said like a native English-speaker. "Welcome to Thailand."

Porter scoffed as he brushed dirt from pants and sleeves. "Call me Dan. And yeah, it's been one hell of a welcome."

Nok stopped in front of him. The men in grey suits positioned themselves on either side of her. One of them held Porter's suitcase.

Porter stepped back into a defensive stance. "Bloody hell, Nok, you know these blokes? They followed me through the airport. Them and some other goons just tried to take me out in the restroom."

She spoke to the men in a language Porter assumed to be Thai.

They laughed then took turns replying to her.

Nok laughed with them.

Porter hissed through gritted teeth. "Something funny?"

She tilted her head to the side. "These two are Thai police officers attached to the Dignitary Protection Unit. They're here to ensure you go unharmed and to clean up any mess."

Porter looked the battered cops up and down. They were the mess. And were they there to protect, or watch him?

"It's a good thing these two were following you," Nok said. "Those Russian guys in the toilet would've killed you."

"Russians? Why? Bloody hell, I just got here."

"That's something we'll need to solve together…" She pointed to the road then to one of the Thai cops. "And you're lucky this guy was here to save you from the car. It could've been a nasty accident."

Porter grunted to acknowledge the cop's help then recalled a similar incident from a couple of months earlier. He'd been jogging near Crooked River in the Australian outback when a speeding SUV had tried to take him out. "That was no accident just now. I mean, how could that pickup not see me on this pedestrian crossing? It's lit up like a day-nighter at the MCG."

"The MC what?"

"Don't worry…But I reckon that bastard tried to run me down."

Nok sighed. "I'm afraid it's normal driving here in Bangkok. Zebra crossings are nothing but lines on a road to be ignored…The pedestrian who dares rarely wins." She smiled. "Trust me, if that car wanted to hit you it could have. Let's go, I'll take you to your apartment."

Porter grabbed his suitcase and followed her. He wasn't convinced. Someone had tried to kill him, or warn him at least. The same mob the Russians in the restroom worked for? Who?

Ten minutes later he sat in a BMW coupe as Nok drove it fast along an elevated motorway towards Bangkok's skyline. Brief chit-chat ended and he gazed out the window. It was his first time in Southeast Asia and the oriental sky was like no other he'd seen before. Mysterious. Enchanting. Its red hue turned purple while the sun sank into a blanket of smog. Lights flickered atop towering buildings as day became night.

A tingling sensation rose from toes to the back of his neck. It had been a crazy start to his assignment with a welcome worse than he'd expected. But could he somehow enjoy his time in this mystical place? He scanned the vanishing horizon and nodded. Yeah, he reckoned he could.

Nok followed the motorway for ten kilometers then took a tollway exit that descended into jam-packed city streets.

Porter watched in awe as motorbikes whizzed by and zigzagged through traffic. Ancient buses blew toxic exhaust fumes as they travelled too fast and forced other vehicles out of their way. Cars surged forward, braked hard to avoid hitting the car in front then surged forward and braked again. He marveled at how close they drove to each other in the lines of traffic and reckoned the panel beaters must've made a fortune. He'd driven in dangerous situations, in places as perilous as the Middle East, but this was total chaos.

The BMW rolled to a stop. Nok checked her cell phone.

Porter peered ahead. "Is the traffic always this bad?"

She kept eyes on the phone. "Monday nights during peak hour? Yes."

"How'd you know it was me when you called my name at the airport? I couldn't have been the only white fella who looked lost?"

Her forehead wrinkled. "Your Dragon Slayer taskforce locked up how many corrupt Interpol agents in recent weeks?"

"Worldwide? More than a hundred. Why's that?"

"Your picture's been in every Interpol bulletin since the arrests began. That's how I recognized you. And now you've joined us, the new bosses in Europe have made you their golden boy and the patron saint of the anti-corruption movement. And I must admit," she paused as though unsure how much to divulge, "I searched Google for more images...You know what, Dan? You kind of look like that Gerard Butler guy. The actor. Same hair and all that..."

In better days Porter had been told of his resemblance to Russell Crowe in 'Gladiator.' He could live with the Butler comparison too and shot her his cheekiest grin. "You mean like in the movie '300' when Butler plays the ripped Spartan warrior?"

She frowned. "Um, no, I haven't seen that movie. I was thinking more of his chubbier version, like in 'The Bounty Hunter' with Jennifer Aniston."

He made a sad puppy face.

She giggled then flicked another interior light on and proceeded to re-apply lipstick.

In the bright light he noticed she was slightly older than first thought. Thirty-two he guessed, thirty-four tops. Her hair she'd styled short like that of the rock star Pink. And she'd colored it the same platinum-blonde too, in contrast to her thick black eyebrows. She wore minimal make-up on a smooth, tanned face and puckered naturally full lips. Porter grinned, because he knew women who'd paid a small fortune for the same bee-stung look.

Nok was stunning and held herself with the confidence of a woman who knew it. She must've sensed him staring because she glanced sideways and smiled. A wide smile with perfect teeth. She seemed comfortable with someone watching her, used to being the center of attention and no doubt loving it. Unlike him, who over time had become the complete opposite.

He averted eyes and feigned interest in pedestrians crossing the road at traffic lights. When he turned back, she hummed along to a song on the radio and tapped fingers on the steering wheel. Long fingers with manicured nails.

'Blood-red' was Jane's favorite nail polish color too. It reminded him that as soon as he reached the apartment he needed to call and let her know he'd arrived without drama. It would be a lie but Jane would sleep better for it.

After forty minutes they arrived at a high-rise building. Nok explained they were in the Asoke area in the heart of the city, just off its main thoroughfare, Sukhumvit road. Interpol and other government departments took up office space on the first ten floors of the building and the remaining thirty consisted of residential apartments. She parked in the underground garage and they took an elevator to the 24th floor.

She stopped outside an apartment and handed him a set of keys. "This is your room."

He unlocked the door and pushed his suitcase inside. "Cheers, Nok, for picking me up and all." He checked the silver Tag Heuer watch Jane had gifted him before his flight. "It's just gone seven but feels like midnight. What's the plan?"

"Are you hungry?"

"Nah, I'm too knackered to eat and reckon I'll hit the sack if there's nowhere else I need to be."

"Yes do, you've got the panda eyes happening…We've a meeting in the office at 8am. I'll drop by just before and escort you down."

"Don't go to any trouble, sweet. I'll find it, no worries."

She smiled and placed a soft hand on his forearm. "It's not a problem. I'm here on the 27th and most of our agents live here too. Interpol owns half the building."

He backed into the doorway. "I'll see you then."

She frowned. "Are you sure you'll sleep okay? Need pills to help?"

"Nah, I don't do pills."

"Okay, sleep tight and lock the door to be safe."

"Safe?"

"Yes, I'm afraid certain members of the Bangkok elite would prefer that you don't see tomorrow."

# FIVE

Porter rose with the sun on Tuesday, thankful to face a new day after Nok's parting words the night before. He made coffee then trudged onto the apartment's balcony. Despite the early hour heat thawed the air-conditioned chill from his body. He looked down then out to watch a blue-and-white metallic snake glide along an elevated train line. The line formed a concrete canopy over awakening city streets and was held aloft in the arms of gigantic Y-shaped beasts. He followed the skytrain until it disappeared under a station's sloping roof. He waited for it to re-appear then watched it wind through a haze covered valley surrounded by mountains of mirrored glass.

He looked down, far below, to where ants emerged from the safety of communal nests then scurried off to work. He gazed straight ahead and saw towering office blocks hiding the sun, monstrosities in all shades of white, silver and grey. And through gaps he spotted a shimmering horizon, a dirty-pink stripe beneath a pale orange sky.

He sipped coffee then scrunched his nose as a harsh smell wafted to it. Disinfectant? He listened. A scrubbing-brush? Next door? It reminded him of a clean bathroom. His line of thought jumped. Squeaky tiles. Airport restroom. The Russian blokes who'd wanted to kill him in it. Why Russians? Mafia? Not one Russian national had been arrested by the Dragon Slayer taskforce but he would task Claire, its intelligence analyst based in Sydney, to check for possible links with those who had.

Nok's warning from the night before echoed. Who the hell were the so-called 'elite' who didn't want him in Bangkok? He knew for certain he couldn't wait for them to come to him because that would make it too easy. He would track them down and ask the question - what did they have to hide?

At 7.55am he followed Nok into the Interpol unit's open-plan office on the 6th floor. She led him down a corridor and into a meeting room. A meeting room with tacky carpet and tackier pictures hanging from yellow walls. Two Asian men in suit-and-tie sat on the right side of a rectangular conference table. One wore black, the other navy-blue. An older man sat at the head of the table. Nok sat on the left alongside a red-headed Caucasian woman.

Porter nodded to the man in black as he sat next to him.

He returned a blank stare.

Nok waved a hand. "Everyone, this is agent Dan Porter from our newly-formed Sydney office." She indicated the older man. "Dan, our boss - Chief Superintendent Sawatri."

Sawatri leaned back with hands clasped atop head and studied Porter through eyes as beady as a crooked Magistrate's. He had a lop-sided mouth on a wide, ordinary face. Thick, dark-brown hair had been combed from front to back and looked greasy from too much gel. Something about the clump of hair didn't look right and Porter suspected it might've been an expensive wig.

Sawatri's pink business shirt hung loose on a wiry frame. He appeared to be in his late-fifties or thereabouts. His pale, waxy complexion and thin nose made him look more Chinese than Thai. His smile was tight, almost arrogant. "As Nok said, I am the boss and manage all Interpol operations here in Southeast Asia." He jutted his chin when he spoke, in a posh accent somewhere in-between Ban Ki-moon and James Bond. "Steve Williams speaks very highly of you, Dan...And you must respect him greatly, to have followed him across to Interpol from your state police force?"

"Yeah, I respect Steve's knowledge and investigation skills. And he's stuck by me when other so-called mates couldn't scamper away quick enough."

"Well, I'm absolutely delighted you've joined my team."

"Cheers. And I've gotta say, mate, you speak the English lingo better than I do."

"Why, naturally... I'm half-British, luk khrueng as we say here, and you're Australian. My mother, bless her soul, was quite an accomplished surgeon in London. And, I studied at Cambridge."

Porter considered calling him a pompous wanker but thought better of it on first meeting. "And I despised grammar classes so much I joined the army to avoid writing boring essays at uni."

No-one laughed.

Porter smirked, twirled a pen between fingers then dropped it onto a notepad.

Sawatri introduced the agents. "There you have it, Dan, every member of operation Lost Angels. Questions? What's Superintendent Williams told you?"

Porter resisted a frown as he swept eyes around the table to acknowledge awkward smiles. Too right he had questions. Every member? Four agents? Only four investigators to locate multiple missing girls in a city of eight million people? Was Interpol fair dinkum? "I know twelve Australian girls have disappeared from either Bangkok or Poipet in the past month, the most recent being Lisa Baxter eight days ago, and I've been sent here to find 'em."

Helen Chapman had been introduced as the team's Intelligence Analyst. She wore fiery red hair in a ponytail with side bangs framing a heavily freckled but pleasant face. She was plump in the cute way the kid's Cabbage Patch dolls used to be and Porter guessed she was thirty. Light-blue eyes twinkled when she smiled at him. "Yes, twelve Australian backpackers. The youngest is eighteen and the eldest twenty-two."

Porter picked Helen's accent as Welsh. He'd worked with a few Welsh blokes over the years and her voice rose and fell in the same melodic way. "Yeah, cheers, that's about the extent of what I've been told already."

"But what you don't know, because very few do, is that over the past month twenty-two other girls of similar age have also disappeared. Fifteen from Bangkok and seven from Poipet."

Worry thudded against Porter's chest. Thirty-four in total. In only a month? He gulped as dread pounded his chest. He forced a smile and urged her to continue.

Helen spent the next ten minutes relaying the background information and circumstances surrounding each girl's disappearance. But she could've told Porter what he needed to know in two sentences. One, they had zero suspects. Two, an important witness still hadn't been questioned - Carly Newman, Lisa Baxter's friend who'd waited for her to arrive at a Bangkok bus terminal and had reported her missing when she didn't.

"Does anything suggest these particular girls have been targeted?" he asked Helen. "Or are they innocent disappearances of random young girls who've wandered too far and will show up safe and sound soon enough?"

Helen glanced to Sawatri, who dipped his head as though allowing her to answer. "The only patterns to emerge thus far – every girl is Caucasian, very attractive, taller than average, and blonde. Girls missing from Bangkok were last seen leaving nightclubs, and not in one condensed area but from all different parts of the city…And as you've just heard they're of various nationalities but Australian and Russian girls make up more than half of those who've disappeared."

Russian? An image of the Russian bloke at the airport with a bullet through his eye- socket flashed through Porter's mind. Was there a link? And why hadn't the Russians or any other nations sent their own federal cops to investigate? Or maybe they had?

"A total of thirty-four missing and every single one's blonde Caucasian?" Porter waited until Helen had nodded in reply. He turned to Sawatri. "These girls aren't simply, missing, and you have to know it…So why name this operation, Lost Angels?"

Sawatri tilted his head to the side.

Fon, in the black suit next to Porter, leaned forward. "It's simple… Bangkok's the city of angels. And these girls, innocent angels, are lost in it."

Fon wore a men's suit and had short spikey hair like a bloke. But when Porter heard the high-pitched voice he turned to study the ghost-white face. It was plain but too pretty to be male.

He smiled at her. "I don't reckon these girls are lost...Or maybe it's just coincidence they're all tall, blonde and very good sorts?"

Fon squinted. "Lost? Abducted? Does it matter? One way or another they've fallen victim to the orient. It's no place for naïve western girls fresh out of school, Dan. It's a place of deadly illusions where nothing and no-one are as they seem."

Porter met her intense stare. Her irises were grey-blue, too large and alien-like for the eyes wearing them. Colored contact lenses? He glanced at her thin neck. A men's tie but no Adam's apple. "Yeah, I know what you mean..." He addressed the group. "And listen, it does matter, 'cos it makes a huge difference to how we go about this investigation."

Nok adjusted her blouse to cover ample breasts too perky to be real. "Dan, don't listen to Fon. She watches too many of those silly Asian horror movies."

Fon poked her tongue out. They giggled like stoned teenagers.

Sawatri scowled. "Enough, the both of you. Show some professionalism."

The female agents straightened, facial expressions glum with hands rested on the table.

Sawatri turned to Porter. "Yes, I do suspect these girls have been abducted. And our bosses in Europe fear the same, that Dragon Slayer's success in dismantling the Knights of Alba's global network has led to quite a considerable number of unfulfilled orders for sex-slaves. It could be, in the worst scenario, that Southeast Asian crime syndicates have seized the opportunity to expand their human-trafficking business to meet that demand."

Porter loosened his tie and wished he could ditch the jacket. "That's a worry. And plausible…" He thought back a few months to when multiple Aboriginal girls had been abducted from Sydney and delivered to sex-fiends across the globe. "With so many girls feared abducted, can it be the work of a lone psycho who's keeping 'em for himself? Nah, I reckon they've been taken by one or more syndicates and sold to customers with white-girl fetishes. Customers based only in Asia, or worldwide? We'll find out soon enough if these girls start turning up dead. And if local mobs are controlling the syndicates responsible, who's leading 'em?"

"As Helen's indicated, we know very little thus far," Sawatri said. "Our bosses hope your expertise can change that. It's why you've been assigned to this difficult task."

Porter frowned. Difficult? Yeah, but Sawatri was making it harder than it had to be. "Let's make sure we're all on the same page here… Lost Angels' brief is to investigate the suspected abduction of foreign tourists by local human-trafficking syndicates. Right?"

Sawatri's head rocked from side to side. "No, not quite."

Porter recoiled in the seat. "No? But you just said th--".

"You must understand…Situations of this type are handled differently here. Those in power and the Royal Thai Police hierarchy refuse to acknowledge something very sinister is afoot. Admitting thirty-odd girls have been abducted, that Thailand's a dangerous place to visit, would be quite damaging for the nation's image. Not to mention the extremely detrimental effect on tourism…"

Porter sucked a quick breath because he'd heard it all before. He fixed eyes on Sawatri then let the air out in a huff. "Are politicians and police bosses the same everywhere? Gutless, with no idea…Look, if you don't bl--."

"We in this room know we're investigating abductions," Sawatri told him curtly. "But local and international media outlets, and those meddling NGO's, have started asking difficult questions. They've been informed that our operation is searching for missing persons." He addressed the group. "They will remain none the wiser, because none of you is to speak to them. And after all, methods in the early stages are quite similar for both types of investigation."

Porter scoffed. "Serious? Mate, the first girl was reported missing a month ago. Trust me, you've missed the 'early stages'… And if we've got multiple victims we could be hunting a large organization with multiple suspects." He glanced around the table. "So why have only four agents been assigned to the job?"

Sawatri sighed as though bored by him. "It is a balancing act. If the media and our political enemies learn we've formed a large investigation team, more questions get asked. The truth quite often sparks panic."

"Truth? Panic? In cases like this panic can be our greatest ally… And don't we have an obligation to these girls and all the others at risk to get the truth out there? As a warning to be vigilant and careful?"

Sawatri shrugged. His eyes smiled as though amused.

Porter leaned back and blew hot air at the ceiling. Boiling blood vessels threatened to burst.

"Dan…" Nok said in a soothing tone. She waited till his eyes met hers. "Such problems are sometimes best ignored until they fade away."

His head wobbled. "Ignorant bliss, eh? Bloody hell…" He shifted his stare to Sawatri. "You can't place your reputation and ego above the need to save lives."

"I do indeed agree, but you're shooting the messenger. This is Thailand and our leaders don't take kindly to embarrassment."

"Mate, they'll be more than a little embarrassed if they stuff up this investigation." Porter grunted. "Tell these leaders of yours to get with the program and give you experienced investigators, as many as we're gunna need. If you wanna locate these girls alive, you have to."

Sawatri sighed. "I've been informed we aren't to receive any more agents and I'm not expect--."

"Sir, forgive my interruption," said Jaru, the male agent next to Sawatri. "I will not allow this falang to further criticize my country and colleagues. We are doing our best." His handsome face was the darkest in the room and flushed crimson. In his late thirties he was solid but not fat and had a prominent chin that exaggerated the flatness of his nose. Serious black eyes bore into Porter as he swiveled towards him. "Enough of this ridicule, Porter." He spoke English with an Asian inflection and not as fluently as the others. "And stop speaking so slow, as though we are stupid Thais incapable of understanding you. You're being a condescending fool. For what?" He scoffed. "Can you speak and understand Thai?"

Porter grinned at him, glad someone in the meeting had finally shown some balls. "I listened to a few lessons on the plane but still don't understand a word. Plus, I'm tone deaf…" He sniggered at his own joke. "Listen mate, get off your high-horse 'cos I'm not meaning to offend anyone… If I didn't slow my speech you'd be stuffed by my accent. Besides, I'm a country boy and we always talk slow in the, coun-try." He winked at him as the others laughed. He glanced to Nok. "This word… Falang? What does it mean? Cos it's only fair that I know if I've been insulted. Right?"

Nok glared at Jaru then smiled at Porter. "In English you would spell it with an 'r'. Farang…It's the Thai word for a westerner. Some Thais have problems pronouncing the letter 'r' and replace it with an 'l' sound… Don't worry, it's not an insult."

Porter grunted.

Sawatri growled, cuffed Jaru across the head then shouted in Thai. "Dan, ignore Jaru's insolence… He's but a simple country cop who's joined us for a year on secondment. He's been raised a simple country boy and educated at a simple university in the simple North-East." He grunted at Jaru again.

Jaru leaned forward and faced Porter. He bowed his head and joined palms together as though in prayer. "My apologies, Agent Porter."

They made brief eye contact before Jaru broke it.

"Ah, no worries champ…" Porter saw no sincerity in the apology. And he understood he was an outsider, new to the crew, and that Jaru didn't like him. But he was there to get a job done, not to be popular, so couldn't give a rat's ass.

Helen must've sensed the friction. "Personally, Dan, I love your accent. It's got a bit of Crocodile Dundee about it. And that's one of my favorite movies ever."

"Oh, yes indeed. Thank you, Helen, it's exactly who he sounds like. Paul Hogan from Crocodile Dundee. Hilarious…" Sawatri chuckled. He attempted a guttural Australian accent. "That aint a knife…." He picked a pen from pocket and gripped it as though holding a large dagger. "This is a knife."

Porter cringed on the inside but laughed aloud. All but Jaru laughed with him.

Sawatri waited for silence. "I can confirm the pairings…Nok, you and Dan are Team 1. Fon and Jaru are Team 2."

Nok smiled.

Fon huffed and crossed arms over a slight chest. "Why boss? Not fair, I never get to work with my sis…"

Porter noticed Jaru glance at Nok, who met his look with smiling eyes before averting them.

Helen had printed up color photos of Lisa Baxter. She spread a few over the table while explaining they'd been pulled from Lisa's Facebook page. She said they were the most recent of her, uploaded the same day she'd left the Cambodian primary school. Lisa's bank and email accounts hadn't been used since, and Helen hadn't been able to track her phone.

"Dan, your thoughts?" Sawatri said. "Where do we take the Lost Angels investigation from here?"

Porter plucked a photo from the table and studied it. Lisa posed with a Cambodian child. She had the warm smile of an eighteen-year-old in love with the world around her. Thick strawberry-blonde hair framed a beautiful, unblemished face. Large, turquoise-blue eyes sparkled with wonder. She reminded him of Olivia Newton-John in 'Grease.' Sweetness personified.

"We all agree these girls have been abducted. Yeah?" Porter waited for nods. "At the same time, we need to treat each case on its merits. Consider all possibilities and all potential suspects. And with the limited resources available we'll have to narrow our scope… I reckon we concentrate all efforts on finding Lisa Baxter and go from there."

Sawatri's thick brows furrowed. "Why her? Because she's Australian?"

Jaru scoffed. "That's ridiculous. She was the last to disappear."

Porter had been instructed to focus on Lisa Baxter but hadn't been told why. He pushed the thought to the back of his mind. "You're spot on Jaru, and that's what makes Lisa's trail lukewarm when all the others are frozen. It's the only one we're a chance of catching a sniff of…" He looked at Helen. "You mentioned Lisa's friend. Carly? Any info from her?"

Helen nodded. "Carly's still in Bangkok and has been avoiding investigators for some reason, but I managed to speak with her briefly over the phone and have passed her contact details onto Nok… She told me about Lisa's intended journey from the school in Siem Reap into Thailand. Tourists usually need to change buses at the Poipet border crossing but the one Lisa travelled on goes non-stop to Bangkok."

"How does Carly know that?"

"She took the same bus a day earlier."

"Strange…Friends volunteer at the same school but don't leave together. Have we spoken to anyone at the school and asked why?"

"I've arranged a meeting with Carly at lunch time," Nok said. "We'll ask her then."

"Can't ask over the phone?"

"She seems worried about something, almost paranoid. She'd rather speak in person."

"Fair enough…Anything else about the bus trip, Helen? Has anyone spoken to border cops? The bus driver?"

"Yes, Nok and I viewed surveillance footage supplied by the Thai-Cambodian Border Co-ordination Office. They say it was given to them by immigration police from both sides, which is interesting because our official requests for it were ignored. The footage shows Lisa getting off the bus and walking towards a nearby casino. She carried a small item in her hand. It looks like a book but it's difficult to be certain. Then the screen goes blank."

Porter frowned. "Why?"

"I spoke to the guy who sent us the file and asked the same question," Nok said. "Apparently they had a blackout not long after Lisa got off the bus. All cameras were out of action for the rest of the day. The exact same thing has happened every time a girl's gone missing from Poipet."

"How bloody convenient…" Porter recalled his run-in with police at the airport. "More dodgy immigration cops are the last thing we need."

Jaru sniggered. "So now you're accusing the Thai border police, Porter?"

"Nah, I'm not accusing anyone but won't discount 'em as suspects either."

"I was able to get the buses number and registration," Helen continued. "Nok spoke to the bus company and then the driver. His story lends weight to the theory that Poipet border immigration police may be involved."

"How?" Porter said.

Nok leaned forward. "The driver assumes Lisa went into the casino to use the restroom. When she didn't return, he wanted to park the bus and look for her. Cambodian soldiers refused to let him off the bus. Immigration police from both sides demanded he drive across the border immediately."

"Soldiers? Strange…"

"Not really, the army runs Cambodia…The driver said some young guy on the bus got angry when he started to drive off without waiting for her. The guy made him stop and open the luggage compartment, then grabbed his suitcase and didn't get back on the bus. The driver thinks the guy was a friend of Lisa's, travelling with her."

"Who is he?"

"That's another question for Carly. And the short bit of footage with him in it, only shows him walking towards the casino with a suitcase. Nothing afterwards… I've spoken to the driver of the next Bangkok-bound bus as well. He wasn't helpful. Said he drives that route seven times a week, fifty-two weeks a year and can't remember any passengers."

"Seems Carly's the only person who can tell us if this young bloke took a later bus to Bangkok…" Porter shifted eyes to Helen. "You said the footage showed Lisa holding something. A book? Or phone?"

"Yes, and I asked Carly about it…It's most likely Lisa's travel diary. Carly said she takes it everywhere with her and there was no diary in her backpack when we searched it. And no phone either, so she probably had that in a pocket."

"Good job," Porter said. "Someone's switched on…"

Helen beamed.

Nok mumbled incoherently.

Sawatri propped elbows on the table. "Despite what you may think, Dan, we are all 'switched on'. Correct procedures have been adhered to for every missing girl. Immigration checks, financial checks, phone checks, social media checks. We've interviewed family, friends, and staff where the girls had stayed. We've checked CCTV footage from public transport, last locations seen, all surrounding streets...The lot."

Porter saw frustration on Sawatri's face. He felt a lump in his throat and swallowed his own. "Fair enough...Well, Carly Newman and what she might tell me and Nok is the best hope we have for now. I suggest Team 2 head to Poipet tomorrow. Shake up a few immigration blokes and the army. Speak to casino staff and check surveillance footage. Did Lisa actually enter the casino? If not, where else could she have gone? Did anyone else notice the young bloke getting off the bus at the same time? Has immigration or the bus company got a list of all tourists who travelled on that bus? The border crossing sounds like something out of the wild west. We need to know who's really controlling it and what they're trying to hide."

"I agree," Sawatri said. He ordered Fon and Jaru to travel to Poipet on Wednesday. "Any further questions? Comments?"

"Yes, boss," Fon said. "It's Nok's birthday and you're all invited to her party. It starts at eleven tonight in Soi Cowboy."

Sawatri nodded. "I'm sure we'll all be there...Dan, anything to add?"

Porter made brief eye contact with everyone around the table. His jaw clenched then relaxed. "We've got a hard slog ahead and the four of us in the field will need to do the legwork of twenty…Time is of the essence and experience tells me we're losing the race against it. The sick bastards who buy sex-slaves usually keep 'em for a month before disposing of 'em, three months at most. If we don't catch up, and soon, we won't find these girls alive."

# SIX

Porter glanced at the illuminated clock on the dashboard of Nok's sleek BMW. 12.15pm. They'd exited the garage at midday and crawled a kilometer since. He studied the map on the car's Navigator screen and realized the Bang Lumphu area of Bangkok was only eight kilometers away. But the Navigator said the trip would take another forty minutes in torturous traffic and they were due to meet Carly Newman in Khaosan Road at 1pm. He didn't want to be late and risk not speaking to her. In his mind she was a crucial witness, and if she couldn't provide fresh information he feared Lost Angels would stall before it got started.

Thirty-four young women abducted in a single month but Steve Williams had only mentioned the twelve Australian girls. Strange… Why hadn't he briefed him about the twenty-two others? Had he withheld information? If so, to serve what purpose and whose agenda?

Porter gazed out the window and tried to clear muddied thoughts. A row of zombies waiting for a bus stared back and he envied them because time was not something they seemed too concerned about. "Is there a quicker route to this meeting place?"

"I'm afraid not." Nok kept eyes on the road. "But chill, Carly will show up."

"Let's hope you're right…You know, I reckon I've heard of this Khaosan road before. It might've been on a cooking show Jane was watching."

She faced him. "Jane? The first I've heard of her…Wife?" She turned back to the front.

"Soon to be…She loves those shows where they try all the local cuisines."

"Well, Khaosan definitely has plenty of street food." She visibly shuddered. "Not that I eat it or go anywhere near the place unless I have to."

"Not a fan, eh?"

She scoffed. "It's full of scum. Vultures who feed off wide-eyed backpackers like Carly. Any self-respecting Thai isn't seen dead there."

"Sounds beaut, can't wait to visit…I had a decent chat with Sawatri after the meeting. He came across a bit snobbish at first but he's not a bad bloke once he lightens up. Said he likes his rugby and a beer or two, so he's alright by me."

"Yes, the boss is okay. Just don't expect too much support from him."

"Why's that?"

"He's rarely in the office. He's from a very wealthy family and this job is more like a hobby to him. He flies to southern Thailand at least twice a week. He says he has business there. Charity work that benefits Interpol. Merit making…"

"Great, our fearless leader sees international law enforcement as a game…He 'says' he has business. You reckon he's telling porkpies?"

She shrugged. "Why would he lie?" She giggled. "He most likely has a mia-noi hidden away down there."

"A what?"

"Mia-noi. A second wife, a mistress... Many Thai men keep one and then discard them without thought. They're

43

usually younger and prettier than the wives who gave them children."

Porter detected bitterness in her voice and wondered if she'd been a mistress scorned. "Where exactly does he go?"

"No-one knows, he never says much about it. And such things aren't for a junior agent to ask nor care about really."

"Fair enough… Jaru can't stand the look of me. What's his problem?"

"Jaru's a Royal Thai Police detective who's spent most of his career chasing buffalo thieves in villages far from Bangkok. Our team had six corrupt agents arrested by your taskforce and got him in return. You're a good-looking foreign investigator with an awesome reputation… Of course he's going to be intimidated by you."

He thought back to the meeting. "Intimidated? Or jealous? I saw the way you look at each other. Something's going on."

She waved a dismissive hand. "I think he's cute but he's married with two kids. At least he apologized to you."

"Yeah, 'cos Sawatri forced him to. But no skin off my nose… And why'd he do that thing with his hands, like he was praying?"

"Oh, my Buddha." She tut-tutted. "That was a wai. A show of respect. And in this case, also an apology. The higher the hands are held in front, the higher the respect shown."

"You mean he wasn't worshipping me like I'm some kind of policing god?"

"Hmm, I'd say that's in your mind only, that you're a god..."

He smirked. Sarcasm didn't translate well and it would take more than a few hours for Nok to grasp his sense of humor. "I'm kidding, and take the piss at my own expense far too often to be full of myself... Fact is, my mate Jaru's angrier than a meathead during a 'roid rage and I don't reckon that'll be the last time we butt heads."

"Ignore him. He's taking his frustration out on you but I'm the one he's pissed-off with. I've refused to have dinner with him because I don't do married guys. Not the poor ones, at least..."

"Speaking of 'guys'...What's young Fon's story, dressing and acting like a bloke? Is she a dyke or just butch?"

Nok's mouth gaped in exaggerated disbelief. "You can't use that word anymore."

"What? Dyke? Who says? It's what I was taught to call women who are into other women."

She shot him a bemused grin then shifted gears and accelerated. "Political correctness isn't your forte, is it?"

"Nah, I'm too old school for my own good sometimes and prefer to call a spade a spade."

"Well in Thailand we refer to girls like Fon as a 'tom'. Short for tomboy."

"Ah, okay. Same as back in Oz growing up, it's what we'd call the butch girls. There were plenty of 'em in the State cops too, and some as hard as any bloke you'll meet. So, if I can't say dyke anymore...Is she a lesbian?"

"No, Dan, I don't think Fon's a lesbian. I've seen her with guys...She's just more comfortable dressing and living her life as a man. She's a lovely person, like a younger sister to me."

"Don't get me wrong, she seems like a gem of a kid. But tell me this, what's with those freaky eyes of hers? Is that normal over here?"

She watched the road ahead as the BMW slowed then stopped at an intersection. She leaned towards him and stared. "Don't be so mean, not everyone's lucky to be born with lovely green eyes like yours."

He grinned on the inside, because she thought his eyes were lovely. Then an image of Jane with a scowling face whizzed through his mind. He gulped and forced himself to think of anything but the opposite sex.

Five minutes later Nok parked in front of a McDonalds at the western end of Khaosan road.

Porter stepped from the car, into a puddle. He swore as he looked down at a gutter littered with empty Styrofoam coffee cups, cigarette butts and floating noodles. He sniffed. Four-stroke engine exhaust fumes filled the moist air. Smells of curries and chili powder wafted from an Indian restaurant. Smoke from incense sticks tickled his nose. Then a foul stench. Discarded coffee, or tea? He sniffed. No, bloody hell, it was stale piss in the gutter. He rubbed leather soles against a cracked paving block to dry them.

He stepped off the road and stood with arms folded over chest. A tour tout shoved a laminated picture in his face. It promised a wondrous experience of temples, palaces and jewelers with welcoming smiles. He waved the bloke away and ignored the shrieking choir of beckoning tuk-tuk drivers that followed. Deep bass sounds from a nearby pub beat against his chest.

Nok glided towards him.

A stocky Asian man ran from an adjacent coffee shop to intercept her. "Who you?" Then he barked at her in a language Porter didn't recognize. "This parking my customer only."

Nok barked a reply, twice as loud. It sounded like the same violent language.

The man proffered a wai as he backed away. He turned with tail between legs and scurried back into his shop.

Porter smirked. "Impressive…What'd you say?"

She flicked a dangling hair from forehead. "He's a typically rude Korean, shocked when a Thai returns abuse in his own tongue…I told him who I am and if he didn't want his shop to mysteriously burn to the ground overnight, he should get out of my face."

Porter waited till she reached the pavement. Then it came to him, the uneasy sense of being watched. He spun to his right and saw tourists meandering down the middle of the sparsely crowded road. A woman prayed to a spirit house on the corner.

He turned to his left, where a line of bright colored tuk-tuks and their spitting drivers blocked his view on one side. He shielded eyes from harsh rays that'd somehow managed to break through the constant layer of smog. He scanned the street, as far as he could see towards the T-intersection at the end. He saw nothing and no-one suspicious.

Who was watching him? The Thai 'dignitary protection' cops? The Russians? Those who'd tried to run him down at the airport? Thugs working for members of Bangkok's elite Nok had warned of? Whoever they were, they were bloody good at their jobs and well-hidden.

Nok placed a hand on his forearm. "Everything okay?"

He nodded.

She led him into the McDonalds behind them. She ordered coffee for both and a burger meal for him. They sat in fake leather chairs close to a bay window in the front corner with an un-interrupted view of the street.

Porter chortled. "Can't believe I've come all the way to Thailand to have my first restaurant meal in Micky D's…"

Nok laughed with him. "Carly suggested it. She's staying in a hostel close by." She checked her watch. "Ten past one already…" She plucked her phone from handbag. "I'll call and see where she is."

Porter's eyes swept up and down the street as he bit into a Big Mac. Signs and billboards of all shapes, color and sizes jutted out from above. They advertised silver shops, massage parlors and 2-star guesthouses. Stalls selling fake 'brand name' shoes, bags, sarongs, dresses and polo shirts spilled onto the pavement.

A pasty skinned, middle-aged couple in matching elephant-print pants and 'I love Thailand' t-shirts strolled past the window. A group of older Asian women went the other way. They wore elegant dresses and wide hats more suited to a day at Royal Ascot than a trot down one of Bangkok's dodgiest thoroughfares. Three Hispanic-looking blokes in shiny soccer jerseys skipped past them.

A diminutive teenager with dreadlocked hair plodded along the uneven pavement. She stopped and pulled straps to heave a humungous backpack higher on her shoulders, a baby turtle with a full-grown shell. She squinted and spun three-sixty degrees then continued in the same direction.

Two twenty-something blondes entered the scene from the right and stuck out like dog's balls. Legs up to armpits. Tiny denim shorts. Skimpy tops showed more breast than they covered. Designer sunglasses propped on tanned foreheads framed model-like faces. Scandinavian girls, Porter guessed, because they reminded him of Lagertha from his favorite tv series.

He looked beyond the Viking wenches to the opposite side of the street and fixed eyes on two human specimens from a very different world. An elderly couple huddled in a shuttered shop-front, their dark skin barely visible in shadow. They wore spoiled rags for clothes and had limbs as thin as starving children Porter had fed in Afghanistan. Their smiles were toothless and desperate as skeletal hands reached out to pedestrians, some of whom dropped silver coins at their feet.

Nok placed her phone on the table. "Carly will be with us soon." She must've followed his gaze. "Tourists shouldn't give those beggars money, it encourages more of it."

He swallowed the last piece of burger then turned to her. "I dunno about that...Does it really do any harm? It's human nature to help others less fortunate. Mostly..."

"Yes, it's harmful to the rest of society. Numerous studies have shown it."

"Studies by who?"

"An anthropologist from Singapore wrote a well-received paper on it. A professor of mine."

"You went to uni there?"

"Yes, at the National University." She raised her chin. "I majored in criminology...After uni I spent six years in the RTP, working CI around Nana and Asoke. I've been with Interpol for the past four years."

"Ah, so you're an academic type?" He smirked. "You prefer to form your opinions around what others tell you?"

"No, not at all…They've been formed around theories, backed by scientific research and what I read in reputable news sources."

He laughed. "Reputable news sources? Bloody hell, they disappeared when the internet arrived…The days of ethical journalists and scientists are long gone. Now they're all working for something or someone and promote the highest-paying agendas."

Her eyebrows arched. "Is that so?"

"Yeah…Look, you're entitled to your opinions but I prefer to base mine on personal experience. Things I've seen and done. And trust me, your professor's research paper will do sweet f all to put food in those stomachs over there. But fifty cents, chicken feed to a tourist, that will, and right now I reckon that's all that should matter." His scanned the area near the beggars across the road. "And what about him, the bald bloke in the orange robe who's just set up in front of 'em? A monk? Why's he allowed to collect money in his fancy bowl but the hungry old people aren't?"

She leaned forward to look. "Yes, he is a monk but he's not begging. He's accepting donations for the local temple."

He scoffed and shook his head.

"I sense you aren't a religious person, Dan?"

"Nah, but at the same time I've got nothing against those who are. And one can still have beliefs without being religious… One of mine is that organized religion's mostly about money these days."

"I'm not sure about that… And we Buddhists see it different again. We're taught to follow the middle path, to avoid the extremes of indulgence and self-mortification and all the problems they bring." She pointed to the monk and the beggars behind him. "In this case, wealth versus poverty and the strong-minded versus the weak."

"Listen, I understand the need to clamp down on scammers and traffickers who run begging syndicates, but sometimes people are just fair dinkum hungry." He felt his face tingle, flushed with hot blood. "Let's agree to disagree."

"You're angry? So, past experiences have molded your belief system yet haven't refined your behavior?"

"What psycho-babble criminology bullshit is that?"

"Well, like in the meeting earlier when you lost your temper…" Her perfect features projected calm. Her tone of voice, sarcasm. "Have your worldly experiences not taught you how to control it?"

"I know what you're doing." He smiled. "And I aint gunna bite."

"I'm trying to help… I can see you're very passionate about this job and helping these missing girls, but here you must manage your emotions. Thais see anger as a weakness and won't respect you for it."

He dipped his head. She had a valid point.

"Good. Control it, Dan, and avoid conflict."

He recoiled. "No decent cop's ever avoided conflict. It comes with the territory…" He grinned. "But I will make a conscious effort to be more, diplomatic, as per the visa in my passport."

"Good to hear. Take the middle path and be calmer for it."

"You mean like Sawatri did when he lost his cool and whacked Jaru across the head?" He smirked. "Weren't real Buddhist of him, was it?"

"That, is different."

He broke eye contact and watched the street. *Hypocrites, the world's full of 'em...*

A few minutes later Carly arrived. She apologized for being late and took the chair in between them. She had a punk look going on, a female Johnny Rotten. Aside from her scraggly pink hair, everything was black. From her black eye shadow to the black Doc Marten boots. She wore a black ring through her nose. Black studs and rings lined the length of both ears. She snarled when she smiled and Porter wondered if she'd been asked to leave the Cambodian primary school because she'd scared all the kids.

Nok introduced him then cut straight to the chase. "Carly, time's running out for Lisa. You need to tell us everything you know, every detail, and you need to tell us right now."

Carly leaned back. Eyes widened as she exhaled with a whoosh. "Like what?"

"You and Lisa have been friends for a long time." They shared a smile as though acknowledging the bonds of sisterhood. "You travelled from Sydney to Thailand together and then volunteered at the same school in Cambodia. But you didn't return to Bangkok together. Why?"

Carly opened her mouth then closed it.

"Carly?"

Carly sighed. "Alright…We had a massive argument about this hot guy teaching at the school. I liked him but he liked Lisa. As usual…"

"And that's the only reason you came back a day before she did?" Porter said.

"Aha…But actually, we both left the school a few days earlier than we should have."

"Why?"

"I'd had enough of the heat and shitty food but Lisa got spooked by the school's headmaster. Mr Saysamone. He got drunk and tried to pash her at a staff party. Was creepy. They say his bosses are furious and he might lose his job."

Porter saw a veil of worry fall over Nok's face.

"The bus driver mentioned a guy who Lisa might've been travelling with," Nok said. "Who would he be?"

"Hmm…" Carly looked to the ceiling then back to her. "It was most probably Tim, this American guy who volunteered with us as well."

"Is he about twenty-five, tall and skinny with longish ginger hair?"

"Yep…"

"Matches the description the bus driver gave…Tim's our guy. Tell us more about him."

"I didn't see or talk to him much. He was only there for a week. The last one…"

"Why?"

"Apparently he volunteers there heaps, like ten times a year. But from what I saw he spent more time partying in Siem Reap than teaching kids."

"He drank a lot?"

"No, he was into pills. Eccies. Said he bought them in the town. Strange ones I'd never seen before."

"How were they strange?"

"Really bright colored, stamped with cartoon characters. He tried to get us to do some. He followed Lisa around like a lost puppy, like, really obsessed with her…"

"Is he the guy you and Lisa argued about?"

"Ewh, no way, Tim's ugly as…And Lisa wanted nothing to do with him either, not in a romantic way at least."

Porter cleared his throat. "Did she say why?"

"She thought he was sleazy. He'd always talk about the Nana area and girlie bars."

He glanced to Nok and raised eyebrows.

"Nana's an area with quite a bit of red-light action, not far from our office," she explained. "If you're a good boy I'll take you there."

He grinned then urged Carly to continue.

"Tim's nice enough but a bit weird, some kind of religious freak. Lisa's always been her own worst enemy, too nice to tell creepy guys to rack off." Carly paused. A look of dread soured her face.

Nok leaned forward. "What is it?"

"I, I'm just really starting to feel so guilty for leaving her alone with him…He had a quick temper. I remember he was absolutely raging one night when we joked about some of his religious views and stuff."

Porter smirked. "Sounds like Tim's got a few loose 'roos in the top paddock." Both gave him bemused looks. "You know, like he's a nutcase…Which is a worry."

Carly stared at Nok. "What if Tim's hurt Lisa?" A tear left a black trail down her chubby cheek. "Is he the reason she's missing?"

She straightened. "We'll do our best to find out."

Porter felt a pang of doubt jab his ribs. Something about Carly wasn't sincere. Was she telling porkpies? If so, why? Did she have something to do with Lisa's disappearance? Resentment was a strong enough motive for any crime. But if she was telling the truth, Tim was a definite suspect.

He locked eyes on hers. "So you've had no contact with Tim since the day he and Lisa left the school?"

She chewed on bottom lip and shook her head.

He analyzed her face and body language for signs of deceit. "How long did you wait for Lisa at the bus terminal?"

"When she wasn't on the first bus, I waited for the next one. It came in about two hours later."

"Did this Tim bloke get off either of the buses you saw arrive?"

"No…But they usually make a heap of unscheduled stops once they get to closer to Bangkok. People get dropped off at the side of the road. Tim might've caught the later bus and got off before the main station, anywhere within a thirty- k radius of the city."

"Both drivers I spoke to said the same," Nok told him. "And the buses have GPS but they never turn it on."

"I've messaged Tim through Facebook and checked his profile page," Carly said. "No reply and no activity since the day Lisa went missing. I've contacted other volunteers and Cambodian friends from the school and they've all said the same thing. It's like Lisa and Tim both vanished into thin air."

"It's very important we find Tim as soon as possible," Porter told her. "Did he say where he intended to stay in Bangkok?"

"Actually, he said he's lived in Bangkok for a few years but didn't say where... I've got this recent photo of him. From my Facebook." She pressed her phone screen a few times then handed it to him.

A ginger haired preying-mantis stood between Lisa Baxter and Carly with arms draped around both. His smile was wide but theirs much tighter.

Porter glanced at the profile names tagged in the photo. "Hah, Tim Nazareth...I'd bet my left nut that's not his real name." He opened his iPhone's 'contacts' directory then passed it to Carly. "My phone number here in Bangkok...Please save it and send me that photo."

She fiddled with her phone then handed Porter's back to him. It vibrated as he placed it into a trouser pocket. Message received.

"I'll ask Helen to hack into Tim's Facebook profile and see what she can find," Nok said. "And, Carly, why didn't you mention him over the phone? Is he why you were nervous about saying too much?"

"No, not Tim... I don't know. I guess I've watched too many spy movies where everyone can listen to everything."

"Nah, you're just a smart girl," Porter said. "Because if you're using a regular phone network, just about every man and his dog can listen in..."

Carly seemed to force a smile. "Please find Lisa. She's my best friend and I miss her."

Nok thanked her and promised to keep her informed.

Porter watched her walk onto the street then hurry out of view. "I reckon Lisa's disappearance is somehow different to the others."

"You don't think she was taken by a syndicate?"

"Dunno. Maybe it's because we know more about her…You reckon Carly told us everything?"

"I'm not sure."

"Tim's the key…Why's a young bloke like him using a fake name? What's he got to hide? Anyhow, Helen will check immigration records and we'll get answers soon enough."

"Yes, let's hope so." She stood, took her bag from the table and headed for the exit.

Porter followed. "Where we off to now? This Nana joint?"

She waited until they were seated in the BMW before answering. "Nana's for later…I'm dropping you at the office. There's a meeting I'm already late for."

"Don't go out of your way. I'll come with and hang in the car or go for a wander."

"That's not possible."

"Why?"

"Because you're not welcome where I'm going and I'll be safer alone."

# SEVEN

Nok dropped an indignant Porter at the Interpol office then took the motorway south to the Chao Phraya river. She ignored the guard at the secure entrance to the Khlong Toei Pier shipping terminal and drove fast through a maze of laneways towards the docks. She followed a long, straight road past enormous cargo ships. Towering cranes lowered rectangular containers onto decks as long as football fields to form stacks of giant Lego pieces in red, yellow and blue. She turned left before the Port Authority building and sped to the end of a narrow alley lined with grey warehouses. At 3.05pm she parked the BMW behind a black pickup truck then strode out onto a dilapidated wooden jetty.

She stopped a few meters in front of two Asian men standing in the middle of it. They removed their sunglasses at the same time to reveal menacing dark eyes. Both had thick necks and bald heads that made thirty-year-old faces look forty. They wore polo shirts and jeans too tight for bulging muscles. Their brown leather boots had three-inch heels, as often favored by vertically challenged thugs whose profession relied on intimidation.

The wide river behind them was a mass of swirling, dirty-brown water, navigated by vessels of all shapes and sizes. A passing ship's horn sounded a loud warning. A white stork with glossy black wings squawked then fluttered from the water towards the yellow haze of a cloud-dotted sky.

"I haven't met you guys before, are you new?" she said. "Where's your boss? I usually deal with him."

The taller thug snarled then addressed her in Korean.

She held a hand up to stop him. She said she had trouble understanding his northern dialect, to slow down or speak in English.

He unfolded arms and stepped forward. She was 5'9 in heels and his eyes were level with hers. "You late and the boss busy," he said in broken English. "You deal with me, sexy girl."

Both men moved closer. She noticed a thick scar running down the shorter thug's cheek. He was better looking than the other, who had several teeth missing from a crooked mouth.

"Get Heung-min on the phone," she said. "Let me speak to him."

The taller man's open hand struck her before she saw it move.

She stumbled backwards. Eyes watered. She wiped blood from lower lip with the back of a hand. She glared at him. "Why'd you do that, you pr--."

"Never speak the boss' name! Now, shut up and listen," the shorter thug said in fluent English. He turned to his right and pointed east along the river. "See the small boat there? The one full of gravel, next to the Caterpillar loader?"

She looked in that direction and saw it thirty meters away. A black and white, flat-bottomed river barge, moored against a dusty riverbank littered with dirt and gravel. A tattered Thai flag hung from a cabin at the barge's rear. A yellow tractor sat idle beside it. A cement truck rumbled away from the river then disappeared behind a brick wall.

She turned back to them. "Yes, I see the barge. And?"

"Our methods for transporting cargo from the river to larger ships waiting offshore in the gulf must change," the shorter one told her.

She frowned. "Why? We already have a good system in place."

"Relations with our friends in the Customs Department and the Port Authority have been compromised. We can no longer use shipping containers or the usual dock."

"There must be someone else willing to assist?"

"No. They afraid to take bribe. Everybody talk about corrupt and they not want jail," the taller one said. "Now Customs check everything. Search boat and containers with dogs. Have more Water Police. Check all manifest. Every time."

Nok turned towards the boat. "That's for transporting raw materials and the cabin's tiny." She addressed the shorter guy. "Where will our product be stored on it?"

"Each unit will be put inside an air-sealed metal box about the size of a coffin, then placed onto the deck," he told her. "A loader will cover the boxes in gravel, just enough to conceal them. At the other end the boxes will be removed from the barge and loaded onto the ship. The process gets repeated if they're sending cargo back to us…"

She scoffed. "Crazy…Why would this barge head so far out into the gulf?"

"Don't be concerned with what happens beyond the Chao Phraya river. Customs and the navy still leave us alone out there. And it's not uncommon for large ships to make repairs while sitting offshore, so a barge delivering sand and gravel shouldn't raise suspicion."

"Won't the gravel be too heavy and damage the boxes and the product?"

"The product will be fine. The boxes are strong enough to withstand much more weight than they'll have to."

"I'm not sure about this… How long should we keep the product in stuffy conditions?"

"That's not a concern, and this boat's faster than the larger ones used previously so trip times back and forth will be shorter."

She closed eyes and rubbed her forehead. "I guess it can work…" She opened them. "But as you said, customs officers are starting to do their job and river patrols have increased. What's to say the barge won't be stopped and sniffer dogs put on board to search it?"

"They most likely will be, sooner or later. But, as stated, the boxes are air-tight and will be hidden under gravel we'll cover in a thin layer of effluent sprayed sand. The chances of the dogs picking up a scent are extremely minimal."

She played with her swollen lip. "What's with the cement trucks near the barge? Is the area secure?"

"Yes, our boss owns the cement works and the entrance is guarded 24/7. We'll load and off-load cargo late at night or early morning. The cement company's trucks will transport the product from the river to the secure location in the city."

"Okay, I'll go along with it."

"You speak as though you have a choice…You don't."

"Well you're wrong, because Heung-min still owes me money. That prick's not the only one with huge debts, you know?"

The shorter thug slapped her face.

She gasped then covered her cheek with hand.

"You'll not speak of him that way. Never. Understood?"

She nodded.

"We'll give you a chance for atonement… One of the boss' most trusted business associates has placed a special order and requires express delivery. You will arrange it."

She stopped rubbing her cheek. "How?"

"Deliver two units of product, Friday night at twelve, to this jetty…"

Nok shook her head. "I'm the same as you guys, I want to get as much cargo out of Thailand while foreign customers are paying premium prices. And before law enforcement tightens its act. But I'm being watched very closely at the moment and it's too risky. I can't do it."

"We know all about this foreign investigator. Dan Porter. Don't worry about him. He'll be removed from the equation before long."

"He's not the only problem… Our entire Interpol unit's under the spotlight. The media and NGO's follow our every move. No, I really don't like the idea of supplying product at the moment. I need a couple of weeks at least, to let things cool a little."

"You have exclusive access and there's no-one else to make the delivery. The bosses won't be pleased if you fail to show."

"But I have to work on Friday night…"

"Our boss predicted your lame excuses and told me to pass on a message."

Her brow furrowed. "And?"

His cruel eyes gleamed. "The boss says…Young Nok, there are hundreds of crooked cops in Bangkok ready to take your place and deliver what we need. Don't make us clip your wings, little bird, you are far from indispensable."

# EIGHT

Porter had been keeping a close eye on the Interpol office's front entrance when Nok returned at 4.39pm. He led her directly into the meeting room, eager to share what he'd learned in her absence. He waited for her to sit then spread pages covered in handwritten notes over the table.

He glanced at her then frowned. "You've got blood on your lip. And it's swollen...You okay, sweet?"

She nodded.

He sat then leaned forward in front of her. "Some bastard's whacked you? Who?"

"It's personal and nothing to do with work. I'm fine." She pointed to the scribbled notes. "What have you got?"

He studied her red face. Was Nok too ashamed to admit someone was beating her? That she had an abusive lover? Was that why he couldn't go along to her 'meeting'? He fought instinct and decided to let it slide and mind his own business. But he would only do it once.

"Me and Helen called the Cambodian school," he said. "One of the admin staff spoke excellent English and answered our questions."

"What's the latest with the crazy headmaster?"

"Carly was spot on... Saysamone got into strife and resigned in shame. Helen's looking into an address in Chiang Mai. A house his mother might own...This bloke hasn't been spotted since the day Lisa disappeared and it's a worry."

"Yes, in more ways than you know…When an Asian man loses face the way he has, is humiliated, he'll often act irrationally. Saysamone possibly blames Lisa for his troubles. If she hadn't gone to the school, he wouldn't have been tempted and then disgraced." She paused, her forehead wrinkled. "He's a definite suspect with a vengeful motive."

"I agree. As is our mate…" he made quotation marks with fingers, "Tim."

"What's the story there?"

Porter read from notes. "The school has him on record as Timothy Nazareth, 26, from Los Angeles, California"

"And that's the name on his passport?"

"Dunno, they've never seen it…Helen's initial search of immigration databases on that name came up empty, so I reckon he'd have a fake passport anyhow…She's gone through all the passenger lists supplied by the bus company for two weeks either side of Lisa's disappearance. Nothing. There's no record of a bloke by that name crossing from Cambodia into Thailand on the 17th of September, or any time within the past year."

"Hmm…It's a concern, but as you said, the Poipet border's the wild west and as corrupt as any place on the planet. Just because there's no official record of him entering Thailand doesn't mean it didn't happen."

"Good point…The admin lady confirmed what Carly said, that Tim's volunteered on a regular basis but for never more than a week. He organizes his own visa from what they know, and the only ID they've ever seen is his Thai driver's license. And again, Helen wasn't able to find any record of Cambodia issuing a visa to anyone of that name…She's trying to access his Facebook profile.

But what's it gunna tell us? Info about some Tim Nazareth bloke who doesn't really exist?"

"Yes, true, and it's very weird he only stays for a week each time…So, it's as we suspected?"

"Yeah, the last person seen with Lisa Baxter is bogus and reeks to high hell." Porter plucked a photo from the table, the one where Tim stood between Carly and Lisa. "If he's not our man and there's some other explanation for him using an alias, why's he ceased all contact with Carly and so on? If he got off that bus in Poipet and couldn't find Lisa, why didn't he report her missing to local cops or an embassy?"

Nok took the photo from him and placed it in her handbag. "They're definitely the actions of a guy with something to hide and Carly seemed afraid of him."

"Yeah, she reckons the bloke's a weirdo but there's gotta be more to it."

She stood. "Carly said Tim likes to hang out in the Nana area. Let's go and ask around."

Porter sighed as he followed her out the door. "It's worth a shot but I reckon the odds are about the same as finding a virgin bargirl in Pattaya."

"What are?" she asked over her shoulder.

"The chances of finding a fraudster in Bangkok who doesn't wanna be found... Sweet f all."


Ten minutes later they exited a taxi near a police box on the corner of Sukhumvit and Soi 4. Nok explained that a 'Soi' was a side-street. They scurried across Sukhumvit road at a pedestrian crossing.

Porter hopped onto the pavement and read a blue street sign on the corner opposite. Soi 3. He looked up while pausing to catch breath, thankful he'd ditched the tie and jacket. He saw more of the concrete beasts he'd marveled at in the morning. They supported the elevated train line he now knew as the 'BTS' and shaded him from the sinking sun. Beyond the concrete beasts a model with a flawless complexion promoted beauty cream on a giant TV.

"That's the first crossing I've seen in this whole city where cars actually give way to people," he told Nok.

She nodded and swiveled to her right. "This way…"

He stepped alongside her, soon dizzy from dodging fellow pedestrians. An elbow-linked couple stopped to study a map in the middle of the pavement. Cocky teenagers walked four abreast as though they owned it. Giggling students circled a phone, oblivious to everything and anyone else around them. Marching men in business suits threatened to trample all in their way. Petite girls in office uniforms window-shopped then wandered off aimlessly in a dream.

They came to an alleyway entrance on the left. An old lady barbequed chicken. An Indian tout tried to sell Porter a suit and shirts to go with it. Thai blokes in numbered orange vests, motorcycle taxi riders, lazed across bikes. They whistled as they ogled Nok, who ignored them with her usual elegance.

A few meters past the alleyway, Nok ducked into an alcove near a row of ATM's and gestured for Porter to join her. He did, glad to escape the rush.

She pointed with eyes, ahead to the left.

Twenty or so women leaned against glass shopfronts, spread out over thirty meters. Porter didn't need to be a cop to know they were hookers. Some stood in small groups, the others alone. Most were Asian. Those who weren't were black and chunky with terrible wigs, except for two white girls in the middle who looked Eastern European. They both had short purple hair and wore tight dresses they shouldn't have.

Two blond blokes, one wearing a red jersey, the other in black, stopped to chat with three Asian girls. The tallest hooker hugged the bloke in red, shook him about then squeezed his cheek. The men shared a joke then laughed and carried on walking.

Nok waited for the men to pass then nudged Porter and strode forward.

He followed then stopped beside her, in front of the Asian girls. Other hookers lined along the wall scampered.

Nok held out a flat palm. "Kwang, hand it over."

The tallest hooker pouted. Glazed eyes blinked, their lashes longer than Cruella de Vil's. She reached into a clutch bag then handed Nok a brown wallet. Her friends skulked away.

Nok turned towards the blokes in the jerseys, who waited to cross the road. "Hey, red shirt," she called out. She waited for him to look then held the wallet up. "You dropped this…"

He ran back and sheepishly took his wallet from her. "Ta, love, I owe you one. Bleedin' lose everything after a few pints…"

Porter picked his accent as being the same as scouse mates he'd met in Afghanistan. They were excellent soldiers and salt of the earth blokes who loved a beer and a good yarn.

Nok watched him walk away. "I didn't notice his football top until he came back." She smirked. "I'm Man U and if I'd known he was Liverpool, Kwang could've kept his money…"

Porter snorted a laugh. "Why'd that young bloke hug her?"

Nok and Kwang conversed in Thai.

Nok giggled. "She says the guy liked her big tits and wanted a feel."

"Fair enough…" He studied Kwang. Black hair in a ponytail. An attractive face but a bit unusual, almost plastic-looking with too much makeup. Full, pastel-pink lips. A tight leopard-skin dress barely contained mammoth breasts. Some sort of padding around slim hips. Skinny calves and gold, high-heeled shoes that made her close to six foot. "Kwang's a nice-looking bird," he told Nok. "But she's got more silicone and rubber going on than the dummies we use in CPR training…"

Kwang huffed and glared at Nok. She squawked when she talked.

Nok held hands up as though to calm her. "Kwang got the gist of what you said, Dan. She's offended."

"My bad, I didn't realize anyone dressed like this at five in the arvo could be such a prude…You gunna lock her up for taking that young bloke's wallet?"

Nok explained that Kwang was her best informant in the Nana area. She'd started working the streets at 16, ten years ago, and what she didn't know wasn't worth knowing. Most of the hookers along Sukhumvit were petty thieves with drug habits to support. They usually targeted drunk tourists who they'd tranquilize with barbiturates during romps in short-time hotel rooms before robbing them.

Nok told him she'd recovered hundreds of stolen phones, wallets and gold chains from hookers and donated them to the local orphanage. The orphanage sold the goods to buy food for hungry children.

Porter frowned. "That's beaut helping the kids and all, but what about the blokes who want their stuff back? The victims?"

"They never report the thefts," Nok said. "Local cops refuse to listen, and what are they going to write in an insurance report and tell wives or girlfriends? I was getting a blowjob from a street whore, who put me to sleep and nicked me phone...Really?"

Kwang laughed, deep and loud.

Porter looked at her and for the first time noticed manly features. He'd dealt with plenty of transvestite streetwalkers in Kings Cross over the years but most had been Polynesian rugby players in drag, as feminine as Hulk Hogan. "Wait," he said to Nok, "Kwang's a bloke?"

Kwang slapped him hard. Nails scratched his cheek. "I had Aussie boyfriend before..." Her voice screeched, with the last syllable of each word spoken in a rising tone. "I know what 'bloke' is."

Porter's right hand curled into a fist. He eyed Kwang's square jaw.

Nok placed a hand on his. "Dan. No." She waited for calm then removed it. "We have three genders here in Thailand. You must refer to a person in the one they themselves identify as, and not in the way you perceive them to be."

Kwang shouted at Nok in Thai.

"She's very upset and says she won't tell us a thing until you apologize."

"Alright..." He addressed Kwang. "Sorry, mate."

Kwang tried to slap him again but Porter grabbed her wrist. He won a brief show of strength then grinned and let go. "Sorry…Sorry, sweet."

Kwang stepped back and revealed the small flick-knife in her palm. "It lucky I like you…" She blew him a kiss. "I not cut your handsome face off."

Porter adopted a defensive stance as Kwang's vacant stare bore through him. He didn't doubt it.

Nok sighed. "Okay, good, we're all friends." She took the photo of Tim posing with Lisa and Carly from her handbag and passed it to Kwang. "Have you seen this guy around? He calls himself Tim…"

Kwang studied the photo. "He look like I can remember, but he ugly and I not remember ugly guy too much. But maybe, yes… Maybe near Nana Plaza. Night time."

Nok told Porter about Nana Plaza, a nearby red-light complex. Three levels of sin she described it as, jam-packed every night with curious tourists, deviant sex-fiends, wily old foxes in cocktail dresses, paralytic drunks, brown-skinned rice farmers' daughters, spaced-out ladyboy tramps, and bikini-clad go-go dancers who'd popped too much ecstasy.

He stood with back to the wall as he listened, for the best view in all directions.

"When do you think you saw him?" Nok asked her, tone impatient.

Kwang flicked hair back then squinted at Porter. "You big guy. How tall you?" She stared at his crutch and winked. "I bet it's nice one. Can see?"

He gave her a quick 'Fuck you' glare then focused on the street.

"Kwang," Nok snapped.

"Okay, okay… I think I saw that guy in photo mayb--
."

"Over there!" Porter strode forward. He pointed to the corner diagonally opposite then ran back towards the intersection with the pedestrian crossing. "In front of the service station, over near the McDonalds where we crossed over before," he told Nok as she came alongside him, "white bloke in white shirt, speaking with the two in tracksuits."

They slowed as they reached the intersection.

"It does look like Tim," she said. "Same long hair, tall and skinny. But let's stay here a minute. We don't want to spook them. Others are watching us and will alert th--
."

Nok's advice came too late. Loud, short but sharp whistling noises pierced the air. They came from the black hookers who'd returned to their place in the parade.

The two black men in tracksuits spun towards the whistled warning. One tossed a package to the white bloke. Both then sprinted away from him, south on Soi 4.

The white bloke froze.

Porter weaved through traffic at the intersection and ran towards him. He heard Nok's clunking footsteps not far behind.

The bloke in white hadn't moved, as though guilt had pinned him to the pavement.

Porter focused from five meters away, certain he was Tim from Carly's photo.

He wore clothes similar to a Mormon missionary - thin black tie, black trousers and shoes. He stared at Porter, mouth and eyes wide, then transferred the package to the other hand and ran.

Tim took awkward strides like Jar Jar Binks in a Star Wars flick. He headed for the McDonalds restaurant then swerved left. He galloped down an alleyway to the rear of a 7/11. He halted with an exchange booth in front, driveway to the right, and a high wall on the left. He spun to face Porter.

Porter stopped five meters from him. He sucked dense air in a vain attempt to soothe burning lungs. "There's no need to run, mate."

Nok joined him. She carried high-heeled shoes. "Don't be afraid, Tim. We just want to talk."

Tim swiveled to his right. "Fuck off." He sprinted to the wall then disappeared.

"Bloody hell." Porter grunted. "There's a frickin' gap in the wall."

He chased him back towards the intersection of Sukhumvit road and Soi 4. He heard Nok swear. She called out and urged him to keep up the pursuit.

Tim ignored the red pedestrian light near the police box and crossed over Sukhumvit.

Porter followed him onto the busy road, stopped within inches of a speeding taxi then leapt from lane to lane. Brakes and tires squealed. Car horns blared. Headlights flashed warnings. A pot-bellied traffic cop in a uniform three sizes too small blew a whistle in his face. He saw Tim veer to the left then right into Soi 3.

Tim was younger and faster, but despite wearing leather shoes Porter settled into an easy pace and was prepared to outlast him. He ran past shoe stores and Egyptian coffee shops. Fat blokes wearing long white robes and kafis on heads chatted as though blissfully unaware they hogged the pavement. They fell silent as they parted to let Tim pass then yelled and shook fists at Porter. He shoved them out of the way and continued on.

Tim peered over his shoulder. Surprise covered his face when he saw Porter had gained on him. His running gait had changed. He looked tired and his eyes fearful.

Porter glanced back and saw Nok nowhere in sight. He chased Tim down a narrow alley with tattered awnings and faded signs written in Arabic. Blokes with dark faces chewed kebabs and stared. Aromas of grilled lamb and garlic hummus wafted to his nose and made him hungry. He passed a group smoking from shisha pipes. Cannabis fumes tickled his throat and made him cough. His eyes watered then focused on Tim, only meters in front.

He reached out to grab him by the neck but Tim darted to the right and through a doorway. He turned and followed him into a crowded Egyptian restaurant. Patrons dressed in black and white murmured. Tim stumbled and knocked a table over. Cutlery clattered. Veiled women shrieked.

Tim shouted in Arabic, too fast for Porter to understand. A waiter yelled a reply. Chair legs screeched on tiles as men stood.

Porter chased him through the kitchen and into a small courtyard at the rear, a square surrounded by high walls topped with razor wire.

Tim kicked the far wall then turned to face him. Narrow shoulders slumped. "What the fuck do you want, dude?" He voice was mid-pitched and nasal, its accent American. "I don't know any Tim."

Porter took deep breaths while he gathered thoughts. His brain always worked faster when his heart beat slower. He stopped panting and stepped forward.

"Listen, mate, you're probably running because of the drugs stuffed down your pants but I couldn't give a rat's ass about those…Just tell me where Lisa Baxter is."

Tim shook his head. "Dude, I don't know any bitch called Lisa Baxter, so piss off and leave me alone."

Porter heard excited male voices coming from the kitchen. The door creaked behind him, the only exit to the courtyard. "C'mon, mate, talk to me. You aint in trouble yet."

Tim glanced at the door. A wry smile. "No dude, I'm not. But you sure as fuck are."

# NINE

*They opened the one and only window in this room for the first time this morning. It's in the middle of the concrete wall and has metal bars to stop anyone from getting in or out. Not that I could climb out anyhow, because the window is about three meters from the floor and I can't see out of it even when I stand on my bed. But at least there's some cool air and natural light.*

*Sometimes the air smells like the ocean. Like seaweed. But sometimes it almost smells like dirty water, musty like a stagnant pond or river. Last night I heard a horn tooting. Maybe a ship's horn. And birds that sound like seagulls and water crashing, but then only lapping, and sometimes I think I feel like this room's swaying or rocking. But that could just be the heroin messing with my head, or when I'm rocking myself to sleep, so I really don't know if I'm on a ship, or in a house, or what.*

*This morning I thought I heard a bell ringing, and then guys shouted in some weird language. Maybe it was a town bell ringing the time. Or a church bell, I mean temple, is what they have here. Maybe a ship's bell. Who knows. Sometimes I think I hear cars or trucks and sounds of traffic. And then another time I thought I heard a cow or a buffalo, and then dogs barking. So weird. And this morning it was like people talking on TV. They sounded like Americans but it was too faint to be certain. And then people laughing and stopping suddenly, and that confused me even more.*

*My forearm is getting sore from where the guy injects me in the same place every day. But I don't complain because the heroin calms me and I feel so good afterwards. Heaven in hell, if you know what I mean.*

*The guy did something weird to me this morning. He tied me to the bed on my back, still with the sack over my head so I couldn't see a thing. And then he opened my robe and sniffed my naked body. I hated it. It made me feel dirty. But how can I stop him?*

*I hope my family never have to read this. I miss you and love you. Very much.*

# TEN

Porter swiveled on the courtyard's concrete surface to face the restaurant's rear door. Three men brandishing knives rushed through it towards him. The black men in tracksuits he'd seen on Sukhumvit road growled as they approached from his left. The Arabic waiter snarled with menace to his right. They waved long blades in figures of eight as they stepped closer.

Tim scampered to the doorway. "Dudes, what took you so long?" He turned to Porter and grinned. "I was gonna say, until we meet again…But hey copper dude, I doubt we will."

Porter watched him disappear into the kitchen then backed away from the blokes with knives. Fight or flight? Fight, whenever he could. He reached for his Glock, fingered an empty holster, then cursed Sawatri for not allowing him to carry a gun. Flight? He analyzed the courtyard's high walls. Even if he made it to the top without getting stabbed, the razor wire would tangle and rip him apart.

Fuck it. Fight it was…

Porter ran at the black man in the middle, the largest of the three wielding knives, and made the distance before he could recover from shock. His left foot kicked the knife from hand. His right fist put the bloke to sleep.

The two remaining thugs turned inwards on either side of him.

He lunged and plucked the loose knife from the ground. He front-rolled a few meters then sprang to his feet. By the time he turned the men were almost upon him.

The waiter was small and quick, a weaselly ninja, and his shiny blade whooshed towards Porter's throat.

He swayed to avoid it and the second man's blade sliced his shoulder. He grimaced and tightened fingers around the handle, desperate not to drop the knife. He shifted it into an overhand grip then stabbed downwards to bury the blade deep in the black man's thigh before yanking it sideways. Muscles ripped and tendons were sliced from bone.

The young man squealed. His face turned purple. He dropped the knife then staggered into the wall and slumped to the ground screaming.

The waiter slashed at him again.

Porter weaved back just in time. The blade missed his throat but cut the same spot on his left shoulder. He winced because it stung like hell. He front-kicked the waiter's chest and sent him reeling.

The waiter backed against the wall. His eyes narrowed.

Porter advanced and was a meter from him when the eyes widened then darted to the left. He reacted too late. A brick-like fist pounded his temple from behind and knocked him down. Porter dropped the knife.

The same huge man pinned him to the ground. He wore a white robe, had a bald head and brown face flushed with blood, a vulture's beak for a nose, and a thick black beard. Evil, blood-lusting eyes stared down.

Air rushed from Porter's lungs as the man's full weight, what seemed like half a ton, straddled his chest. A heavy fist thudded into his cheekbone. His vision blurred as he rocked his head from side to side to avoid more punches. When it focused he saw three more men in white robes kicking his torso and legs from the side. Adrenaline flooded his body as animal instincts and the will to survive took control. Pain disappeared and energy levels re-booted.

The waiter hovered above Porter. A wicked smile revealed a gold tooth as he aimed the blade at his throat. It edged closer, inch by inch.

A kick caught Porter on his bottom left-side rib, the same he'd cracked playing rugby years earlier. He managed not to yelp as searing heat shot up his spine and sapped strength. Strength he desperately needed. Because if he couldn't throw the huge man off him the punching and kicking wouldn't stop and he'd be beaten to death.

He reached out on both sides. Trembling fingers searched for the knife. Nothing. Another punch. His nose broke. Again. Eyes watered, the huge man's face blurred. A kick to the side of his head. Consciousness slipped away. He returned Jane's smile and told her he loved her. Eyelids wanted to close. He resisted, then his whole body shook. Fists and boots pounded him. Maniacal, high-pitched screams reached a crescendo. Eyelids slowly fell down like curtains being drawn on his life.

Boom! Boom! Boom!

Frenzied shouting stopped. Silence.

Porter heard a 'crack'. He opened eyes and blinked to focus.

Another 'crack' as Nok's pistol slammed against the huge man's skull a second time. He fell off Porter and slumped to the ground. Still.

Porter shook fog from his head. He staggered to feet and wiped warm blood from his mouth. He pinched the bridge of his nose between thumb and forefinger then sucked a breath as cartilage wriggled back into place. His ribs ached but they'd been worse.

The men in robes tried to kick him again.

Boom! Boom! Boom!

Nok fired her pistol into the air and shouted in Thai. They retreated.

The waiter and one other supported the injured black men and they hobbled into the kitchen. The two remaining men sneered at Nok and moved towards her. She levelled her pistol at them and shouted.

The huge man on the ground groaned and rubbed his head. He called out in Arabic and the men helped him stand.

He glared at Nok and they argued in Thai.

He pointed at Porter then ran a finger across his throat as though slicing it with a knife.

Nok shouted a reply then levelled her pistol again.

The Arab men fumed as they raised hands above heads. They sat, slowly, cross-legged in the middle of the courtyard.

"Come on, Dan," she said. "We have to leave…"

Porter's jaw clenched while he glowered at the trio. "Hang on, aren't we gunna ta--."

"Dan! Now!"

"But we need to interview these blokes. They can lead us to Tim."

"No." She strode forward and grabbed his elbow. "Listen to me…We're in the Arab part of Nana, their territory. If we try to arrest this big guy, their boss, they'll swarm from everywhere and we won't leave here alive."

He shook her hand away. "That's bullshit…Whose city is this? And what's to say they won't follow us?"

"I'll explain later, and no, they won't follow." She shouted again in Thai then moved to the door. She bent to put shoes on. "Let's go."

Porter followed her. They walked briskly through the restaurant, down the alleyway and turned left into Soi 3. Nok hailed two motorcycle taxi riders. The taxis picked them up, drove along the pavement and two minutes later dropped them where they'd left Kwang on Sukhumvit road.

Kwang rushed to Porter as he hopped off the bike. "Darling, what happen to you?" She led him off the pavement and into an alcove. "Let me see. Where have blood?" She handed Nok her handbag then rolled Porter's blood-stained sleeve to the shoulder. She shrieked and covered her mouth with a hand.

Porter studied the cut. Ten centimeters wide but not deep. "Calm down, it's hardly a scratch…I'll clean it up when we get to the office."

Nok frowned. "Sure you don't want to go back now?"

He nodded and tightened the sleeve around the wound.

She examined his face. "Your nose is swollen but at least the bleeding's stopped."

He scrunched it. "That was never in doubt…This mangled snoz of mine's already lost enough blood for ten lifetimes."

Kwang rubbed his forearm. "Not worry, darling, you still very handsome."

He winced then rubbed his ribs. "Now, Nok, tell me why we're not rounding up those Arab blokes and asking questions about Tim."

"It's complicated…Let's just say, well, they're protected."

"What? By who? They can lead us to the last bloke to see Lisa alive but we can't frickin' talk to 'em?"

Kwang huffed. She rubbed a thumb and forefinger together to indicate money. Greedy palms being greased?

"I reckon Kwang's spot on. Are those bastards paying local cops to turn a blind eye?"

Nok sighed. "Do they run their own Middle-Eastern hookers, illegal shisha bars and drug dealers in that very small part of Nana? Yes…Does the local police boss allow them to, for a fee? Yes. But do I think Tim's working for them, or vice versa? No."

Porter scoffed. "Then why'd he run to 'em for help?"

She shrugged. "Maybe he supplies Soi Arab with product the Middle-Eastern dealers don't want to touch? Ya-E or ice? And he's most likely friendly with some of the younger guys."

"Ya-E?"

"Same same ecstasy." Kwang told him, still irritating as hell with her screeching voice. She turned to Nok. "Falang not make deal anything with Alab. Falang give to black guy and then black guy sell to Alab. But only ganja, a little bit, when Alab dealer no have. And yes, ecstasy too."

"So that's it? End of?" Porter asked Nok. "We just ignore the fact the waiter and the black dealers are Tim's mates and probably know where he lives, which could be where Lisa Baxter's being held? You've gotta be kidding me?"

"No, we don't ignore it but we can't go back into Soi Arab…I'll speak to Sawatri, who'll speak to the Police

Colonel in charge of Nana. He'll then speak to Big O, the Arab boss, the massive guy you met."

"The guy I met? Bloody hell, the fat bastard almost squashed me to a pulp…Alright, but if you don't talk to Sawatri about it, I sure as hell will."

"The Arabs won't risk a good thing to protect a white guy. I seriously doubt they know anything worthwhile about Tim but if they do they'll give him up."

Porter nodded, unconvinced. Did she understand Tim's importance to the investigation?

Kwang prodded Nok. "When I see Dan chase that skinny falang I remember where I see him before…" She opened her handbag, pulled out a yellow piece of paper and passed it to her. "He give me this. About three night ago. He stand at front of Nana Hotel and give same to every girl who work in Plaza too."

Nok told him the Nana Hotel was directly opposite the Nana Plaza red-light complex. She studied the paper. "It's a flyer…GAIT?"

Porter took it from her. He read aloud. "GAIT…God's Angels in Thailand. A non-profit organization run by the Anglican Church whose mission is to save young Thai women from a life of sin. We aim to assist them in starting new lives, away from the evils of drugs and prostitution." He read the remaining two lines to himself then handed it back to Nok.

She frowned at him. "So basically they're just another nosey, do-gooder NGO…The type Sawatri spoke of."

"Reckon so…And strange there's no address or phone number. Only a website."

She nodded as she read. "GAIT.com. I'll have Helen check it out."

Porter turned to Kwang. "How many times have you seen the bloke who gave you this?"

"Hmm…Him, only two or three time. But have more guy, work the same and look same him."

"There's more than one handing out flyers? And they all wear the same outfit, the thin black tie and so on?"

Kwang frowned.

"How many guys have you seen?" Nok asked her.

"I think I see three or four different guy…Maybe? They all the ones who give drug for black guy to sell and they boss for black girls too."

"What?" Porter leaned towards her. "These white blokes supposedly working for this NGO act as suppliers, and pimps for the African hookers?"

Kwang's face crumpled in a look of confusion.

"She doesn't understand the question," Nok said. "And I think she could be embellishing the truth to please you, to tell what she thinks you want to hear."

Kwang sulked. "Pee Nok, I not lie you. The black girls told me like that, about this white guys."

Nok frowned at her. They had a brief conversation in Thai.

Kwang eyed Porter sideways then raised her voice.

Nok shouted at her.

Porter thought he heard the English words - 'monkey house'.

Kwang whimpered and folded arms.

Porter wasn't a fan of being excluded, especially when both Thais could speak English. "Monkey house? What's that about? What did Kwang just say?"

Nok exhaled, loud and as though deliberate. "The 'monkey house' is Thai slang for a 'prison', and I just told Kwang she'll be going back there if her disrespect continues." She glared at her. "She says these white guys, god's angels or whoever they are, seem to have some kind of control over the African hookers and dealers. She's asked the girls what it is but they don't want to talk about them."

"As I said…Are these blokes using the NGO as a front? To supply amphetamines and African hookers? Here in this, what is it again? This, Nana area?"

Nok spoke to Kwang in Thai.

Kwang nodded.

"Yes, she's certain they have a monopoly on supply in Nana," Nok told him.

Porter watched the endless stream of traffic while he paused to think. He turned to look along Sukhumvit road, to where they'd seen the parade of hookers earlier. The black girls were gone. "Kwang, do you know what country the black girls come from?"

"Niger?" She frowned. "Niger Lia?"

He nodded. "Nigeria…"

Kwang beamed and tried to jiggle her boobs, as though proud of herself.

Nok thanked her then hailed a taxi.

When they were both seated in the back, Porter said, "Should we check the emergency rooms at nearby hospitals? I sliced that bloke's leg pretty deep and he'll need stitches for it."

She shook her head. "Big O will get him treated by one his private doctors."

"Fair enough, but I'm coming back later to look for his mates and the hookers. Gunna threaten to send 'em to the monkey house if they don't talk and promise to leave Thailand. It's where they'll end up if they don't."

"They're most likely here on expired visas and someone's paying local cops and immigration to leave them alone. Tim maybe?" Her brows furrowed. "You don't like them, do you? Black people..."

He smirked and pulled his wallet from back pocket. He handed her a passport-sized color photo.

Nok studied it. "She's beautiful. And very dark."

"Yeah, she grew up in London with Jamaican parents."

"Who is she?"

"Jane, my fiancé." He grinned.

She nodded as she sighed. "Okay, I get it, you don't hate blacks...The tone in your voice threw me because it seemed full of disgust whenever you spoke about them."

"Don't worry about my tone, sweet, I've only got one." He winked. "Look, I'm angry at the bastards who use 'em for their dirty work, not the kids themselves. And I was interested to learn they're Nigerian because it means they could be Christians, same as the blokes from our dodgy NGO."

She averted eyes.

He saw her face flush red. Embarrassment?

"Tim working for a church sponsored NGO makes sense after what Carly told us. About him being a religious freak..."

Porter grunted. 'Yeah, it does. And it's got me even more concerned about his involvement with Lisa Baxter."

"In what way?"

"You aware of the two Kenyan girls abducted from a Bangkok nightclub a few months back?"

"Yes, the corrupt agents removed from our office were working on the case. Freelance hookers, right?"

"Yeah, they were." He recalled the girls had been branded with 'KA', victims of the Knights of Alba. He decided not to divulge the fact. "They were found dead in Germany a month later."

"You're saying it happened to the Kenyans and fear these Nigerian girls are in the same danger?"

"Maybe…" Porter stared out the window. Was there a link? A link between those responsible for trafficking the Kenyan girls to Germany and those now running the Nigerian hookers in Nana? Had the Dragon Slayer taskforce's swoop through Asia missed a KA associate operating out of Bangkok, one not named in the Cumal Files? "Even if this GAIT mob aren't planning to send these Nigerian girls elsewhere, they're still involved in organized prostitution. And this Tim bloke seems to run it."

Nok stooped in front of him to force eye contact. "Are you afraid of what I am? That GAIT could be associated with Southeast Asian human-trafficking syndicates who've decided to broaden their operations, like the ones we suspect abducted Lisa and the others? Could Tim be working for a syndicate as a spotter or similar? Is that why he volunteered at the Cambodian school?"

"Good point and worth keeping in mind…But nah, I'm not worried Tim's working for 'em…I'm worried him and his mates at GAIT are the actual syndicate responsible. After what we've learned from Kwang about Tim's contacts' I'm convinced he's a suspect for all the abductions."

"I agree, and have him as our main suspect. Although something about Mr Saysamone doesn't seem right…And where's GAIT based here in Bangkok? If they have taken the girls, where are they holding them?"

"Dunno…And don't forget the girls who've disappeared from Poipet. Who says they're in Bangkok?"

"True, they could've gone in multiple directions from the border. Let's hope the GAIT website gives us a clue."

"I doubt it but you never know… This is a huge city and apart from the Nana area we've no idea where to start searching."

"Then it's best we focus on finding Tim and friends. Correct?"

"Yeah…They'll be spooked after today and probably lie low for a bit. But we'll hit Nana every night until they're spotted again. And if we can grab someone working for Tim we'll hold 'em for as long as we can and make him sweat about what they might be telling us. We need him to panic and make a mistake."

"I like it... But I know Sawatri and he'll be concerned about our approach being too 'visible' to the public. So how much do we tell him?"

Porter didn't reply. He stared at the driver's seat.

"Dan, what's wrong? Is your nose painful? We're almost at our building and I'll get you something for it… Oh, I forgot, you don't do pills."

"Nah, it aint that." He growled and swept rigid fingers across his forehead. "We've focused on where these girls might be held and by who, but neglected equally pertinent questions."

"Such as?"

"If they're no longer in Bangkok or Poipet and they've been sold by Tim's blokes or whoever… Where have they been sent to? And how?"

# ELEVEN

Porter took the elevator to his apartment after the short taxi ride from Nana. He showered to wash a dirty city from rough skin then cleaned and dressed the cut to his shoulder. He changed into a blue polo shirt, a pair of 501 jeans, and his favorite New Balance sneakers. He reckoned he had more fights and foot pursuits ahead so wanted to be as comfortable as possible.

At 7pm he returned to the office. Helen met him with a radiant smile then said Superintendent Steve Williams had phoned and wanted him to call back. He heard laughter from the meal room and walked down the corridor towards it.

Sawatri stepped from the room as Porter tried to enter. "Woah…" Sawatri swayed back. "Someone's in a hurry." He frowned. "Oh dear, Nok said you had some trouble but I didn't quite expect your nose to be spread all over your face… Are you okay, Dan?"

"No worries, it'll be fine."

"Of course, I forget you're a hard-headed rugby union fellow. You're most likely quite used to the knocks and scrapes."

"Union? Nah, I'm a League man." Porter shuffled sideways through the doorway and nodded to acknowledge Nok and Jaru seated at the table. He turned back to Sawatri. "Where I come from, only blokes who couldn't make it in the NRL play Rugby Union." He grinned.

Sawatri made googly eyes then continued out the door.

Porter took a bottle of water from the fridge then sat next to Nok. Jaru sat opposite, head stuck in his phone.

Porter pointed to the piece of paper in her hand. "What are you reading?"

Nok passed it to him. "It's a summary Helen prepared...She collated intel reports of known drug dealers operating along Sukhumvit. There's no mention of guys working for GAIT...She's also requested information from government databases regarding the various NGO's based in Bangkok and who runs them. We should receive a response in a day or two..."

Porter sighed. He wouldn't hold his breath waiting for a bureaucrat to supply useful information.

Jaru stared at his swollen face then laughed.

Porter was in no mood to let it go. "Something funny?"

Jaru's malicious smile revealed yellow teeth. "You're asking me a question? But I thought you already know it all?"

Porter stopped drinking from the bottle. "What's that supposed to mean? Stop talking in riddles, mate."

Nok placed a soft hand on his arm. "Dan, ignore him..."

Jaru's nostrils flared. "Well, Porter, I can see you've lost a fight. Surely a cop of your prestige and experience knows better than to chase an offender into a strange place in a strange city?"

"It was three then seven against one, and I did--."

"No need for explanation, your ugly face says more than enough." He placed a forefinger to pursed lips. "Clearly you're not so smart after all, but just another co--."

Nok slammed an open palm against the table. "Jaru. Stop it."

He drove a clenched fist into it and sent water bottles tumbling. He glared at her. "Shut up. You don't tell me how to behave. Remember?"

Porter hissed as he snarled. "You gutless mongrel." He thrusted a finger at him. "You're the one who hit her, aren't ya?"

"No, Dan, you're wrong…" She held his elbow then pulled his arm down. She shot them both a look of disdain. "Calm down, you're acting like children."

"I am calm and just waiting for Fon to return…" Jaru leaned back. "And as I was saying, I'm enjoying the sight of this falang's banged up face. A typically cocky falang who obviously has no idea what and who he's dealing with and failed to take due precautions."

Porter leered. "Mate, I've forgotten more about police work than you'll ever know. And I'm smarter than you'll ever be too…I just prefer to keep plenty up my sleeve so dimwits with bad attitudes, blokes like you, don't feel so miserable about themselves…And don't ever mistake my easy-going nature for naivety. It'll come back to bite ya big time."

Jaru chuckled.

Nok groaned.

Porter noticed Sawatri and Helen. They stood in the corridor and watched the scene through the doorway.

Jaru dismissed him with a wave of a hand. "As I said, Porter, you're just a typical falang."

Porter leaned forward to lock eyes on him. "Tell me, where's your hatred of foreigners come from? What's caused it? You angry 'cos your soccer team never wins, or what?"

Jaru snorted. "I had a young and beautiful girlfriend once who was just like Nok. I was crazy about her and we planned to marry and make a family...But a rich, smooth-talking falang came along and promised her the world. She dropped me like a slime covered stone."

Nok shook her head. "Jaru, you don't need to te--."

"But I want to, since he asked..." He turned back to Porter. "That falang used her in disgusting sex parties, shared her with his filthy friends then left her without a cent."

Porter nodded to suggest he continue, because he still hadn't heard a decent explanation.

"She was forced to become a go-go dancer in Soi Cowboy," Jaru told him. "Forced to sell her body to fat, ugly old white men. Drunk, obnoxious fools..."

Porter scoffed. "She was forced to work there, against her will?"

Jaru shook his head.

"Or did she make a bad life choice?" Porter asked him. "Because, you know, they are two very different beasts."

"Is that so?"

"Yeah...I'd like to have more cash. I could rob Citibank tomorrow, live like a king and travel the world. But I won't."

Jaru huffed. "There you go again, trying to apply your warped western values to how the rest of the world lives...And I doubt you've ever been desperate for money."

"You reckon? I weren't born with no silver spoon, champ. My first job after school paid me stuff all to shovel chicken shit for twelve hours a day in forty-degree heat. How about yours?"

"Pfft, you did a shitty job for shit money. Pass my violin…It doesn't mean you understand Thailand."

"I'm not saying it does, mate, and I don't want or expect empathy. But some do deserve it…Like the cleaner Nok and I saw in the elevator this morning. A gorgeous young girl with a cracking body who could be raking it in as a sex worker. Nok told me she'd be getting paid twenty bucks to scrub toilets and make beds for ten hours a day, seven days a week."

Jaru grunted. "What's your point?"

"No doubt that cleaner would like to have more money, and she could get it by selling her body. But she's still got her dignity, which is priceless… And she's made a choice to stay loyal to her morals and the ethical code she lives by. Similar to the reasons why I don't rob a bank."

Jaru's crimson face twitched. "You're wrong. Again. My ex was forced into prostitution when that falang left and now she's hooked on ice. He's ruined her."

"You don't get it, mate…Girls like these abducted ones we're trying to find, they, are forced into it and don't get a choice. They aren't the same as the cleaner, or your go-go dancing ex-girlfriend who's decided drugs are the answer."

Jaru sat silent for five seconds. "Since you speak of making choices…Nok told me about your black fiancé." He sniggered facetiously. "Why'd a handsome man of the world like yourself choose her? Considering her type are beneath us all, even you falang..."

Porter growled as he stood. His chair cannoned backwards into the wall.

Jaru stood and stepped to his right to meet his charge.

Porter stopped in front of him, inches from a collision, seething as he stared down. He saw a glimmer in his black eyes. One of fear?

They stood chest to chest like two silverback gorillas refusing to cede ground.

"I won't have you using your girlfriend's sob story as an excuse to disrespect my missus." Porter prodded white knuckles into his chest. "Got it, you racist fuckwit?"

Jaru smirked as he looked up into his face. "No, I don't, get it…"

Porter eyed the pig-like nose. He wanted to smash it and spread it all over his smug face. Then Sawatri stepped between them and shouted something. But Porter didn't pay attention to him because in his mind he saw Nok smile and he tuned-in to her soothing voice. *'Take the middle path, Dan, and be calmer for it.'*

Jaru shoved him in the chest.

Porter's hands curled into fists but Nok's whispered wisdom echoed. He relaxed them and addressed Sawatri. "Sorry, mate, that was unprofessional and won't happen again." He waited for him to nod then strode through the doorway.

He turned into the meeting room, kicked a chair out from under the table and flopped onto it. He waited a minute for the fire in his chest to smolder then called Steve Williams from his private cellphone.

"Port, thanks for getting back to me," Williams answered the call. "I gather you arrived okay?"

Porter decided not to tell him about the fun and games at the airport, or his scrap with knife-wielding drug dealers, or his recent stand-off with a xenophobic Thai detective. He didn't want to worry him and risk he'd tell Jane.

"Yeah, my flight got in on time. No worries."

"You okay? You're breathing hard and sound on edge."

"All's good mate. It's been an interesting twenty-four hours but nothing I can't handle."

"Excellent. How you liking Bangkok?"

"I still don't know whether to thank you for sending me or to wring your bloody neck."

"Hah, give it time. It'll grown on you."

"Maybe…I mean, the women are great. Polite and pretty like you said. But most of the blokes are rude, arrogant wankers. The traffic's a bastard and the whole city's a mass of never-ending concrete. And it's hotter than the Simpson bloody Desert..."

"Seriously, you'll never change, Port. You can take the rascal out of the country but you can't take the country out of the rascal."

"Very funny…The humidity's insane too. I'm sweating more than a corrupt judge during his first night in the slammer."

Williams chuckled. "And apart from all that?"

"Ah, Bangkok's not a bad joint. So far…" He told Williams about the lunch meeting in Khaosan road, that his first meal in Thailand had been a Big Mac with fries, and about Nok threatening to burn a Korean bloke's café to the ground.

He waited for Williams to stop laughing then spent five minutes briefing him about the investigation and suspects identified thus far.

Williams whistled, low-pitched. "You've certainly got your hands full. This Tim Nazareth guy's a concern. With his alias and so on…"

"Yeah, and if he is our crook, has he acted alone or as part of an organization?"

"Time will tell."

"And we don't have much of it, not if Carinya taught us anything."

"Exactly. If the girls are still in Bangkok they won't be for much longer."

"I told Sawatri and his crew the same. But I don't reckon it sunk in."

"Probably not. From the limited conversations we've had, Sawatri doesn't strike me as being the sharpest tool in the shed… Seems you've already got an important decision to make. What's your gut feeling?"

"Tim's our man… His syndicate, under the guise of GAIT, abducted Lisa Baxter and probably the others." He hesitated and remembered what he'd wanted to ask earlier. "Listen, mate, why didn't you tell me about the twenty-two other girls who've disappeared? Why'd you only mention the Australian girls?"

"Why?" Williams paused. "Because I only learned of them this morning…"

Porter had known him for fifteen years and detected the pitch-change in his voice. It usually accompanied a mistruth. "You didn't know of 'em before today?"

"No." Williams coughed. "Now, you were talking about this Tim guy… Who could his syndicate be selling the girls to? How might they be transporting them?"

Porter allowed him to change the subject and filed his next question for later. "I've no idea regarding the transport. Bangkok's a hub with planes, trains, boats and automobiles leaving in all directions. We'll keep looking into it… And we've had no luck with who the buyers are but Sawatri said there's plenty of demand after we shut KA down."

"Yes, that's the word… Listen, you have to go hard after Tim and GAIT. Today."

"Agreed, and with the limited resources available they're the one and only mob we can focus on… But then if I'm wrong and Tim's only responsible for Lisa's disappearance, I worry we'll lose any chance of tracking the rest of the girls."

"Come on, Port, you've been around long enough to know it's the game we play… It's the nature of these investigations where we've fuck-all evidence or witnesses… We place our bet on a qualified hunch and hope for the best.

"Yeah, I know, but I don't have to like it."

"And when you say, 'limited resources'… What's the issue?"

"We've got four agents and one analyst on the job."

"What? Sawatri promised twenty investigators and a large support team."

"Well, we aint gunna get 'em…" Porter pulled more questions from the file register in his brain. "Why's the Australian embassy so quiet on this, mate? Why aren't our Federal coppers stationed in Bangkok getting involved? Why aren't foreign law enforcement sending their own investigators? It's like no-one wants to touch it."

"Yes, because they don't."

"Meaning?"

"It's become a diplomatic shit-fight…Thailand's current leaders have a weak hold on power, the nation's political landscape is beyond shaky, and its economy can't afford another blow to investor confidence. They've told every foreign nation with an interest in Lost Angels to stop meddling and let them handle the situation."

"Which is why they don't want me here…And from what I've seen so far they aren't handling the, 'situation'." Porter scoffed. "Sawatri said his government doesn't want this story out there because it'll scare off tourists and be bad for its image."

"Yes, and it's a military-led government under increasing Chinese influence. Thailand holds a strategic position in the Asia-Pacific region and other nations in it, Australia included, are very wary of pissing them off and pushing them closer to Beijing."

"Are you lot back in Oz and all the others who should be interested in this but aren't, gunna allow incompetence to risk innocent lives? For the sake of protecting pride and maintaining diplomatic harmony? Bloody hell, mate, you can't."

Williams sighed. "It's out of my hands and well above my pay grade...And as I said, we're not the only ones being frustrated by apparent apathy. The Brits, Americans, Russians…We've all been told to mind our own business."

Porter thought back to his arrival in Bangkok when everyone at the airport didn't seem to want him there. Were influential members of Thai society who'd told foreign powers to stay away the same Nok had warned him about? Did they see him as a threat, worried his presence as a foreign investigator would draw the international media attention they dreaded?

"Steve, the truth… Have Aussie politicians already placed this situation in the too-hard basket?"

"I'm afraid so."

"Gutless bastards…" Porter exhaled hard through his nose. "Nok told me about Thai blokes not wanting to lose face. It's like their entire government's paralyzed by the fear of embarrassment and refuse to act. And it must be contagious because just about every other politician suffers from it too."

"What do you want me say? I agree… Tell me about Nok and what she's like when she's not threatening Korean shop owners. Is she a good sort?"

"Mate, it's a good thing I'm engaged and behave myself because she could get a bloke into a lot of strife…You know Pink the American singer? She's a Thai version of her. She's a real stunner."

Williams laughed. "And so is Jane, who you love dearly. So be a good boy."

Porter laughed with him. "No worries there, mate. I've told you before no-one scares me like Jane does."

"Speaking of lovely ladies, I sent Lyn Foster to Los Angeles yesterday."

"Yeah, what's the job?"

"Three Vietnamese-Australian girls went over there on student visas two months ago. They only intended to stay a fortnight but their families haven't heard from them since."

"Bloody hell…But no fear, Lyn's a great investigator and I'm sure she'll sniff 'em out."

Williams started to speak then stopped. Silence.

Porter sensed he was withholding information again. He decided to put it on him and retrieved the question he'd stored for later. "Why'd you tell me to pay particular attention to Lisa Baxter? Why's she special?"

"She's not…With a lack of evidence it's merely best practice to focus on the most recent victim."

The expertly calibrated bullshit detector in Porter's brain sounded the alarm. Revolving lights flashed. "Steve? C'mon…Piss-weak bosses over here are trying to sabotage this investigation and I don't need you fucking me around too. What's the real deal with Lisa?"

Williams cursed then cleared his throat. "Alright, but this stays with you."

"That goes without saying…"

"Lisa Baxter is John Fitzgerald's step-daughter."

An image of Senator Fitzgerald's proud face sped to the front of Porter's mind. When Prime Minister Tate had proposed amendments to legislation in response to demands Porter had made at the conclusion of the Carinya investigation, Fitzgerald had helped get them passed. He'd then supported the establishment of taskforce Dragon Slayer, the global law enforcement operation that'd dismantled the Knights of Alba's human-trafficking networks and sentenced hundreds of evil men, including corrupt members of his own party, to life imprisonment. He was one of the few politicians Porter trusted.

"I can't believe you kept that from me. It creates a whole new dynamic for the investigation and a longer list of suspects."

Williams sighed. "It was Fitzgerald's idea not to tell you, to avoid unwanted media attention and causing more friction with the Thais. Hardly anyone knows and even Carly Newman's been instructed by our embassy not to name him as Lisa's step-father…And you're right about possible suspects...Has someone taken Lisa in revenge? Is her disappearance, as you suggested in summary just now, an entirely separate case from the thirty-three others?"

Porter recalled the lunch meeting with Carly where he'd sensed she had more to tell. Had she guarded Lisa's secret? "Fitzgerald helped us send a heap of crooks to the slammer...So yeah, payback and vengeance are definite motives to hurt him." He thumped the table. "And bloody hell, mate, I should've been told about it."

"Alright, I know, I fucked up...And I'm concerned there's more to this, that sick fuckers totally separate to GAIT have decided to join the game. Is this situation worse than we already think?"

Porter shook his head at the ceiling. "How could it be?"

"Either way, whoever's responsible for these crimes is professional and very well organized. And that's got me thinking... Did Dragon Slayer miss a major player in Southeast Asia? Has a KA associate formed a new human-trafficking syndicate that's operating out of Bangkok?"

"Earlier I thought about those Kenyan hookers abducted from the nightclub and wondered the same... Dragon Slayer locked up more than thirty of KA's blokes here in Thailand, but did one or more of 'em slip through the net?"

"Well if they did, Port, we need to find them yesterday. We owe it to the girls and ourselves. We can't allow the 'Knights of Alba', that nightmare, to start all over again."

# TWELVE

Porter ate dinner with Nok and Fon, who'd ordered delivery from a restaurant in the nearby 'Terminal 21' mall. He ate a spicy dish with beef and rice then drank plenty of water to douse the flames in his throat. Afterwards he sat at his desk for an hour and made notes, trying to link what he knew with the who, where and when. But he couldn't concentrate, because those who might've been able to answer his many questions weren't in the office. They were over a kilometer away, selling themselves along Sukhumvit road or dealing drugs in Nana's dark backstreets.

At 9pm he made for the exit.

Nok looked up as he strode past. "Where are you off to?"

"Going for a wander along Sukhumvit." He turned when he reached the door. "I'm tired of sitting and being inside. Gunna have a look around for Tim's mob and those Nigerian hookers."

She checked her watch. "They won't all be on the streets yet. We'll look later when my party's over. Between 2 and 4am will be best…Stay and we'll put some music on."

"Nah, I'd rather head out now."

She frowned. "Fon and I have an appointment at the hairdressers in thirty minutes but if you need us to come too, we can cancel."

"She'll be right, you ladies go and pretty yourselves up…I've already marked where the party is and I'll meet you there later on."

He took the elevator to the ground floor, turned right towards the Nana area then joined the column of worker ants marching along the cracked pavement parallel to Sukhumvit road. After a minute he broke ranks and dawdled. He wanted to experience as many of the fresh sights and sounds, and the not so fresh smells, as he could. And despite his slow pace and the constant flow of pedestrians and zigzagging motorbike taxis, he covered ground faster than the cars trapped on gridlocked streets.

After fifteen minutes he approached a familiar intersection and passed the police box with the pedestrian lights on its right. He stopped on the corner next to a souvenir shop, swiveled to scan three-sixty degrees then wandered south along Soi 4. Lights in many different colors shone in his eyes from every direction. Some shaded, some dimmed, but mostly too bright. They illuminated alcohol-fueled revelers darting across pot-holed streets and casted shadows on crumbling brick walls.

Hundreds of nocturnal creatures scurried about him then ducked into pubs and beer bars. Music blared from dingy, smoke-filled dens. He guessed most single men in the red-light area sought comfort from scantily clad hostesses with warm Thai smiles. And he assumed the foreign couples drinking in its crowded bars were mostly tourists seeking a sense of safety amidst Nana's undeniable seediness.

He came to a gap between bars and the rows of green umbrellas lining the footpath. Pedestrians in front meandered so he stepped onto the edge of the road between food carts to avoid them. He looked up and smirked. 'Nana Plaza', said the sign spanning the driveway. Large white letters covered a black banner dotted with yellow flashing lights. Red silhouettes of sexy girls wrapped around poles danced on either side of it. Above the banner a luscious lip and sparkling teeth formed half of a sensual smile. And the red and white message below it claimed the three-level complex to be - 'The World's Largest Adult Playground.'

Porter decided he'd wait to explore the Plaza with Nok. He crossed over Soi 4 to stand with his back to the Nana Hotel, in the same spot Tim had given Kwang the GAIT flyer a few nights earlier. He surveyed the street in both directions and saw no-one matching the description of those he sought.

He enjoyed the amusing parade of workers and customers entering Nana Plaza for ten minutes then walked back towards Sukhumvit road. Girls in beer-bars opposite waved and called out - 'Where you go sexy maan?' and 'Come back handsum maan.' He passed the hotel's carpark, turned left through the gap in the wall then right into the alleyway he'd chased Tim down. He stopped, hidden by shadow. He watched the front of the McDonalds restaurant and the service station next to it. Nothing suspicious. No drug dealers in tracksuits.

He took the pedestrian crossing over Sukhumvit to the corner of Soi 3 then walked to the alcove near the ATMs. He pressed himself against the wall and peered towards well-lit shopfronts where the black hookers had earlier plied their trade. Thai girls and the Eastern Europeans still hovered but the Nigerian girls were nowhere in sight.

He approached a group of motorcycle taxi riders near an alleyway entrance and pretended to be under the influence. "Ya-E?" he said to the youngest looking bloke with a slur. "Where can buy Ya-E?"

The Thai man stared back as though confronted by an alien. An older one barked something in Thai.

The young one snarled at Porter. "You ting-tong falang. Fuck off." He flicked his head towards the older bloke. "He say you falang police."

Porter patrolled Nana for another hour without luck then walked briskly back along Sukhumvit road towards Asoke. He followed directions on his phone and made his way to Soi Cowboy.

At 11.10pm he wandered down an alley glowing in neon-pink and found the 'Baccara' go-go bar. A bikini-clad glamour stood by the door and he accepted her invitation to enter. He stepped inside and had shuffled forward through a dense crowd for a few paces when Nok grabbed his arm and led him to a raised, semi-circular booth. He nodded to the others then sat at a round table littered with bottles of Johnny Walker, ice-filled buckets, soda mixers and a half-eaten birthday cake. Sawatri, Helen and Fon smiled back. Where was Jaru?

He swept eyes around the room, over the two-stories of topless dancers and the mostly Asian clientele. Too many years of hard liquor had pickled his liver so he ordered a bottle of Leo, a locally brewed beer. He'd found one in the office fridge after his argument with Jaru earlier and had liked the taste.

Nok sat next to him and smiled. Glazed eyes twinkled. "I'm so, so glad you made it," she shouted above the music. She squeezed his bicep in two hands and squealed with glee. "We wanted to show you a good time on your first night in Bangkok so decided to start here in Baccara. It's one of the best go-go bars in the city."

He tapped a foot in time to the booming bass beat. "This joint's amazing...I've been to strip clubs before but they're nothing like this."

He told the group about his interesting walk around Nana then listened as they took turns explaining the intricacies of Bangkok nightlife. He nodded while guzzling chilled Leo.

'Paradise City' by Guns N' Roses blasted from the hi-end sound system, an all-time favorite from the soundtrack of his youth. He hummed the lyrics while he watched Nok out the corner of his eye. He wasn't sure about the grass being green in Bangkok city, but the girls were definitely very, very pretty.

When the song ended a new line-up of topless dancers in glittering bikini-bottoms glided onto the narrow stage. Nok waved to the nearest girl who stood gripping a pole then beckoned her to join the group. The girl smiled and flicked long black hair from a golden-brown face. She hurried over and wedged herself between them.

Nok introduced the dancer as Som from Buriram province in the North-East. She said Som was like a younger sister and soon to be twenty-one.

Porter hadn't yet bought Nok a birthday drink so ordered tequila all round. Sawatri then Helen followed suit. After three shots he felt a warm buzz soothe his soul. He felt free of jetlag and relaxed for the first time since landing in Thailand.

Nok and Som had chatted loudly for ten minutes but when Porter shifted eyes from the stage back to them, Som leaned close to Nok's ear and whispered.

Nok placed her glass on the table while nodding as though listening intently then fished for something in her handbag.

He kept one eye on the stage and the other on Nok. He saw her pull a clenched fist from the bag and pass something to Som.

Som placed a closed hand down the front of her bikini bottom then pulled it out flat and empty. She smiled at Nok, then they kissed with slippery tongues entwined.

Nok cupped Som's pert breast in one hand and circled its dark areola with a finger from the other.

Porter gulped. The kiss lingered so he sculled half a bottle and forced himself to watch the pole-dancing.

Was Nok into chicks? Or just teasing him and all the other blokes who enjoyed the impromptu show? He watched them kiss again, unable to take eyes from Nok's glistening lips. If she was teasing, she did it well.

Som left the booth, stepped onto stage and wrapped herself around a pole as though she'd never left it.

Sawatri pretended to fan himself. "Phew, that was quite sizzling hot stuff to watch."

Fon grinned then leaned across to hi-five Nok. "You're a naughty girl but we love you for it."

All but Porter laughed.

He turned to Nok. "That wasn't the usual sisterly peck on the cheek."

"Just a bit of fun...I'll tell you more later but she gave me some great info, that guys matching the description of Tim and co have started selling ecstasy here in Soi Cowboy." She grinned. "I merely rewarded her for it."

He nodded, wondering whether the passionate kiss or the object she'd handed to Som had been the reward.

An hour later the group left 'Baccara' and Sawatri took his leave. Porter wanted to take a taxi to Nana and search for the GAIT blokes but Nok said it was still too early and persuaded him to party for another hour. After a short stroll the girls dragged him into the 'Glow' nightclub. A bouncer met Nok with a smile then cleared a path to a reserved table. Shortly after the manager said happy birthday and that all the group's drinks were on the house.

The DJ played 80's retro hits and Porter tapped a beer bottle on the table while he stood and watched the three girls wriggle on the packed dancefloor. When the fluted opening bars of Men at Work's 'Down Under' filled the room he squeezed through the crowd to join them. He sang to the disco ball hanging overhead, played an imaginary drum kit and rocked from one heel to the other. He'd forgotten how much fun a night on the town could be.

Fon and Helen waved to acknowledge Jaru's arrival and went to join him at the table.

Nok glided closer to Porter. He glanced towards the others to avoid her stare.

Helen frowned as she watched them dance, arms folded over her chest.

Fon clapped and cheered.

Jaru's cold eyes shot poisonous darts.

Nok swayed in front of Porter, a hungry cobra eyeing her prey. She turned and thrusted firm buttocks against his groin. She placed his hands on her hips then leaned backwards with lips slightly parted as they came towards his.

A sinister concoction of beer, tequila shots, nostalgic tunes, seductive perfume and luscious pink lips almost made him kiss her. But Jane appeared and willed him to resist temptation, so he grinned and playfully pushed Nok away.

She laughed then sauntered back to the table as though it had only been one of her teasing games.

Porter shook his head and followed. Had it been?

He ignored Jaru's snarled greeting, jiggled on the spot with his beer and watched the girls dance around the table. Three gym junky young blokes with crew-cuts joined their conga line. The tallest one gripped Nok's waist and moved up close behind her. She winced as she came past Porter, smiled then winced again. The tallest bloke turned to share the joke with his mates as he pinched her on the ass.

Porter slammed his beer on the table then lunged forward. He grabbed the tall bloke's wrist and twisted it upwards behind his back.

The tall bloke grimaced as he tried to break free.

"Apologize to the lady." Porter glared up at him. "Now!"

"Piss-off you old bastard," he told Porter in an Aussie accent as raw as a dingo's dinner. "Fuckin' let me go…"

Nok nodded, so Porter eased his grip.

The tall bloke wriggled free. His two mates came alongside with chests puffed like pissed-off peacocks.

Porter analyzed them. He knew the look, the attitude. "You soldier boys should know better."

The stockiest one stepped forward. "How'd you know we're army?"

"I just do…" Porter exhaled through gritted teeth. The young grunts had ruined the party's fun vibe and upset a lady. They needed to learn some respect. "I reckon one of you blokes should whack me."

Nok grabbed his elbow and tried to pull him away. "Dan, come back to the table."

He leered at the tallest bloke. "Come on, tough guy…Like you said, I'm just a harmless old bastard. Don't be scared. Go on, free hit…All three at once if you like."

The bloke frowned. "Why the fuck you want us to king hit ya?" He sneered. "Judging by your bruises you've already copped one floggin' today."

Porter smirked. "Cos when you whack me and then I clean you all up, it's gunna look like self-defense." He indicated the CCTV camera staring at them from a nearby wall. "And that's beaut, because I doubt you've got travel insurance and I can't afford to pay your hospital bills."

The tallest soldier chuckled to his mates then nodded at Porter. "Can you believe this silly old dickhead?" He cocked a fist.

Nok smashed a bottle over his head. Eyes lolled as the tall bloke slammed against the floor.

His mates lunged at her then froze, because Fon and Jaru aimed Glocks at their temples.

Helen squealed and ducked behind Porter.

Nok shouted at two bouncers in Thai. Four more rushed to the table. The six of them dragged the soldiers through the crowd then disappeared.

The Interpol agents let out a collective sigh, resumed their places at the table and drank.

"That's how we deal with drunken assholes," Jaru told Porter.

Porter ignored him and turned to Nok. "What did you tell the bouncers?"

She gulped whiskey then smiled. "I said, take them out to the back lane and mess up their pretty-boy looks."

Porter placed a sticky-note on the right side of his brain as a reminder to never piss her off then sculled the rest of his beer. He checked his watch. 2.19am. A vision of Jane flashed and she demanded he stop drinking, to protect his dodgy liver. Steve Williams hovered above her and told him to start searching for Tim and the other GAIT blokes, something best done sober.

And Williams was spot on, because the Nana area would be buzzing with creatures of the night. But the beers were going down far too well. Ah stuff it, Porter decided, he had time for one more.

An hour later he left the table and headed for the restroom. He swayed too far to his right and almost fell. Strange, because he'd only drank fifteen beers at best. He felt an arm wrap around his and lead him to the dancefloor. Bright lights blinded. The room spun around the disco ball. He looked down, curious to know who he danced with.

Helen smiled at up at him. Blood-shot eyes sparkled with a strange look of lust and her dress' plunging neckline revealed too much of a plump bosom.

Porter swayed again. His head seemed impossibly lighter, and he loved the world, and when Helen reached up and shoved her hot tongue down his throat, he kissed her back.

Two seconds later he reeled away from her. Like a tranquilized rhino he fought to remain standing but his brain rocked against his skull and he crashed to the sticky floor. He floated across the room. Strange faces scowled down at him while others laughed. Orange strobe lights flashed then his world turned black.

# THIRTEEN

When Porter's eyes flickered open he had no idea how much time had passed since they'd closed. He threw the sheet off, rolled onto his back and peered towards the thin ray of light at the bottom of curtains. Stinging eyes focused. He realized he was in his apartment. But how had he got there?

He turned on the bedside lamp and saw he was naked except for grey boxer shorts. But he'd worn black briefs under his jeans when he'd headed out, hadn't he? Strange…He groaned as he rubbed a throbbing temple then trudged to the balcony door and drew curtains. Fierce sunlight jolted him as it flooded the room.

He tried to recall last night's events while waiting for the kettle to boil. How long had he slept? Where were his keys and phone? He didn't think he'd drank too much, so why did his head and body ache as though he'd pulled an all-night bender? A thousand images from the past twenty-four hours whirled through his mind but none provided answers. Then a picture of Helen beaming up at him on a packed dancefloor kept flashing. Bloody hell, no…Had she put him to bed? Or had he bedded her?

He slammed a palm against his forehead. The sharp dagger of guilt plunged into his heart. *Fuck, Porter, what've you done? You bloody idiot...*

He checked the bedsheets. Nothing unusual. No used condoms on the floor or in the bathroom waste-bin…His jeans hung over a chair in the corner. He fished his phone and room keys from them then returned to the kitchenette and plonked them on the bench.

Why couldn't he remember anything after kissing Helen? And why could he only remember scant details prior to that? He remembered feeling dizzy and the nightclub spinning. Had some bastard dropped a pill in his beer? Was that why he'd passed out? The theory made sense...But who'd done it? And why?

More blurry images from his night out appeared. A rogues' gallery of suspects became clearer. He focused on the young soldiers he'd argued with. They had motive to spike his drink and plenty of time to do it before they'd been dragged out by bouncers. But the spiteful Jaru had motive too and had lingered near his beers for hours. Fon? Nah, she'd been having too much of a good night to be bothered with ruining his. And why would she?

Helen? She'd been at the table when he'd left his drink unattended and had frowned at his dirty dancing with Nok. A jealous frown? Had Helen spiked his drink, brought him home comatose and then...? Eyes slammed shut. He sucked a long breath. Bloody hell...Helen.

He shook eyes open then checked the time. His phone showed 10.13am on Wednesday the 26th. Eleven missed calls. Most of them from Jane. Guilt stabbed his chest again, this time laced with confusion. Was his guilt about kissing Helen and what else they might've done? Because he couldn't stop thinking about Nok? Or because the wedding was less than three months away and his behavior suggested he didn't want to go through with it?

He'd never been unfaithful to Jane before. Was last night just a blip, a one off? He tried to convince himself

115

it was someone else's fault, that an altered state of mind had made him do it. He huffed and called himself an idiot…Who was he trying to kid?

A finger hovered over the phone's screen. He had to call Jane. He needed to say how much he missed her and Amber, that he loved them both and looked forward to the wedding.

The phone buzzed. A message from Nok. Fingers tingled as he opened it. 'Hi Mr sexy eyes. Meet me at the private jet terminal, 2pm, and bring your passport.'

At 2.35pm they took off from Bangkok's Don Mueang airport bound for Cambodia. Nok explained that Helen had been contacted by Detective Inspector Veasna from Phnom Penh's Organized Crime Squad in response to an Interpol alert she'd circulated regarding the foreign girls abducted from Poipet. Veasna had a Cambodian suspect in custody and thought Lost Angels investigators would want to interview him.

Two and a half hours later they were greeted by Veasna at the entrance to Phnom Penh's central police station. He looked close to forty, wore a cheap grey suit over a slim physique and had combed silver-flecked black hair from front to back. He drew on a cigarette then let it hang by his side, a darker version of the suave detectives in Porter's favourite 1950's crime flicks.

Veasna dropped the cigarette then stated his policing credentials in perfect English. He led them inside the French-colonial building, up flights of stairs then stopped at a doorway on the third floor. He asked Nok to remain where she stood, walked five meters from her and beckoned Porter to join him.

"What's going on?" Porter said.

116

Inspector Veasna pulled him closer. "I'm sorry," he whispered. "But your partner cannot be present when you speak to my suspect."

"Why's that?"

"We don't trust Thais. Especially their police and definitely, no offence, definitely not Thai Interpol agents."

"None taken, I get it…But Nok's come a long way and I can vouch for her."

"It's out of my hands. The order came from above."

Porter walked back and told Nok. Her face reddened. She scowled and turned to Veasna as though about to abuse him but didn't. She smiled at Porter, said she'd expected as much and would wait in the foyer.

He watched her start down the stairs then followed Veasna into a gloomy interview room. It had dirty walls, a dirty floor, and a dirty shirtless man handcuffed to the only chair in it. A uniformed cop guarded him.

Porter coughed as cigar smoke tickled his throat. He sensed someone else in the room and swiveled towards the opposite corner, uncomfortable with having his back to the unknown.

"Agent Porter…" Veasna said, "may I introduce General Chea of the Royal Cambodian Army."

Chea stepped from the smoke cloud, past a small desk and into the light. He looked sixty and was taller than most local men Porter had seen in Phnom Penh. He had a thick mustache, broad shoulders and a giant belly – a Cambodian, Sergeant Shultz from Hogan's Heroes. Three chins hung below a sagging, pock-marked face. Black shoulder boards on his immaculate olive-green uniform displayed four gold stars. The front of his jacket was dotted in gold buttons and lapels of different shapes

117

and sizes. Rows of multi-colored service ribbons covered the left side of his chest. His right hip bulged under the jacket where he carried a pistol. He removed his cap to reveal a smooth, bald head, squashed the cigar under a well-polished boot then placed the cap next to a shiny metal box on the desk.

Chea shouted at the Cambodian cop in a harsh language Porter assumed to be Khmer. The cop scurried from the room and closed the door.

Chea squeezed Porter's hand as he shook it and fixed narrow, black eyes on him.

Porter returned the stare, suspecting those eyes had witnessed more death and suffering than most.

"Pleased to meet you, Agent Porter…" Chea said in fluent English.

"Same…" Porter said. He wondered why the cop, low rank aside, had taken an order from a soldier. Then he remembered what Nok had told him, that Cambodia had a military controlled government. And from what he'd read in the Bangkok Post in recent days, Thailand did too. "I detect a bit of a twang in your voice, General… Where's that come from?"

Chea raised his chin and peered up at him. "Ah, you're referring to my refined New York accent? I lived there for a few years… And I graduated from West Point back in the 80's, one of only three Cambodians to have done so. That's why I lead the twelve commando battalions of the 911 Special Forces regiment and why my soldiers are as good as you'll find in any army."

Porter had served in the SAS and knew to the contrary but decided not to wound the General's ego.

"You must be wondering, Agent Porter," Chea continued, "what a four-star general wants with a piece of filth like this?" He stepped forward and whacked the suspect's face with a cuffed hand.

The suspect winced. He wiggled his mouth then spat blood onto the floor.

Porter cocked his head. "I'm still waiting for one of you blokes to tell me."

Chea smirked at Veasna.

"Do you understand our language?" Veasna said.

Porter chuckled. "Bloody hell, I'm struggling to say hello in Thai let alone understand your lingo…No mate, I don't speak Khmer."

Veasna nodded then pointed to the suspect. "This man works for a gang operating out of the Poipet casinos. My informant at the border told me they were loitering on the same day Lisa Baxter disappeared. They usually detain Thai girls with gambling debts and send them overland to brothels in China. I'm concerned they decided to take a few white girls too."

Porter's chest tightened. Had Lisa Baxter and the others missing from Poipet been abducted and transported the same way, north to China? Had he missed the obvious, that separate groups were responsible for the Poipet and Bangkok disappearances? He removed a page from his imitation-leather briefcase and handed it to the skinny Cambodian handcuffed to the chair. It showed photos of the girls missing from Poipet.

The man glanced at the page then spoke to Veasna and dropped it.

"He says he hasn't seen any of them," Veasna told Porter. "But he also said all white girls look the same to him…"

Porter studied the gangster. His face and body were riddled with scars and cheap tattoos. He gazed up at him with the dull eyes of a man not easily frightened. "I know he's a tough guy and all but isn't he just a tad worried what you blokes are gunna do to him?" he asked Veasna. "Tell me more about this mob he works for."

"You're correct, he should be worried, but this code of silence is beat into these men from a young age… His gang are well-organized, ruthless criminals, who also aid drug smuggling into Thailand from sources in Vietnam. They're employed by corrupt Cambodian politicians who the General and I hope to expose. Me, because I despise them. And the General, well, because the Poipet border crossing comes under his jurisdiction."

Porter glanced to the General. If Poipet was the wild west, he was its sheriff. "So, what's our crook here said about the missing foreign girls?"

"Only that his gang aren't responsible," Veasna said. "I've waited for you to arrive before pressing him further."

"Cheers…So if he reckons his mob didn't take 'em, who did?"

Veasna spoke to the suspect in Khmer. The man shook his head and said nothing.

General Chea grunted then whacked the gangster's face. He pulled a pistol from under his jacket and aimed it at his head. "Let's test this 'code of silence' rubbish…Ask him again what you want to know," he instructed Veasna.

Veasna spoke to the suspect, who said nothing.

Chea stepped to the metal box on the desk. He removed a silencer and shouted in Khmer while the man watched him screw it onto the end of the pistol. Again the man shook his head, so Chea forced the pistol into his mouth. Eyes widened and the man's rapid breathing reached a crescendo before he nodded. Chea removed the pistol. The suspect ranted for two minutes unabated.

Veasna wrote in his notebook then turned to Porter. "He says Korean loan-sharks are taking the barang, the foreign girls. He says they send them to Bangkok to settle huge debts. And from there they're shipped to human-trafficking syndicates elsewhere."

Porter frowned as he made his own notes and mumbled to no-one in particular. "Koreans? Transporting 'em to Bangkok? And then on to where, and to who?" The information punched his guts and winded him, because the gangster's story was plausible. Sex-slave victims recovered by the Dragon Slayer taskforce had been transported to overseas buyers in shipping containers. "Do you believe him?"

"On the one hand, no, because he'll say anything to protect the scum he works for," Veasna replied. "But on the other, yes, because Korean loan-sharks led by a degenerate named Park Heung-min have been known to abduct girls from Poipet before. Only three months ago they detained a young Thai girl and held her family to ransom. I've heard Heung-min has gambling and cocaine addictions, so it's feasible that yes, he and his men needed a massive payday and saw your foreign girls as a means of getting it."

Chea growled. "My soldiers at the border also suspect Heung-min's crew have expanded their operations. This filth here," he pointed to the suspect, "knows I'm prepared to blow his head off and I think he's told the truth. Park Heung-min's a prime suspect, Agent Porter. You'd be wise to target him."

Porter dipped his head. "Fair enough." He faced Veasna. "How are the Koreans transporting the girls to

Bangkok? And it's a big joint, so where exactly are they shipping 'em out from? And to who?"

Veasna spoke to the suspect, who gave a short reply.

"He says he doesn't know about the transport to Bangkok. But they usually use medium sized trucks owned by criminal associates so I'd say it's what they're doing with these girls too…He has no idea who they send them to or where. He only knows they use a large shipping terminal south of Bangkok."

Porter inhaled then let air out in a huff. He needed Nok because he had limited knowledge of the geographical area referred to. "South of Bangkok? There's a lot of water south of Bangkok isn't there? That could be anywhere…"

Chea sniggered. "I think our simple fool meant to say the terminal's in the south of Bangkok…Not simply, south, of Bangkok…I lived there for several years, close to the river. The Khlong Toei shipping terminal is its largest, and, is in the south of the city."

Porter nodded. "Sounds like the one then…I'll look into it, hopefully after I've spoken to this Park Heung-min bloke."

General Chea gave a tight smile. "Excellent…Now, it's time for me to ask the questions." He went back to the box then returned to the suspect holding a large zip-locked bag. The bag contained crystal meth, ya-ice as the Thais called it.

Chea pulled the gangster's shorts down at the waist, dropped the bag onto black pubic hair then pulled them up again. The man's eyes darted about the room. He tried to wriggle in the chair and release the drugs from his shorts but couldn't. He suddenly had something to say for thirty seconds before Chea placed the pistol against his temple.

Chea shouted at the man in Khmer. The man shook his head.

The process repeated, over and over, louder and more aggressive each time.

"What's he saying?" Porter asked Veasna. He wondered if that was the true reason the Cambodians didn't want Nok in the room. Were they afraid she understood Khmer and would hear information they didn't want her to?

Veasna didn't reply. He stared at the General's interrogation.

Porter stepped closer and yelled in his ear. "Oi, Inspector, I asked you a question. What's going on?"

Veasna faced him. "Sorry…Ah, the General's telling the suspect to name his bosses, the corrupt politicians, and to sign a statement he'll prepare for him. He's refusing to, because they'll murder his whole family if he does."

"I've got one more question, about the smuggling route from Vietnam into Thailand he mentioned…Ask this bloke who runs that drug syndicate. Thais, Vietnamese, or Cambodians?"

Veasna nodded then spoke to the man.

The suspect spoke three syllables in reply before General Chea shot him twice in the back of the head.

Porter stepped aside just in time, avoiding the splatter of blood and brain. The gangster slumped forward in the chair with half his head missing. Porter stared then closed eyes, because a vision of Andrew Dawes' face had replaced the dead Cambodian's. Andrew Dawes, the raw SAS Lieutenant who'd panicked during a firefight in the Afghan desert and died after running into Porter's line of fire.

Porter exhaled, shook the image from his head then opened eyes. "What the fuck, General…Why? This bloke could've given further information."

Chea laughed in his face. "No, Agent Porter, this filth was a disgrace to our nation." He took the bag of crystal meth from the dead man's shorts. "And he was obviously dealing in this ghastly poison, the penalty for which is death." He turned to Veasna and laughed again. Wicked eyes glistened. "I save our taxpayers a fortune, Inspector. I'm the investigator, the judge, the jury and the executioner all rolled into one…Now, I must be going. You get this mess sorted away." He took his cap and the metal box from the desk, inclined his head towards Porter and strode from the room.

Porter thanked Veasna and said he'd be in touch.

Veasna leaned close to him. "Be careful," he whispered. "I sense there's something very unusual about Lost Angels. And I can see you're a dedicated cop so I'll give you my friendly advice… If you want your investigation to succeed and hope to survive it, trust no-one there in Thailand, both Thai and foreigner alike."

# FOURTEEN

Porter loosened his tie as he strolled down Sukhumvit Soi 18, one of the leafier streets he'd visited during his short time in Bangkok. Karen from 'Google Maps' told him he'd reached the Thai restaurant Helen had chosen for their midday lunch meeting. He thanked her, dropped his phone into breast pocket then stepped inside and scanned the dimly lit room.

Helen hadn't arrived so he took a table in the far corner and blew out the candle in the middle of it. He sat with back to the wall, with a view of the entire room and the narrow street beyond. He yawned then ordered black coffee from the waitress and hoped it'd be strong enough to demist his brain.

It had been close to midnight when he'd returned to his apartment from Phnom Penh. He'd crashed out the minute he rolled into bed and overslept until 10am. On waking he'd read a message from Helen. She'd received a response to the database searches requested of Thai government agencies regarding NGO's based in Bangkok and whether GAIT was a legally registered charity. He'd suggested they meet to go over the information but had more selfish motives for wanting to see her.

During the trip to Phnom Penh he had quizzed Nok about the events surrounding her birthday party on Tuesday night. She said he'd passed out in the club and bouncers had carried him to a taxi. Helen told her she'd gone in the taxi with him, helped him to his room and into bed. What had happened after that was the most pertinent of Porter's questions and only Helen could answer it.

She arrived in a taxi, wearing a low-cut blouse beneath a pant suit and a laptop bag on her shoulder. She waved and mouthed 'hi' as she approached Porter's table.

A grubby street urchin skipped alongside then ran ahead of her. He pulled a chair out and waited for her to sit. He helped her pull the chair in then bowed.

She ordered a pot of tea from the waitress. "Sorry I'm a bit late, the hairdresser took forever." She flicked her fringe back. "Do you like my new style?"

Porter failed to notice any difference but nodded anyway.

The boy faced him. He held out a flat palm, his grin as wide as his dark forehead.

Porter frowned while he fished inside his trouser pocket. He pulled out a ten-baht coin and gave it to him. "There you go champ, buy some water."

The boy ignored the coin and kept his hand out.

Helen avoided eye contact with Porter as she wriggled in the chair. "I think he wants more."

"Nah, not happening," he told the boy. "Off you go."

The boy smiled like an angel at her. He snarled at Porter. "You falang kee nok. No good…" He skipped from the table, dodged a playful smack on the bum from the waitress then waited on the pavement for his next target.

Helen took her phone from laptop bag. She giggled as she pressed the screen. "Farang kee nok," she said eloquently into the phone as though speaking to a hard of hearing grandmother.

Porter grinned. "That's what the kid just said. 'Foreigner', then something…"

She laughed as she read from the phone. "'Nok' is the word for a bird, and 'Kee nok' means bird shit. 'Farang kee nok' is Thai slang." She laughed again. "He just called you a stingy foreigner. A cheap Charlie."

Porter chuckled. "Cheeky bugger. So much for Thailand not having a tipping culture."

"The locals don't tip. And neither did tourists apparently, until American and Aussie soldiers came along during the Vietnam war." She pulled a bundle of A4 paper from her bag and laid it on the table. "Right, first thing…Fon and Jaru's trip to Poipet was a waste of time. Thai and Cambodian officials from the border control office didn't even acknowledge their authority to ask questions. The casinos refused to let them view surveillance footage and Cambodian soldiers threatened then virtually ran them out of the place."

He grunted. "That doesn't surprise me…Tim and his mates haven't been spotted since Tuesday…What's the latest on Headmaster Saysamone?"

She stared at the table. "Still no sign of him. And still no contact between any of the missing girls and their family members. No use of email, phones, bank accounts. Nothing."

"Saysamone remains a suspect. But only for Lisa's abduction because I don't reckon he's involved with the others."

She nodded and cleared her throat. She turned a page then skimmed over the next one. "I only picked these reports up a few hours ago and haven't had a chance to read them all. I'll give you a full written summary

127

later…In short, the searches on GAIT came back a total blank."

"Yeah? They're not a registered NGO?"

"That's what's so very weird about this…They are registered as an NGO, a charity, and a Thai limited company. But there's no record of a director, employees, contact details, or any physical location they're working from."

He wobbled his head. "No paper trail at all?"

She waited for the waitress to pour her a cup of tea and leave. "Nothing, no trails of any sort…And when I searched for an electronic one, I was told that queries on all transactions under the GAIT company name have been blocked by the Bank of Thailand. Even if we did have their financial details we couldn't obtain transaction records under the usual anti money-laundering regulations and so on…The traces I requested on IP addresses associated with their website were denied too, which is weird again, because as of this morning the website no longer exists."

"Bloody hell, the whole lot of 'em are dodgier than FIFA…This info confirms GAIT's bogus and nothing but a front for criminal enterprise. A legitimate organization of their size can't operate without a physical office or headquarters."

"I agree we're up against deeply entrenched corruption across multiple government agencies, because it's taken a lot of work to make all their assets and activity untraceable. Invisible, as though they don't exist."

"Question is, what do these crooks gain from using this dodgy NGO? In a way it brings more attention to 'em, which makes no sense if they're only involved in drug supply…So I reckon Tim and his mates must gain contacts via the fake NGO who then aid their syndicate's human-trafficking."

"These reports suggest they have many contacts. Which ones specifically?"

He paused to think. "Contacts in the Immigration Bureau…Nok said cops in Nana turn a blind eye to African hookers and dealers staying here on expired visas." He nodded to the file in her hand. "What did the searches of immigration databases bring up on GAIT?"

"To be honest I haven't looked at those yet…" She skimmed over pages then stabbed a finger at one. "You're right, there's something here." She ran a finger down the page as she read. "Okay, we have GAIT sponsoring more than forty student visa applications in the past year…But, it looks as though good old corruption has raised its ugly head once again."

"How's that?"

"GAIT sponsored the visas but the only 'contacts' listed seem to be admin staff from the relevant universities."

He huffed. "Typical." An image flashed, of African hookers standing along Sukhumvit road. "And let me guess… All the students are Nigerian?"

She read again then nodded.

"That confirms what we'd suspected," he said. "GAIT's bringing 'em to Bangkok to sell Thai drugs and African bodies… I've got another lead to look into but I'll ask Sawatri to task Fon with stepping up efforts to find these kids. We only need one to say how they got here and there's a fair chance it'll lead us to the bloke running GAIT."

"Or, the woman who's running it?" She smirked. "Whoever they are, they have friends in very high places."

"Yeah, no doubt."

"What's the other lead you're chasing up?"

"How much do you know about the Korean loan-shark mobs operating in Thailand?"

Her eyes darted everywhere but his face. "What makes you ask about them?"

He hesitated while Inspector Veasna's words echoed. *Trust no-one in Thailand, Thai and foreigner alike.* "I remember reading about a Thai girl taken from a Poipet casino earlier this year. The Koreans were suspects then. Maybe they should be for the Lost Angels girls now?"

She shuffled papers and put others into neat piles. She took a few pages from the top of a pile, bound them with a paperclip then handed them to him. "I know quite a lot about the Koreans…I prepared that report last month when foreign girls first started disappearing from Poipet. I forwarded a copy to each of the Thai agents, because like you, I felt the loan-sharks should be targeted. But none of them seemed interested…Nok admitted she didn't even bother reading it because she's so certain they aren't responsible for the abductions."

He nodded, pleased with himself. He'd been wise not to tell Nok what he'd learned from the Cambodian gangster in Phnom Penh. He didn't have complete trust in the other members of Lost Angels, certain they'd kept important evidence from him, and worried she'd share the Cambodian's allegations with them.

He skimmed over the first page of the report. "You certain about this Heung-min bloke being their boss?"

130

"Yes. He's one of the most feared criminals in all of Asia."

Her statement both reinforced what Veasna had said and confirmed his suspicions. Heung-min was their man, at least for the foreign girls abducted from Poipet. "I've heard some of these Korean blokes like to gamble…You reckon we'll locate Heung-min at one of the underground gambling dens you've listed?"

"Aha, and amongst the high-rollers you'll find Thai actors, other famous celebrities, members of the hi-so, politicians, etcetera…The dens are highly illegal in a country where gambling's supposedly frowned upon, underground and exclusive in every way. The most popular one and Heung-min's favourite is beneath 'Babylon', what's supposedly a huge massage parlor but is essentially an exclusive mega-brothel. Judging from the few pictures available, the gambling area is more like a plush casino and unconfirmed reports say Heung-min resides in a luxurious apartment next to it. 'Babylon Towers' houses residential apartments directly above Babylon and numerous intelligence reports suggest that a restricted access elevator goes directly from the tower to the basement level gambling area."

"Interesting…Gambling's highly illegal yet untouchable?"

"Honest cops within the CCD and DSI, anti-corruption crusaders, have tried to close them down but higher powers always stop it from happening. There's just too much money involved for them not to."

"Do the Koreans own some of these joints?"

"Oh, no, they're rich but relative paupers in the company they keep…These buildings are prime real estate along Ratchadaphisek road. Worth billions of baht and said to be owned by the wealthiest of the elite in business partnerships between high-ranking police, corrupt governors, judges, politicians and so on. Even Chief Abbots…"

"Chief Abbots?"

"Head monks, one the largest and most influential temples."

"Bloody hell, these casino operators sound as dodgy as those back in Oz." He recalled an operation a good mate had worked on where criminal-backed casinos had been prosecuted for their involvement in international money laundering. Were the Koreans and other crooks doing the same in Bangkok? Not necessarily trading in cash but other goods? Other niche, in-demand goods like sex-slaves?

Helen called the waitress over and ordered Thai dishes with rice. She packed the reports into her bag then glanced at him as she placed it on the floor. They made eye contact for the first time during the meeting.

He did his best to conceal a gulp then told her Nok's version of how events had transpired on Tuesday night. He asked Helen how she remembered them.

"It's as Nok said, Dan…You passed out and we assumed you'd had too much to drink. The others said they needed to search around Nana for Tim and co. I'd picked your keys from the floor when you fell so volunteered to take you home. I did and then put you straight to bed."

"Cheers for that, it sounds like I was in a bad way…Did you…It sounds crazy, but did you change my undies for some reason?"

"Yes, I put you into fresh boxers." She smirked. "But don't worry, I didn't take a peek downstairs."

He nodded. "So, ah, we didn't…?"

"Shag? No… Not saying I wouldn't have said yes but you were in no state to and I'd never take advantage of someone like that."

He let out a 'Phew', louder than intended. He analyzed her face for signs of a lie, because something about her defensive tone of voice made him doubt her. "You're being fair dinkum, yeah? I need to know the truth."

"Dan, nothing happened and I've no idea how large or small your package is." She smirked as she tilted her head. "But I did notice the tattoos on your chest…The one on the right side, I guess that's military of some sort? And the letter 'B' over your heart. What's the 'B' stand for?"

"Yeah, it's military, my SAS regiment's shield."

"And the 'B'?"

"Listen, Helen, I remember stuff all of what happened on Tuesday night and reckon my drink was spiked…Did you see anyone acting sus around my beer?"

"No, and I've no idea who might've done it. But I'll chase up the club's CCTV footage if you like?" She smiled, leaned closer and took hold of his hand. "Yes, you were very drunk but I know you kissed me on the dancefloor and that our kiss meant something. I could feel it."

He patted her hand with his other then slowly pulled them apart. She watched him closely, as though she wanted to devour every inch of him. Bloody hell, had he led her on without knowing it? Had he enjoyed her obvious infatuation too much?

He met her gaze. "H, I'm sorry if I've sent the wrong signals. The other night was a mistake…I'm getting

133

married soon, to a wonderful lady who I love very much."

Her face reddened in an instant. "Well you should've fucking thought about that before you stuck your tongue down my throat and decided to flirt every day…" She took a bank note from purse and slammed it onto the table.

"What? Listen, I've told you why I acted that way. Not proud of it, but I wasn't in control. We still have to work together… Can't we stay mates?"

"What a pathetic excuse." She plucked her bag from the floor then stood. Her eyes and mouth widened as though a sudden realization had slapped her face. "You arsehole. You think I spiked your drink to get you into bed. You think I'm some kind of psycho stalker bitch? Well fuck you, Dan Porter, and fuck being your mate!"

He blew hot air at the ceiling then watched her storm from the restaurant, knowing he'd lost one of the few in Bangkok who'd been on his side. And if she'd told the truth, it meant someone else had spiked his drink. Who? Jaru hovered and winked at him. He seethed as he imagined punching his smug face to a bloody pulp.

He finished reading Helen's profile on Heung-min's loan-sharks, sat for a further ten minutes to formulate a plan and smiled when it came to him. Roulette was Heung-min's favourite game of chance and according to the report he was in luck, because Thursday night at the Babylon casino was said to be the featured roulette night.

He studied maps on his phone then sent Nok a message. Could she meet him later, 9pm at the entrance to Sutthisan subway station on Ratchadaphisek road? A minute passed before she replied in the affirmative and asked why. He told her to dress up for a night on the town, arrive via taxi, and to come unarmed.

He left money on the table for food that hadn't been touched then dawdled out the front door. He swiveled on the pavement to scan the street in both directions. The Nana area and a search for African hookers beckoned, but the walk there in scorching heat would do nothing for his foul mood so he decided to take a taxi. He spotted one to his right, parked against the curb in front of a white SUV, and headed for it.

The urchin from the restaurant appeared from nowhere. He pointed at Porter and danced around him as he laughed. "Falang kee nok…You very bad man. Lady think no good."

Porter threw him another coin then watched him skip away. "Yes, little mate, as I've already been well and truly told."

He placed a hand on the rear passenger-side door handle and the taxi driver started the car. He pulled the door. Stuck? Locked? He pointed to it and the driver motioned for him to get in on the other side.

Porter strolled around the back of the taxi to the rear drivers-side door. The door didn't budge so he tapped on the window for the driver to unlock it. An engine roared, bloody loud. Too loud to be coming from the taxi. Porter let go of the handle then spun to his left to face the black pickup truck speeding directly at him.

He yanked at the door. Still locked, with the truck now less than ten meters from him. He had nowhere to run so braced himself and prepared to jump out of the way at the last second.

But he didn't have to because the white SUV parked against the curb darted forward and blocked the pickup's path.

Brakes screeched and tires smoked as the pickup skidded then stopped inches from a collision. Wheels spun and it reversed away from the SUV.

Porter glanced to the SUV's front seat. He couldn't be certain through the dark tinted windows but thought he saw a blond, Caucasian man driving it.

He sprinted after the black pickup truck. Its windows were dark and mirrored and he couldn't see its driver. The truck reversed thirty meters, swung into a U-turn then sped off in the direction it had come from.

Porter heard a car behind him and leaped onto the pavement. He looked for a registration plate on the pickup but it didn't have one. And neither did the white SUV as it roared past him then disappeared in pursuit of it.

He sucked moist air into lungs then blew it out with force. He walked back towards the restaurant and found shade while waiting for his heart to stop pounding ribs. It had been another attempt on his life by some bastard driving a black pickup truck. The same that'd tried to run him down at the airport?

The white SUV's involvement perplexed him. It angered him too, because it would've been tailing him all day and he'd failed to notice it. And was its driver Caucasian? If so, someone other than Dignitary Protection cops had saved his life. Who the hell were they? And why?

He stepped up to the taxi and its curbside window slid down. He handed the driver a fifty-baht note. "She's

136

right, mate, I'm gunna take the skytrain... I reckon it's gotta be safer than these bloody roads of yours."

# FIFTEEN

Porter gasped when Nok stepped from a taxi at the Ratchadaphisek road entrance to Sutthisan subway station at 9.15pm. She was a combination of sexy and elegance, wrapped in a blood-red cocktail dress that displayed ample bosom and barely covered her knees. She smiled when she got closer and he stared at her full lips as they glistened in the same seductive color.

"Wow, look at you all handsome in your suit. And what's with the fake moustache and the fancy metallic briefcase?" She sniggered as she studied him. "So this is what Mata Hari and Hercule Poirot's love-child would've looked like?"

He fiddled with the thick mustache and forced himself not to scratch the itchy skin underneath. "You're cracking me up... Look, no-one where we're going should know me but it's just to be sure. And c'mon, it's a decent enough disguise, yeah? I reckon it looks, as Sawatri would say, rather debonair."

She giggled, handed him a clutch bag then bent to adjust her dress. "What are you up to, Dan?" She straightened and her eyes squinted. "Why couldn't I bring my gun? And where are we going that I couldn't drive to?"

He returned her bag. He turned and pointed to an illuminated high-rise building fifty meters away on the same side of the road. "Babylon Towers. I read that its lobby restaurant does great seafood."

She frowned. "There are plenty of seafood places close to our office. Why here? I never come to this part of town and I already ate."

He grinned as he linked an elbow around hers. "No worries, we'll just have a few drinks until you're peckish again."

It took them five minutes to reach Babylon Towers' street-level entrance and take an elevator to the third floor. He managed to keep her engaged in conversation about her day, to avoid a barrage of questions and discourage use of her phone.

He turned right on leaving the elevator and dismissed her protests they'd gone past the lobby. He led her to the end of an expensively finished corridor, a sparkling tunnel of flawless white marble, then stopped in front of a smaller elevator with a single gold-colored door. He bent to press a wall-mounted, electronic number pad and entered six digits. After a few seconds the door slid open. He stepped inside and beckoned her to join him.

Her perfect face crumpled. "Where exactly are we going? This place is weird, like a sleazy brothel or something."

He smirked, because she was spot on. "I told you, it's a surprise." He closed the door once she'd entered then pressed the button for basement level 4. He faced her as they descended. "I came here earlier today for a sticky-beak, following up on some info…I was lucky to find a cleaner who understood I'd pay her a thousand baht if she could find out where this 'special' elevator was and provide me the restricted access code for it."

"And this special elevator is taking us to…? How did you even find out about it?"

The elevator whirred to a halt and the door opened to reveal a golden corridor more impressive than the white one. A thick-set Asian man in tuxedo held the door open and waved them forward. They joined a short queue of similarly dressed, glamourous couples. Porter was the only 'farang' man waiting to pass through the narrow doorway fifteen meters ahead and all but two of the nine Asian men had a gorgeous blonde on his arm.

Nok pulled him close. She pointed to the granite covered wall and a glittering sign written in Thai. "That says 'Babylon'…You do realize what this place is?"

"Yeah, it's a dodgy casino beneath a dodgy brothel."

"And you didn't care to say we were coming here…Why?"

"Would you have, if I'd told you? There's a bloke inside I wanna chat with."

She glared at him then peered ahead and wriggled with excitement. "Oh my Buddha, my favourite actor's here. And famous singers, hi-so, celebrity plastic surgeons, other members of the elite…So the rumors about exclusive gambling dens are true?" She paused and stared at the ground as though deep in thought. "No, this isn't good, it's too dangerous for you to be here. For both of us to be here…I just saw a few police bosses and high-ranking politicians go in. We have to leave, because if they catch you trying to sneak in who knows what they'll do. It's happened to Special Branch guys before. They came looking for these gambling dens and haven't been seen since." She tried to pull him back to the elevator.

He stood his ground. "Relax, no-one's gunna recognize me with this fuzz under my nose. And yeah, you might know them but have they got any clue about you?"

She sucked a breath and shook her head, visibly flustered.

"Good, then there's no reason to get your knickers in a knot." He glanced to the entrance. "Follow me." He held up the metal briefcase. "Tell security at the door I'm a high-roller who's here to repay a debt to one of their regular customers."

Bemusement masked her face. "This is crazy."

"Just play along and get me inside." He bypassed the queue and strode towards the entrance, ignoring her whispered argument and snarls of disgust from those in line.

He approached the middle one of three men guarding the doorway. He gave his most arrogant smile then pointed to Nok as she stopped alongside him.

She huffed as though to compose herself then spoke in Thai.

The security man replied, his demeanor calm but firm.

"He wants to know the name of the guy you're indebted to," she told Porter.

He returned the man's serious stare. "Tell him it's private but has been pre-arranged, and that the bloke I'm meeting is gunna be pissed-off if he doesn't get his play money tonight."

The security operative listened as Nok relayed the message. He took the briefcase from Porter and weighed it in one hand.

Porter held his breath and hoped he'd packed enough old magazines inside for the man to believe it full of cash.

He eyed Porter up and down then returned the briefcase. He grunted to the other security men, who frisked them for weapons. They nodded when they were done and stepped aside.

Porter took Nok's arm and they strutted through the doorway, down stairs and onto the illegal casino's main floor. He sensed suspicious eyes watching so led her away from them, along a red-velvet walkway with four rows of gaming tables on either side. The gamblers murmured inquisitively and shot glances of disdain at the newcomers.

Porter turned his back on the far wall when he reached it. Nok did the same. Despite the high ceilings, cigarette smoke hung thick in the air and stung his eyes as they scanned the expansive room. He glanced to a row of Craps tables on his left. A blonde woman threw dice then shrieked at a win. Onlookers clapped and cheered in feigned delight. Her overly charming date pecked her cheek. Losers groaned and slithered away from the table.

He analyzed the whole room and guessed there were two-hundred people in it. Then he studied those crowded around the nearest table. He'd never seen so many false smiles, fake cleavages and genuine Rolexes in the one place.

"We shouldn't stay too long," Nok said. "If looks could kill I would've died a hundred times already…Let's go check out the other side, behind the Craps tables."

She walked to their left then returned to the wall when he didn't follow.

"You look like a vegan who's been locked in a butcher's cool-room all night…And you haven't stopped fidgeting since we got here, which isn't like you. What's up?"

She hesitated. "Yes, I'm stressed out…Some of the country's most influential people are in this room. You think they want Interpol agents sniffing around, that they want the adoring public to know what they really get up to after dark?"

"Who says we're Interpol agents? Right?"

He pressed the fake mustache against his face then fished phone from pocket and selected a photo. He memorized the face in it, replaced the phone and shifted his gaze to the row of roulette tables on his right.

Bingo! First time. Porter saw him standing at the head of the third table, surrounded by four thugs in suits. He was solid and looked more muscular than fat. He wore a short-sleeved dress shirt two sizes too small and baggy trousers. He howled at the ceiling like a crazed wolf while three gorgeous Asian girls pretended to adore him.

"Dan, this is ridiculous…Who are we looking for?"

Porter pointed at the howling Korean then smirked as he realized who his high-cut hairstyle and chubby face reminded him of. "That bloke there, Park Heung-min the Korean loan- shark boss. The Kim Jong-Un on steroids…"

She spun to face him with brow furrowed. "What? Why?"

"Because him and his crew have taken girls from Poipet before, they're regulars here and probably had gambling debts to settle. They might've settled 'em by grabbing a few white girls and I reckon they need to be questioned…If you'd bothered to read Helen's report on 'em you might already know that."

He watched all color drain from her face. Did she already know?

He stepped towards the roulette tables.

She yanked him back by the elbow. "Don't give me that nonsense, that Helen's intel reports led you here…Those pricks in Phnom Penh nominated the Koreans, didn't they?" She leered. "Why didn't you tell me? It's because you don't trust me, isn't it?" She scoffed. "You're no different from Veasna and his bigoted crew, making assumptions all Thai cops are crooked."

"They did mention Heung-min, but Hel--."

"Yes, the Cambodians dangled the loan-sharks as bait, to throw you off their own scent. And you gobbled it up."

He took a deep breath then let it out in a rush. She made a valid point, because it was feasible the Cambodian gangster had lied for that very reason. He led her into a deserted corner, away from prying eyes and ears. "Listen, we can't go around discounting information just because its source's motivation, might, be tainted…It's part of the art of cultivating and using informants…Didn't they teach you any of that in criminology 101?"

She poked his chest. "This is my city, my country, and we'll do this my way…It's too dangerous to approach Heung-min here in his comfort zone. We're unarmed, remember, and we'll get no help if he and his men turn nasty. Let me speak to him alone and arrange for an interview in our office."

"With tea and scones? Bloody hell, Nok, why would one of Asia's top crooks just waltz in for questioning when he knows we've got stuff all on him? Don't be so bloody naïve…Listen, I've done things your way for three days now and it's gotten this investigation frickin' nowhere…From here on I'll do it my way, whether you like it or not."

He stepped past her. She tried to hold him back but he broke her grip and strode towards Heung-min's table. He got to within three meters of it when a stocky young thug with a thick scar down one cheek intercepted him. A second thug came alongside and they blocked his path to the table.

The stocky thug glanced sideways to Nok and smiled at her. He snarled up at Porter. "We haven't seen you here before," he said in perfect English. "Who are you and what do you want?"

"My name's Provan and I'd like a word with your boss. In private."

"Regarding?"

He held up the briefcase. "A business proposition…"

The thug grunted then walked back to Heung-min.

Heung-min nodded while he spoke into the thug's ear. When finished, he huffed like a spoilt child then glared from Nok to Porter then back to Nok. He led his gaggle of whores and henchmen from the casino via a guarded side-door.

The stocky thug returned. "Mr Provan, my boss said to please enjoy the casino's bar for half an hour as his guest. I will then come and take you to him."

Porter nodded then watched him leave through the same side-door. He turned to Nok. "I'm sorry, sweet, that got out of hand…You gunna hang around?"

She faked a scowl then playfully punched his arm. "You can be a real prick sometimes, Porter." She smirked. "And yes, I'm going with you to meet Heung-min. But only to stop you from getting your arrogant ass killed because I don't care for the paperwork…And Provan? Where did you pull that name from?"

"I dunno, it's the first that came to me. He was a footy player, a Dragon's legend."

"A what legend?"

"Doesn't matter…Now where's this bar? I need a beer or three."

An hour later they followed the stocky thug from the casino through the restricted access side-door, down a long corridor and into a luxurious apartment. He locked the front door, nodded to the thug guarding it, then led them into an enormous open-plan living area.

Porter smiled at three Asian girls who drank from champagne glasses while they frolicked in a bubble-filled jacuzzi on the left side of the room. He assumed they were Heung-min's companions from the casino. One wiped soap away then flashed jangling naked breasts at him. The other two giggled and followed suit.

The stocky thug moved to a leather sofa on the right side of the room and sat on one end of it.

Park Heung-min was seated on the other end. He snorted lines of coke from a coffee table. Porter knew from reading his profile that he was forty-two but up close he could've passed for thirty. His skin was pale, with a wax-like sheen that made his black eyes look like bottomless round pits on an otherwise spotless salt-lake. He looked up and sniffed as he wiped his nose against a thick forearm. He leaned back into the sofa with hands on his head and flexed bulging biceps in tandem. He told them to sit on the sofa opposite.

Heung-min eyed Nok then smiled like a deviant. "You're one of the prettiest whores I've seen in a long

146

time. Very tasty, high-class…" He'd been born in the North Korean city of Pukchong but educated in Seoul. He spoke fluent English in a guttural tone. "And while I'm hoping Mr Provan will share you at some stage, we won't get you out of that lovely dress just yet."

Nok didn't reply. She cocked her head and smiled as though she hadn't understood.

Heung-min looked to the jacuzzi and shouted in a language Porter thought was Thai. A naked woman in her early twenties stepped out of it, grabbed a towel from the wall and trotted to the sofa. She gave the towel to Heung-min. He dried her flawless brown stomach then picked her up with ease and laid her across his lap. He prepared a line of cocaine from her navel to the hairless mound between her legs then snorted it. She giggled, sat up and pecked his cheek. He slapped her buttocks as she trotted back to the jacuzzi.

Porter frowned, unsure what Heung-min had tried to prove. Then he glanced to the stocky thug sat opposite and noticed him smiling at Nok. He turned to watch her. She averted eyes from both of them.

Heung-min fixed his stare on Porter. "Now, Mr Provan, what's this business proposition you have?"

"Maybe you'd prefer my lovely date gave the sales pitch?" Porter said to Nok as much as Heung-min. "I mean, I've got a feeling you've all met before…"

Heung-min grinned as he stood and sauntered forward. He stood in front of Nok, cupped her chin in an open hand then lifted her face. "Do I know this lovely little bird of yours, Mr Provan? I've never seen this whore in my life but there's little doubt she knows who I am, as do all the pieces of flesh for hire who frequent these burrows of sin…And unlike those pompous posers

147

in the casino next door, my celebrity status comes courtesy of being feared as one of Southeast Asia's cruelest monsters." He stooped to bring his lips close to hers.

Her face trembled.

Heung-min spoke slowly. "You know me? You see me before?"

She shook her head.

Heung-min gripped her chin and twisted it.

She winced then shifted her wide-eyed stare at Porter. She blinked once.

He took it as a signal that she was okay and needed him to remain calm.

Heung-min shouted at the stocky thug, who took a handgun from the coffee table and passed it to him. Heung-min snarled down at Nok, holding the pistol in one hand and her crumpled face in the other.

"Seeing as we're both gambling men, Mr Provan," Heung-min said, "let's play a little game of chance." He placed the barrel against her temple.

Porter lunged forward then stopped, because Nok shook her head as she sucked frightened breaths and the stocky thug had aimed his pistol at him.

"You've fooled no-one with your high-roller impersonation." Heung-min sneered at Porter. "You see, I have a very good nose for bacon, and not only do you smell like a cop…" He reached across and ripped the mustache from Porter's face. "But you look like one too." He laughed at the ceiling. "I know exactly who you are but want you tell me…And why the fuck did you come here to embarrass me in this my private den?"

"Alright, mate." Porter held hands up. "I'll tell you whatever you want but leave the lady alone."

Heung-min nodded. "Yes, you will…And if you tell the truth only you have to play the game. But if you lie?" He let go of Nok's face and swept fingers across her heaving chest. "First I'll let my men have their way and then I'll splatter her lovely head all over this wall."

Heung-min sat then clicked fingers.

The young thug left the room. He returned a minute later and placed two bottles containing red liquid on the table in front of Heung-min.

"To win this game of chance, Agent Porter, you must tell me exactly why you're here…And then, if you wish to save this pretty whore's life, you'll drink from one of these bottles." A wicked gleam filled Heung-min's eyes. "I suggest you choose very carefully…One bottle contains lao khao, a foul but harmless rice whiskey. The other? Well, that's whiskey too, but laced with enough fentanyl that a mouthful of it will kill you."

# SIXTEEN

*Diary      Thursday 27 Sept. (I think)*

*I counted eleven bells ringing not so long ago. From somewhere not too far away. So I think it must be close to midnight now. And I'm scared. Scared that I've made the guy very angry and he'll stop giving me what I need. The heroin.*

*This morning was different from the others. The old lady came first and cleaned me all over and she even washed my hair. She made me stare at the wall the whole time so I couldn't see her. And then she brought me a gorgeous white dress and told me to put it on. That's when she spoke for the first time. Her voice was old and her accent was a bit like the Cambodian teachers I worked with. She said I looked beautiful and was ready for the 'big day'. What fucking big day? Weird.*

*And then I had this strange feeling that I know the guy who's keeping me here. I started thinking about the day I got taken at the border crossing and I remembered that I thought I'd seen the headmaster, Mr Saysamone. I've had crazy thoughts that I'm here locked away in his house and maybe the sicko freak wants to marry me. Is that the 'big day'? My god, please someone get me out of here.*

*Today the guy, My Saysamone or whoever he is, came later than usual. Sometime in the afternoon. And I hate him because he made me wait. He usually injects me first thing but he made me lie on the bed in my robe. And he kissed my body all over and then he. Licked me. You know. Down there. I'm ashamed that I let him but all I wanted was that needle in my arm and the escape it brings. I couldn't risk making him angry and not giving it to me.*

*But then he did get angry. When he pulled the sack up to my nose and tried to stick his stinking penis in my mouth I just couldn't let him. I gagged and almost vomited. Then he pulled the sack down and slapped me across the head and untied me. And then he left the room and hasn't come back.*

*It's confusing. I need the heroin. My body craves it and can't stop shaking. But I think I need him too. His touch and the human contact. Even if he is violent. I hate being alone.*

*I can't sleep and hope he comes soon. When he does I'll tell him I'm sorry and I'll give him whatever he wants.*

# SEVENTEEN

Porter watched Heung-min unscrew caps from the bottles. He noticed a thin brown snake infused in each, coiled from top to bottom.

Heung-min took two shot glasses from the young thug and placed them on the table. "In this form the rice whiskey's known as snake wine. We've poured a tasteless red dye in each bottle to remove the slight color difference…" He smirked at Porter then filled each glass from a different bottle. "It's said to have medicinal properties…"

Porter stared at the red liquid. "Yeah, except when it's mixed with pure fentanyl… I've seen what that stuff does to junkies and it aint pretty."

"A painful death never is…" Heung-min pushed the shot glasses across the table, closer to Porter. "Now tell me, why did you come to Babylon?"

Porter eyed Nok. "Let the girl go, she knows nothing. It's only me you want."

Heung-min chuckled. "That may be true, that she's harmless…But protecting her is your only motivation for playing my game of chance. I can see it in your eyes that you don't fear death. Those same eyes also tell me that you have feelings for this whore."

Porter sucked a long breath through his nose. It hissed as he let it out through gritted teeth. "Listen, you already know who I am and who I work for. And my bosses know I'm here. You reckon they won't come looking if I don't leave this place?"

Heung-min leaned back and met his gaze. "You're lying...Your superiors have no idea you're here because they'd never allow you to come in the first place. The existence of some things, the Babylon casino for example, are too embarrassing for the rich and famous involved to admit to. And besides, very few know this apartment exists. It's one of the most secure locations in Bangkok and you'd never be found, even if your imaginary friends did come looking for you. And as I said, I want to hear the truth from you...Why exactly are you here?"

"Alright...Young backpackers are missing in Thailand and I've been sent here to find 'em."

"See, isn't the truth liberating, Agent Porter? And that's wonderful news for your whore, as now only you must choose a glass to drink from."

Porter winced. "I came here tonight because you've been named as a suspect. Because your men were spotted in Poipet when girls were taken. What can you tell me about that?"

"Ah, Porter, look around...What part of this scene, with my man's gun aimed at your head, suggests that you're in a position to ask the questions?"

Porter stared at him.

Heung-min smirked. "Every game of chance must offer reward. And I being the generous man that I am, will offer you two... If you drink from a glass I promise not to harm your pretty whore. Then if you survive the game, I'll tell you everything I know about the missing white girls."

Porter leaned forward. Trembling fingers curled around the nearest shot glass.

Nok pulled his hand away from it. She stilted her speech. "No. He will not shoot us."

A fiendish grin spread across Heung-min's face. He yelled at the stocky thug in Korean then leaned back on the sofa with hands clasped behind head.

The thug marched to the jacuzzi and shot the middle girl in the shoulder. She screamed and cowered behind the other two. White bubbles became red.

Nok gasped.

Porter scoffed. "You blokes are insane."

The thug sat next to Heung-min then levelled his pistol at Nok.

"Drink, Porter," Heung-min said, "or your pretty whore is next."

Porter didn't doubt him. To drink was his only chance at survival and learning the truth. He frowned as a vision of Jane flashed through his mind. He grabbed a glass and raised in to within an inch of dry lips. He closed eyes, said a quick prayer to no-one in particular, then forced the putrid liquid down his throat.

It burned as he swallowed. After a few seconds he gulped. He opened eyes. Nok and the men stared at him with stunned disbelief etched on their faces.

She leaned across him to force eye contact. "You okay?"

Porter felt the burning sensation flow to his stomach then subside. He nodded.

Heung-min snickered. "You chose well, Agent Porter. The lao khao tastes like shit but the fentanyl would've started to kill you by now. Bravo for surviving the ultimate game of chance." He spoke to the young thug, who lowered his gun then moved to the jacuzzi and tried to calm the whimpering hookers.

154

Porter coughed to remove the last trace of whiskey from his throat. "You like your games and I got lucky… Now, are you a bloke of your word?"

Heung-min nodded. "A cop who'd risk his life for missing strangers is of a rare breed in my opinion. You have my respect and your reward shall be the truth."

"If you blokes didn't take the foreign girls, who did?"

"Firstly, I'm curious to know... Who suggested I've had anything to do with it?"

"A Cambodian crook linked to human-traffickers in Poipet reckons you blokes abducted the girls to settle debts."

Heung-min chortled. "And you believed the word of a desperate criminal? You don't suppose he lied to protect the corrupt politicians those gangsters work for?"

Porter paused to think. "His info was on the money. He told me about the huge terminal in Bangkok and that you blokes are sending girls from it in shipping containers. I'm gunna have those docks searched and Customs are gunna check every cargo manifest. What's the name of that place again?"

"Khlong Toei doc…" Heung-min cut himself short then frowned.

Porter smirked. "Yeah, spot on. The Khlong Toei docks."

"Search all you want. You'll find nothing there to incriminate my men or the Cambodian gangs."

"Then who?"

Heung-min glanced to Nok before fixing his stare on Porter. "Word is, some whacko religious guys from a church backed NGO have lured the girls and sold them."

Porter thought of Tim and God's Angels in Thailand. "Any names been mentioned?"

Heung-min shook his head. "I've heard very little. Only that the NGO send the foreign girls out from Khlong Toei's deep-water docks to buyers in mainland China. Powerful, high-ranking men are involved. Both the suppliers and their clients…"

"China? Any idea who's running the NGO, or who these 'powerful' blokes are?"

"No, Porter, I don't know." Heung-min sighed. "Now, it's time for you and your pretty whore to leave. And kindly don't come back. I'm certain Babylon's owners won't allow a second breach of security, so if you value your companion's life it's best you stay away."

"And its owners are?"

"Even I don't know the answer to that. It's one of the best kept secrets in all of Thailand." Heung-min faked a smile then told the young thug to escort them from the casino.

Five minutes later Nok hailed a taxi on Ratchadaphisek road. Porter joined her on the back seat.

She prodded a finger into his chest. "Don't ever do that again!" She glared. "You nearly got us killed."

"Calm down…We're both okay and mission accomplished. Do you believe what Heung-min said?"

"Yes, I do…How would he know an NGO's responsible for the abductions if he hadn't in fact heard it from criminal associates? And he used the words 'church backed'. Very specific."

"True, I thought the same. It's one crazy triangle of deception going on here…Cambodians name the Koreans, who in turn name the foreign NGO workers."

156

"We suspected GAIT and Heung-min's info confirms it. It's a relief because we can now focus on them entirely, on finding Tim and friends."

Porter leaned back against the seat and let hot air out in a huff.

"What is it?" she said.

"A stabbing pain in my guts, telling me that if these girls have been sent to China in shipping containers the modus operandi reeks of KA because it's exactly how they transported hundreds of sex-slaves around the world... Steve Williams reckons we missed one of their main associates, someone based in Southeast Asia not named in the Cumal Files. I'm worried he's right and they're still very active...And maybe Tim and his GAIT mates are working for 'em?"

"It's possible..." Her phone beeped. She fished it from handbag and fiddled with it. "It's a message from Helen. We have time to go to our apartments and change clothes. Then we're taking a flight up north."

He checked his watch. "What? It's after midnight."

She studied the illuminated phone screen. "Helen says that Saysamone has used his private email account. It's been tracked to an IP address registered to a house in central Chiang Mai."

"But didn't Chiang Mai cops already search his mum's place up there and find nothing?"

"Yes but this is a different address. And I don't trust the local cops so we won't be telling anyone we're coming."

"Fair enough... I doubt Saysamone has Lisa or any of the other girls but it's worth a shot." Headlights from oncoming traffic shone on her face. He watched her as he thought back to their meeting in the casino. "I'll be honest, Nok, there's something nagging me about you and Heung-min."

She faced him. "What do you mean?"

"I've been doing this for a long time and I'm a pretty good judge of non-verbal cues, of how one person reacts to another… Tell me the truth. Do you and Heung-min know each other? Personally?"

She recoiled. "What?" She scoffed. "No, that was the first time I've ever seen the guy in the flesh. What exactly are you accusing me of?"

He met her stare. "At lunch with Helen I learned about the word 'nok', that it's the Thai word for 'bird'…Right? And Heung-min called you 'little bird.' Didn't he? As though he knew your name…And the looks I saw between the two of you and that young bloke working for him, I reckon they were the exchanges of people familiar with each other."

"Dan, 'little bird' is nothing but an expression. False endearment…He doesn't know me. I mean, if he knows I'm an Interpol agent he would've said…Wouldn't he? And they wouldn't have let us into the casino if they knew…Would they?"

He nodded. She'd made a good point.

She leaned closer and ran fingernails along his forearm. "If we're going to succeed as partners you need to start trusting me. Okay?" She gave him a gorgeous smile then licked her top lip while squeezing his bicep.

His whole body shivered. He nodded then gazed out the window.

# EIGHTEEN

*My diary. friday 28. maybe??*

*Only a few hours have passed since I last wrote in here so I guess it's 1 or 2 in the morning. There's yelling and screaming coming from somewhere in the house and I can't sleep. It's been going on for ages. A man and a woman in a language I don't know. And just now I'm sure I heard a second male voice and banging and thudding against walls. It sounds like people beating each other up.*

*Maybe an hour ago I thought I heard a younger voice. It was just before the yelling started. It sounded like a young girl crying. Not far from my room. So it made me wonder. Maybe I'm not alone. Are there others being kept prisoner in this house. Or on this ship. Or wherever I am.*

*I wish the fighting would stop so the guy can come to inject me. I know it's his way of punishing me because I rejected him. And I feel terrible about it. I didn't mean to hurt his feelings. I need him. I'm going crazy without my fix. Of it. Of him.*

*The yelling just got louder. A lady screamed. The old lady maybe. I'm scared and I'm turning off the light now. I'll try to sleep and dream away this nightmare.*

# NINETEEN

At 3.10am Nok tip-toed onto the verandah of Headmaster Saysamone's wooden bungalow in the center of Chiang Mai's old town.

Porter watched her and the side of the house, hidden from the street light's harsh glare by an overgrown mango tree.

She tried the front door handle. She turned to face him, frowned and shook her head.

He joined her by the door and listened. Silence. The only window was covered by a dark curtain. Faint light flickered beyond it. He glanced to the adjacent carport. Empty, same as the driveway.

"There's a path going down the side," he whispered. "Let's check the back door."

She nodded as she drew her Glock from shoulder holster. She shone a torch onto damp grass and led the way.

The path ran alongside a musty smelling stormwater drain that emptied into a concrete canal at the rear of the property. Rushing water spilled into the canal then lapped against its sloping walls. Behind the canal, a small park led to a well-lit street. Late night revelers spilled from a pub and excited voices pierced the still night. Tuk-tuk drivers beeped horns as they circled the crowd in search of customers.

Nok pushed a metal gate. It squeaked open. Dogs barked in a neighbor's yard.

Porter hurried past her and placed an ear against the rear door. Silence. He jiggled its handle. Locked. He looked up and saw a high window in the far-left corner of the house. It was protected by steel bars and light shone through it from somewhere inside. He nudged the thin door with his shoulder. It buckled and could be forced open easily enough.

She nodded as though encouraging him to do so and readied her Glock.

He forced his full weight against the door. Wood around the lock splintered and the door wobbled inwards.

Nok squeezed through the gap and jumped into the first room. She held the pistol and torch to the front in two hands then swept them from side to side.

Porter followed her into the narrow room and stepped to his right. He shone his torch and revealed a small bathroom in the corner. He felt vulnerable without a weapon but ran forward anyway. No-one behind the bathroom door. He flicked the light on. A towel hung from the wall. A disposable razor and shaving cream on a shelf above the wash basin. Black, wispy whiskers lined the basin and water trickled down its sides. Discarded shaving cream hadn't yet hardened. A bloke had shaved in the bathroom, not long ago.

He moved towards her. "Someone's still here, or has just left."

She turned a light on. They stood in a kitchen. A filthy kitchen with used plates, glasses and frypans piled on a dusty bench top.

She shone the torch towards the front of the house. A hallway led to the left and right. "I'll go left. You go right. We'll meet back in the middle…"

He nodded and waited for her to move. He stepped into the hallway and tried the door handle of the room to his right. Unlocked. He pushed the door open, jumped into the room and scanned it with the torch. Nothing but a desk and chair in the corner. A laptop sat open on the desk, its screen glowing florescent blue.

He turned down the hallway and came to an open doorway. He peeked around the corner and saw faint light coming from a bedside lamp. Was that a body lying on top of the bed? He kicked the door and it slammed against the wall. Certain no-one hid behind it, he stepped into the room then swiveled to his left. Nothing and no-one in that corner.

He shone the torch at the bed and saw a body. A female lay still on her back, dressed in a dark gown. He sniffed the stale air. No need for closer examination. She was dead.

He searched an inbuilt wardrobe then turned the light on.

The dead woman was Asian and Porter guessed her close to eighty. Her white hair fell over slight shoulders and her arms had been folded across her chest with hands clasped on her stomach. She looked as though she'd died peacefully, except for the bruising around her throat. Had Saysamone strangled his own mother? Was Lisa Baxter in another room? Dead? Or alive?

He ran to the doorway. "Be careful, I've found something," he shouted. "Stay put, I'm coming to you."

Nok shrieked then spoke in an incoherent panic.

Porter ran towards the noise. "What? Where are you?"

"Oh my God…" Her croaking voice echoed throughout the house. "I'm in the room at the back and I've found something too."

# TWENTY

Porter followed the hallway towards light at the end of it.

Nok stood in a doorway, staring into a room in the rear corner of the house.

He saw a slender, naked body hanging from a narrow window several meters above the tiled floor. A bed sheet had been tied around the window's metal bars and the body's broken neck. He stepped closer to the corpse.

Headmaster Saysamone's swollen tongue jutted from an open mouth. Glazed eyes stared, arrogant and defiant.

Porter saw a bed in the corner and two mattresses on the floor. "Why so many beds?"

"Who knows? Maybe some of the missing girls were here?" She shuddered visibly. "Or Saysamone might've had other family members sleeping here. It's common for multiple Asian families to live in the same house."

"Fair enough…" He bent over the bed and saw a dirty footprint on the bare mattress. "He stood on the bed, tied the sheet around the bars and his neck, then stepped off it."

She nodded then pointed at Saysamone's chest. "Bruising. Like, pinch marks? As though someone's tried to fight him off in a struggle."

"Yeah, his mother. She's dead in another room. I'd say he's strangled her and then done himself in. You did say the shame and disgrace he's brought to his family would be too much to live with."

She frowned. "That's true. But what if he did have Lisa and some of the other girls here at some stage? What if he was working for the Cambodian trafficking gangs and they've come and forcibly taken them from him? He would've been a perfect recruit for those gangsters with his access to young foreign girls."

"Nah, I don't reckon. Lisa's the only girl to go missing from his school." He spun three-sixty degrees. "And aside from three beds, there's nothing in this room or anywhere else in the house to suggest the girls have been held captive here."

"You're convinced Saysamone had nothing to do with Lisa's disappearance? That this is simply a murder/suicide?"

"Yeah, as I said before we came…I doubted Saysamone took Lisa and now I'm certain of it."

"The forensic exam will probably support your theory. But for me, something's still very weird about this."


Porter returned to his Bangkok apartment close to 6am and slept until his cell phone buzzed at 1.35pm. He held the phone at arm's length and waited for eyes to focus on the screen. Jane. He dropped the phone on the side table and let the call ring out. His mind was a jumbled mess and he had to unscramble it before speaking to her.

He yawned and stretched as he rolled onto his back and threw the bedsheet onto the floor. A vision of Nok's smiling face hovered overhead. He smiled back until Jane slapped his face. Guilt drove a hot iron into heart and he reached for his phone.

He unlocked it and read the screen. Nine missed calls, all from Jane. The first had been at 9.30am. He sucked a breath and selected her number.

"Dan?" Jane answered. "Where da hell have you been all morning?"

"Hi babe." He blinked to force eyes open and sat up with back to the wall. "Sorry, I worked until late and just woke up."

"Really? Working 'til late? Is that what you call it?"

She spoke in a tone of voice he'd rarely heard from her, one full of suspicion and doubt. "What's wrong, babe? You sound angry."

Her breathing was loud and labored through the phone.

"Babe?" he said. "What's going on? Are you crying?"

She sniffled. "Yes, I am fucking crying. Because you're an asshole and I'm fucking upset."

He exhaled at the ceiling. "Hang on…What? Seriously, I've got no idea what you're on about."

"Then I'll send it to you to read. To jolt your memory."

"Send me what?"

"An anonymous email I got this morning." Her voice shrilled. "Da one telling me you're fucking your partner there in Thailand…Some whore called Nok."

Her words punched him hard. He shook his head and saw evil snarls on the first two faces that came to him. Helen. Jaru. The only two who hated him enough to stoop so low.

"What do you mean it's anonymous?" he said. "There must be an address of where it came from?"

"Of course I looked for that. But it's blank, as though it's been encrypted to hide all sender information."

He forced himself to ignore Jane's sobs and expanded his thought process. Both Helen and Jaru had motive, but only Helen had the means. As the team's intell analyst she had access to private personnel files that Jaru didn't. A basic search of his profile would've provided her with his next of kin details and Jane's email address.

He spent five minutes trying to explain the fact to Jane. He told how he'd rejected Helen's sexual advances and that her accusations of his affair with Nok were nothing but the devious lies of a woman scorned.

Jane scoffed. "I don't believe you. And I want you home."

"You know I can't leave. I've made a commitment to Steve Williams and this investigation. Multiple girls are in danger and I can't turn my back on 'em."

"And what about da commitment you made to me?" she shouted. "To be faithful. To get married. And to always be here for Amber…She misses you. We both do. What da fuck…This is such typical Dan Porter, always putting strangers before those he's supposed to love."

"You know that's not true, Jane."

"Isn't it? Then prove it. Leave Bangkok today and come home."

He yawned then cuffed his forehead with an open hand as though trying to shock himself from a bad dream. "I told you…I'm here for the long haul and I can't."

"Or you don't want to? Wow, is she really that good a fuck?" A five second silence. "We'll expect you in Sydney by tomorrow. Have a safe flight."

He grunted, hoping to call her bluff. "And if I'm not?"

"There'll be no wedding. No more us…"

# TWENTY-ONE

Porter strode into the Interpol office at 2.30pm and slammed his briefcase onto a desk. "Where's Helen?" he asked Nok.

She hesitated then frowned. "In the meal room. What's wrong?"

He nodded and started in that direction.

"Did you speak to Steve Williams? He rang about five minutes ago and said he would try your cell phone."

He pointed to the briefcase. "It's in there…Did he say what he wanted?"

"No, only that it's urgent."

He thanked her, took his phone out then wandered into the empty meeting room. He dropped onto a chair, called Steve Williams and asked what was urgent.

"You okay, Port?" Williams paused. "You sound pissed-off."

"Because I am…"

"Well, this news won't help…Inspector Veasna in Phnom Penh was shot and killed at his home early this morning."

Porter sucked a hurried breath. "Fuck." He thought of the corrupt politicians Veasna had been investigating and the Korean loan-sharks led by Park Heung-min. "Any suspects?"

"Plenty…Unfortunately hundreds now know what he'd told you."

Porter's heart jumped to his throat. "What? There was only me, Veasna and General Chea in that interview room. And the crook's dead…I only disseminated my intel report to Interpol agents based in Asia, those with a need to know."

Williams sighed. "No, Port, you didn't. When you self-evaluated that report you failed to give it the correct classification and security clearance. It names corrupt Cambodian politicians as suspects in human-trafficking and should've been marked as top secret. But it went through as 'unclassified' and every corrupt cop in Phnom Penh, in most of Asia for that matter, has had access to it."

Porter dropped the phone on the table. He closed eyes and buried his face in open palms. Veasna was a good, honest cop and his fuckup had cost him his life.

He raised the phone to mouth. "How'd you find out about it?"

"General Chea called me a few hours ago," Williams replied. "You said he was present when you questioned the Cambodian crook. Could he have wanted Veasna dead?"

"Nah, I don't reckon. He seemed as keen as Veasna was to put those dodgy politicians away."

"Well it's clear those threatened by Veasna's investigation will do anything to protect themselves. And that means you're in danger… I'm thinking of pulling you off Lost Angels and out of Thailand."

Porter scoffed. "Mate, this changes nothing. I've been in strife from the minute I stepped off the plane."

"How's that?"

"A couple of Russian blokes had a go at the airport…Speeding pickup trucks have tried to run me down."

"Russians? Working for who? Shit, Port, why didn't you tell me?"

"I dunno. Guess I didn't want you or Jane to worry…"

"Jane? Give me a break. She hounds me every day but I tell her nothing."

"And she's hounding me too. Told me to come home now or she'll call the wedding off."

"You're kidding? Why?"

"Later…Listen, I'm not concerned about whoever's trying to spook me. It's a good thing 'cos it means I'm close to a breakthrough and they're worried…Nok's warned me from the start about influential fuckers not wanting me here."

"Yes, as we discussed last time, and it's more reason to pull you out… How do you feel about joining Lyn Foster in LA? She could use some help with her missing student investigation."

A vision of Veasna's serious face hovered before Porter. "Nah, after what's happened today I'm more determined than ever, mate. I owe it to the girls and Senator Fitzgerald. And now Veasna…" He frowned as he said the name. Was finding the abducted girls and avenging Veasna his true motivation for wanting to stay in Thailand? Or did he want to stay for Nok and his growing need to be near her?

"I admire your dedication to the job. But are you really prepared to risk your relationship with Jane? Because I want you to know that I'm not asking you to…"

"Don't worry about Jane, I reckon she's bluffing. She'll be right."

Williams sighed. "I'll let you stay on. But if there's one more threat or attempt on your life you'll be booked on the first plane back to Sydney."

Porter told him he understood. He spent ten minutes bringing him up to date with the investigation then ended the call. He placed his phone on the table and stared at it. He thought about Jane, and Veasna, and Nok. Guilt prodded his hollow chest, because Jane was right to say he always put strangers first. Why was that? Could he ever change? He shook the thought from his mind and shifted his anger to Helen and the vexatious email she'd sent Jane.

He strode to the meal room and stopped in the doorway. Every other Lost Angels member sat at the table.

"Helen," he said. "Can I have a word in private?"

She stared up at him. "You look angry and I'd rather not be alone with you." She glanced around the table. "Say what you have to say here and now. I want my colleagues to witness it."

He smirked. "Alright…My fiancé received an anonymous email this morning in which some weak bastard wrote complete bullshit about me having an affair at work. And Helen, I reckon it was you."

She laughed and broke eye contact. "Really? And why's that?"

"You're the only one in this office with access to my contact details. And contained within those details is Jane's email address."

She shook her head at him. "No, incorrect. I'm not." She looked at Sawatri. "Right?"

Sawatri swiveled to face Porter. "Apologies, I should've told you that all members of our team have

170

access to every other member's next of kin contact details in case of emergency... And why would Helen do such a horrible thing?"

Porter started to answer.

Helen cut him off. "Because we argued the other day and Dan's fragile ego can't handle the fact he was wrong. And oh," she rolled her eyes, "he's deluded and thinks I'm madly in love with him."

Jaru chortled. "A typical falang, always thinking they're irresistible to women."

Porter straightened in the doorway. "I've had enough of your bullshit, mate. Step into the room next door, just me and you. Let's discuss your problem."

Jaru stood.

"Sit down," Sawatri told him. He addressed Porter. "I understand your anger and bad mood. No doubt it's because you've just heard about Inspector Veasna?"

Porter nodded.

"And so you should be angry, and ashamed," Helen told him. "You placed Veasna in danger with the way you handled that intelligence. Your report was the proof those corrupt politicians needed, that confirmed Veasna considered them suspects. You should've sent it through me to be classified correctly. But you didn't because you don't trust me. You let a personal grudge affect your professionalism and a good cop has paid the price."

Porter opened his mouth to speak but didn't. What could he say? Helen was right. He turned slowly then trudged into the office. He slumped into his chair, rocked back and gazed at the ceiling.

Nok had followed him. She stopped in front of his desk. "You want to talk? About Veasna? The email?"

"Nah…" He stood. "I've gotta get out of this building, it's driving me crazy. Gunna go and look around Nana for the Nigerian kids."

She frowned as she sat opposite him. "Sit. There's no need. Those African students who'd been working along Sukhumvit are either dead or won't be coming back."

He sat. "What?"

She nodded. "Around eleven last night Fon and Jaru got called to a hostel not far from Nana Plaza and found sixteen Nigerians tied up in a large dorm room. All died from drug overdoses. Fon found traces of heroin in the room. She thinks the overdoses had been forced, said there was vomit all over the floor and all victims had multiple injection points. Forensics estimated times of death were between about seven and eight o'clock last night. The drug dealer from Soi 4 you stabbed in the leg, he's one of the victims."

"Bloody hell, someone's made sure those poor buggers didn't talk…Any witnesses? Surveillance footage?"

"The Thai lady working reception told Fon the security cameras haven't worked for weeks. She saw two young Arab guys leaving the dorm room but can't remember what time. That's all she'll say."

"What a star witness… Have the kids been identified?"

"Yes. The originals weren't found but the hostel had photocopies of their passport data pages."

"And?"

"All were here on student visas. Sponsored by GAIT."

"As suspected…The mysterious GAIT, who absolutely no-one in the Thai government seems to know about, have brought these kids here to work and then bumped 'em off. Why?"

"They knew too much?"

"Why would drug syndicate bosses expose their operational secrets to these kids?"

"I don't think they would."

"Spot on, they wouldn't…So why would GAIT kill 'em?"

She tilted her head to the side. "Helen told me what her database searches revealed about GAIT…I'd say someone within immigration tipped them off about us asking questions regarding student visas. GAIT has dealt with the risk accordingly, by ensuring the Nigerian kids weren't arrested and forced to talk about who'd brought them here."

He flicked a thumb against lower lip. "Makes sense…You're saying these kids were unlucky to be in Bangkok while we've put the heat on GAIT?"

She nodded.

"Bloody hell." He sighed. "More dead kids on my conscience."

"Sorry…"

He said nothing for a minute then leaned towards her. "The receptionist saw Arab blokes leave the dorm room. Blokes linked to that Arab crime boss? Big O? Protecting his interests in drug supply and hookers. Eliminating competition around Nana?"

"Perhaps…But Tim has Arab friends too don't forget, those guys who attacked you at the restaurant. They could've murdered the students on his order, to protect him and GAIT."

"Yeah, true, because he doesn't strike me as a crook who does his own dirty work…We need to hammer Big O and get names of those blokes working for him."

She frowned. "He won't talk…And we can't go back into the Arab area."

"Why the fuck not?"

"I asked Sawatri if we could pursue them after your fight at the restaurant. He said no and ordered us so stay away."

"That's bullshit. Why would he?"

"Someone much higher ranking than him says Big O and his operations are untouchable."

Porter scoffed. "It's exactly as you said before…Police bosses being paid to protect Arab criminals."

She gave a weak smile.

He shook anger from his head to clear it. Had he missed the obvious?

She leaned towards him. "What are you thinking?"

"That a Christian NGO calling itself GAIT is the perfect front for dodgy Thai cops and Arab crooks to run an organized crime syndicate together…I reckon we ignore Sawatri and go hound Big O. Right now."

"I know it's frustrating for you the way things work here, but I can't."

"You can't or you won't?"

"Now you're just being an arrogant pig…"

He watched her hand as she pulled it away. A gold watch glimmered on her wrist. "I understand you being wary of corrupt police bosses but why are you protecting these Arab blokes?"

"How am I?" She huffed and folded arms. "Is your obsession with them because they attacked you?"

"Hardly... Look, they're into drug supply and could be involved in Southeast Asian human-trafficking too. The recent abductions and so on... Most of KA's clients in the sex-slave market were identified as mega-rich Arabs but relevant law enforcement agencies didn't play ball and Dragon Slayer wasn't allowed to go near 'em."

"Big O and his guys sell street-level drugs and Middle-Eastern hookers." She scratched her chin with long, pink fingernails. "And only those things."

He grunted, unconvinced but with no means of disproving her. He studied her gold watch again. How had she afforded it on a junior agent's salary? How did she drive a new BMW sports car? Was she as corrupt as the others and taking bribes? She'd worked CI in the Nana area and would've made all the right connections. Could he continue to trust her?

"Can you ask Helen for a list of all Klong Toei docks used by large ships heading to China?"

"I can do that," she said.

"Cheers, and we should start searching this afternoon."

"We'll go tomorrow morning. I have a meeting later."

"Me too?"

She hesitated. "No... It's private business. Family."

He saw her mouth twitch. "No worries, tomorrow it is. I'll go for a wander around Nana and see who pops up."

"Tim maybe?"

"Huh, doubt it. Him and the other GAIT blokes have gone well and truly underground... Maybe we should expand our search into other areas of Bangkok where these Arab crooks operate? Question a few who aren't 'protected'?"

"I still don't agree with your theory about the Arabs, and even if I did, search for them with who? What resources? We're it, Dan, four Interpol agents."

He clenched his jaw and nodded. She was right.

"You need to remember what Heung-min told us, that men working for the NGO are abducting the foreign girls," she said. "And the only thing we know for certain, the only common link between GAIT, Lisa Baxter, the Nigerian students and the Arabs is Ti--."

"Tim. Yeah, spot on…But he could be anywhere in Thailand or Cambodia by now." He forced bitter bile down a dry throat and stared at the desk. Too much time had passed. "Hate to say but I reckon our best lead from here might involve one of these girls turning up dead."

"I hope you're wrong…You've said many times that if we get Tim, we get to GAIT's bosses. And my informants suggest he's still around so we'll find him sooner than later."

"Informants? Who?"

"Go-go dancers in Nana Plaza and others. Tim was a regular customer and the dancers refer to any girl he's dated as a 'pii noi'."

"Meaning?"

"A little ghost… Apparently more than a few of his girlfriends disappeared and haven't been seen again. Do you remember my ladyboy informant, Kwang?"

"How could I forget."

"I didn't want to get your hopes up but she thinks she saw a GAIT guy in Nana last night."

"She 'thinks' she saw?"

"Kwang's off her head most the time and never certain of anything…" She smiled her dazzling smile.

"Anyhow, I have a plan, one I hope will draw out Tim and his co-workers."

He eyed her sideways. "And that is?"

"Meet me at nine, at the spot on Sukhumvit road where you first met Kwang. We'll go from there."

"You gunna tell me why?"

"Nope. Life's more fun with a few surprises and you need cheering up."

## TWENTY-TWO

At 6.15pm Nok took stairs to the third level of the Yaowarat District Police station in the heart of Bangkok's Chinatown. She smiled at the female personal assistant stationed outside the largest office. "Hi Pat, Police General Woracha's expecting me."

Pat returned the smile and waved her towards the door.

Nok entered without knocking. She closed the door, stepped to the far side of the room then stopped a meter behind and to the side of the district's police chief.

Woracha tilted a gleaming bald head while keeping his back to her. He wore an olive-brown uniform with silver rank-insignia on shoulder lapels, immaculately pressed but too tight for his bulging middle-aged belly. He was shorter than Nok, despite the heels of his black shoes adding two inches in height. He gazed out tinted windows that ran the length of the room from floor to ceiling, seemingly fascinated by the scene below.

"You're late," he said.

"Sorry, sir…Um, how did you know it was me?"

"I bought you the perfume you're wearing. Hermes 24. Remember?"

She didn't reply.

He twisted towards her but avoided eye contact. "How is your mother?"

"Same as the last time you asked…"

He turned back to the window.

Her hands fidgeted. She shuffled forward half a meter to hear him better because he spoke Thai with a strong southern accent and often mumbled. She looked down. "I've never seen your streets so busy. Restaurants and bars were teeming with customers as I drove past."

"Local entrepreneurs have somehow convinced naïve tourists and wannabe yuppie hipsters that Chinatown's the new place to be seen. It's brought too much attention from the media and I don't like it."

"Because it's harder to keep flying under the radar?"

"What do you think?"

"That you'll just need to be more careful."

"No, little bird, it's you who needs to be more careful," he said louder. He grunted as he lit a cigarette. "When you first joined our CI office in Nana all those years ago I spotted your potential early on. Your ability to manipulate others and get what you want…And up to this point you've realized that potential."

"Why do I sense there's a 'but' coming?"

"Our mega-rich Arab friends in Malaysia and Indo have taken a real liking to our pure white product. Do not let me down now, not with so much money at stake."

"Sir, you taught me well. You've gone from a low-ranking detective to a district boss in the space of four years and I'm well aware of the entitlement and rewards awaiting if my profits and subsequent donations can match yours. Don't be concerned, my commitment to our enterprise is stronger than ever."

His voice grew louder again. "Then why the fuck did you risk everything by taking Agent Dan Porter into the Babylon casino?"

She rocked backwards. "I, I didn't mean to take him…I'd never been there before and he tricked me. We were standing outside the entrance before I knew it and it would've looked too suspicious if I'd forced him to leave."

He scoffed. "Needless to say, many were far from impressed to see him there in his pathetic disguise. I've had to do some serious groveling to save your job at Interpol…And what were you thinking, allowing him to interview Park Heung-min? He's ropable that you put him in such a position."

Her head dipped. "I'm sorry…But like I said, I'd only heard stories about Babylon's underground casino. Heung-min has never spoken of it and I had no idea he was a regular there."

"Intelligence reports summarizing his gambling habits have been widely disseminated. You should have known."

"Yes but Porter tricked him too, into confirming traffickers are using the shipping terminals at Khlong Toei. Luckily Heung-min recovered quite well from it."

"Did he just? How exactly?"

"He told Porter the product's being shipped onto China from the massive, deep-water docks. And they're actually the furthest away from the one we're using…"

Woracha chuckled. "Excellent."

"Did Heung-min tell you we've had to change how we transport the product to larger ships waiting in the Gulf?"

"Yes and it concerns me he hasn't tried harder to find a new Port Authority boss to pay off. Or one from the Water Police, or Customs… Most are corruptible so how hard can it be? Should we get rid of the Koreans and try different smugglers? Utilize another transport option?"

"No. Heung-min and his men are assholes but they're the best at what they do and have the largest distribution network in what is, as you're well aware, a very niche market."

"Alright, I'll heed your advice. Heung-min also told me about the order he's received for two units of our product. You've been told to deliver them?"

"Yes, at midnight to the usual jetty. But I don't think I can, it's too risky."

"The man who placed this order's a billionaire and more influential than he is rich. He's heard our product's the finest on the market and well-suited to his particular tastes. You will deliver it as you've been instructed."

"But I have to work with Porter tonight. It's impossible to get away from him."

He drew on the cigarette then growled as though clearing his throat. "My men wanted to go after Porter when he first arrived in Bangkok but I stopped them. I've thought it best to keep him alive, knowing it wouldn't look good if we allowed a foreign cop to be murdered on our watch... I'm starting to have doubts."

"He's already had a few close encounters."

"I've heard..." He dropped the cigarette onto tiled floor and let it smolder. "Porter has more enemies than he knows."

"Hmm, I'm pretty sure he knows about them. He's just not easily scared off... If you can keep your men at bay and maybe a few of the others, I'll do my best to protect him."

"Good. And stop allowing him to control you when it's you who should be controlling him. If you don't, everything we've built will come tumbling down. This is our nation and we'll continue to do things our way. I'm relying on you to make him understand that."

"Easier said than done, sir. He's a typical farang. Strong-minded and thinks he always knows best. Even here in Thailand where he's far from home."

"Then use your abundant charms. Fuck him if you have to and keep him pussy-whipped as a slave to your will."

She frowned as she gasped. "When was it exactly that I lost your respect? You address me as though I'm nothing but a common street whore."

"Dear Nok, you too have sold your soul to the need for more baht. Are you really any different to them?"

She opened her mouth to answer but didn't. She stared at golden temple spires in the distance.

He turned and gave her a lopsided smile that wrinkled an ugly face. "Harsh words I know, but said in your best interests."

She nodded with pursed lips.

"Stop Porter from progressing the Lost Angels investigation any further."

"You worry too much." She scoffed. "He's got nothing."

"The fact he's been inside Babylon to harass Heung-min and knows about the Khlong Toei docks points to the contrary…" Black eyes bored into her. "I detect it in your voice. You have romantic feelings for this farang, don't you?"

She broke eye contact, looked up and laughed. "Don't be silly… But you're right, I must control him better."

"Yes, or he'll destroy our business and reputations in the process. Your career would be over and family name forever tarnished. And your mother would not be pleased. Would she?"

She glanced at him. "No."

"So, you have a life changing decision to make, little bird. And two options…You can allow Porter free reign and therefore aid his success. And you'll have betrayed me and your nation when he exposes us and disgraces the entire population… But then again, others more powerful than I are likely to take definitive action to ensure that doesn't happen."

"I'd say that 'definitive action' has already been set in motion." She sighed. "And my second option?"

"You hamper his investigation until he's sent back to Sydney as a failure…You see, it's you who'll decide his fate, Nok. Will Dan Porter make it out alive? Or will he go home to Australia in a body-bag?"

# TWENTY-THREE

Porter waited for Nok where she'd told him to, in front of ATM machines where street hookers plied their trade near the corner of Sukhumvit road and Soi 3. He hoped for a foot pursuit in the hours ahead so had ditched the suit and leather shoes. He wore a black polo short with jeans and New-Balance sneakers. At 9.05pm Nok pulled up in a Toyota Camry and called him over.

He entered the front passenger side and told himself not to glance at the cleavage spilling from her low-cut blouse. He felt his face flush with hot blood after disobeying the order from his brain.

She winked as though letting him know he'd been caught taking a peek. "Hi. Wow, amazing what half a day of rest will do. Your face looks much better and nearly all the bruising's gone... Ready for some fun and games?"

He grinned, hoping to hide embarrassment. "Always..." He watched the road ahead as she squeezed the sedan into a line of traffic. "Where's the Beamer?"

"My BMW? Oh, I thought this old piece of junk would be less conspicuous for what I've got planned."

He wanted to ask what that was but knew she wouldn't tell. "Fair enough..."

After five minutes she made a U-turn and drove back along Sukhumvit the way they'd come. She took a left into an alleyway. Cars travelling in the opposite direction flashed lights and beeped horns as they swerved to avoid a collision.

"Are we going the wrong way on a one-way street?"

"Yes," she said. "But don't worry, we're the cops."

Porter smirked and gazed out the window. They turned right onto a narrow street jammed with taxis, tuk-tuks and motorcycles. Tourists of all shapes and sizes wandered along uneven pavements, their wide-eyes sparkling in the bright lights of Nana's red-light district.

Food carts lined the edge of the road and added to the insane congestion. The sedan crawled past a tattoo shop, an open-air bar where dull-eyed girls in cheap cocktail dresses stared at cell phones, and a street vendor selling barbequed meat. A row of orange safety cones lined the gutter for ten meters on the other side of the vendor's cart in a vain attempt to discourage parking.

Nok stopped alongside the cart, wound the tinted window down and spoke to the vendor.

The vendor shook her head then replied in a language Porter didn't recognize.

Nok leaned over him to yell at the vendor in what sounded like the same language.

The woman mumbled as she wiped hands on the front of her apron. She waddled to the edge of the road and removed five safety cones.

Nok scowled at her before winding the window up. "Simple Cambodian bitch…Who does she think she is?" She steered the sedan as close to the curb as possible and parked in front of a laundromat that'd been closed for the night.

Smoking incense sticks and bottles of red Fanta littered a brown spirit house near the pavement to Porter's left. He saw the Hooter's pub ahead and the Nana Hotel's carpark just beyond it. He surveyed the opposite side of the street and saw the entrance to Nana Plaza less than fifty meters away.

"So here we are, parked up nice and cozy in Soi 4…What now?"

She took binoculars from the middle console and handed them to him. "We sit low." She reclined her seat. "We marvel at the endless stream of whores and deviants heading into the plaza, and we wait."

Forty minutes later she nudged his shoulder then brought her seat up. "Binoculars…In front of the 'Big Dogs' bar."

Porter did the same with his seat. Traffic on the street had eased and he was able to focus the binoculars on the open-air bar next to the plaza entrance. "Yeah, got it…Who exactly am I looking for?"

"The Thai girl in the yellow dress. Standing with the blonde farang."

"Yeah, I see 'em. Who are they?"

"It's my friend Som, the go-go dancer you met in Soi Cowboy the other night. And the farang is Bridget, a hot Swedish girl I met at the nightclub afterwards." She gave him a cheeky smile. "She's a great kisser too…" She laughed as he over-exaggerated a gulp. "They're both more than happy to help us."

He zoomed in on them. "Help with what?"

"Like I said earlier, Kwang thinks she saw a GAIT guy out and about last night… Som and Bridget are the type of girls they go for and hopefully they'll pick them up and lead us to their headquarters."

He lowered the binoculars. "You're kidding me? We can't use these girls as bait, it's too bloody dangerous."

186

"Chill, it's an opportunity too good to miss. And how else are we going to find out where these guys stay and might be holding the abducted girls?"

He pulled on the door handle and started to push. "Nah, I won't be a par--."

"Shh...Look!" She pointed to the girls. "The two guys approaching them..."

He closed the door and peered across the street. Two men in white shirts and black trousers chatted to the girls with their backs to him. Both of them turned slightly. He noticed they wore thin black ties, the same as Tim had.

The thrill of the hunt gripped him. He shivered from the adrenaline rush. "They've gotta be GAIT blokes..."

One of the men handed Bridget a flyer and she appeared to read from it.

"Did you see that, Dan? It's definitely the guys we want. Let's just wait for a bit. We might see their car or something…"

"Alright, it's your call. For now…" He watched through the binoculars. "But I'm over there the second those girls look to be in any trouble."

They watched the group chat for five minutes.

Nok snatched the binoculars from him and leaned forward as she looked through them. "That could be it."

"What?"

"A white van with no plates just pulled out from the curb and is heading towards them…See it? It just flashed its headlights. Do you see it?"

His mind backtracked a few months to when multiple victims had been abducted in Sydney by crooks using white vans. The memory punched him in the chest and jolted him into action. He started to open the door. "Call the boys in brown for backup. I'm getting those girls away from there."

She dropped the binoculars into the console and held his elbow. "Wait…" She nodded towards the group. "At least until we see if it is their van?"

He watched the girls. They appeared to flirt with the men but he suspected their laughs were attempts to mask fear. The white van stopped alongside them. Its windscreen was dark and concealed the driver. The men ushered the girls towards the rear. They started getting into the van.

GAIT's van? He had to warn them. He pushed the door open and sprang onto the pavement. He ignored Nok's protests and sprinted towards the van. He was twenty meters away when it accelerated, flashed its lights and drove straight at him. He waved arms above head and stood his ground in the middle of the road.

"Dan, behind you!"

He heard Nok's warning just in time. He glanced over his shoulder and saw a black pickup truck bearing down from behind at high speed. Eyes darted back to the front, to the white van that wasn't going to stop. He spun towards the black pickup, now less than five meters from him, then leapt towards the side of the road. He landed on his hip and rolled to cushion the blow. The pickup truck missed his trailing leg by inches and roared past him. He collided with the gutter, pushed up onto knees and turned to watch it speed to the intersection and disappear to the left on Sukhumvit. A black pickup truck with no plates…

He pivoted to look in the opposite direction, to where the white van had gone. No sign of it. He ran towards the

188

sedan as Nok steered it from the curb. She made a quick U-turn then waited until he jumped in.

She accelerated, drove fast southbound on Soi 4 and weaved the sedan through traffic. She blared the horn. Cars and motorbikes braked hard to let her pass. Shocked pedestrians scampered.

After a kilometer they came to a T-intersection. The sedan skidded to a halt.

Car headlights illuminated her frown. "Which way do you think? If they turned right it's possible to get onto the motorway and they could be far from here by now."

He glanced in both directions. "Go left then make a phone call. Fon was chasing up another lead earlier but she'd be back in the office by now...Get her to circulate the van's description and that of the girls and the GAIT blokes. You and me will keep searching until we find 'em."

She did as he'd requested, ended the phone conversation with Fon then briefly turned to him. "Another lucky escape tonight. The driver of that Hiluxe pickup definitely wanted to kill you. Who are they?"

He grunted. "Russians from the airport? Assassins contracted by the Bangkok elite you warned me about? Goons dealing drugs for that fat Arab bloke, Big O? Heung-min's Korean hoodlums?" He took a deep breath and let it out with a whoosh. "And bloody hell, they're only the ones I know about..."

"It could've been other GAIT guys, maybe even Tim, making sure the white van got away?"

"Possibly...And was that an admission just now that you don't still reckon I'm imagining someone trying to bump me off?" He smirked as eyes scanned dimly lit streets. "It's been a black pickup and that same make and model each time. With no plates or unique markings that make it easy to distinguish from others."

"I'll get Helen to chase up CCTV footage from that area around the plaza. Maybe we'll get a better description of the guys the girls left with? And cameras along Sukhumvit might give us an idea which way the Hiluxe went."

He nodded then tuned out as she kept talking.

"Dan, did you hear what I said?" Her voice rose. "Why aren't you listening?"

"Sorry, was just thinking…I saw Jaru leaving our underground carpark the other day. He was driving the same type of black pickup."

She kept eyes on the road as she scoffed. "You can't honestly believe he's the one who's tried to run you down three times?"

"Why not? He hates me and reckons you and I are getting it on. Jealousy's the strongest motive of all… Or is he acting on behalf of police bosses concerned about what I might find? He could be using his own pickup and removing the plates each time."

"Do you know how many black, Toyota Hiluxe pickup trucks are in Bangkok? Besides, Jaru knows where you stay. If he really wanted you dead he would've killed you in your sleep already."

He recoiled at the thought. "Maybe, but I'm not so sure."

They searched the Nana area for another hour without luck.

Nok moaned. "Sorry but I've got to go home. I'm really not feeling well and think I might vomit."

He checked his watch. "It's only just gone eleven… Can't you hang in there for a few more hours? Chances

190

of spotting that van are much better now compared to in heavy traffic tomorrow."

She groaned and put a hand to her stomach. "I'll drive us back to the office and ask Fon to partner you for the rest of the shift. Sorry."

Visions of Som and Bridget flashed to the front of his mind. Their fresh smiling faces reminded him of Nadia Tindall, the first abduction victim he'd found brutally murdered in Sydney during the Carinya investigation. Guilt punched him in the guts. He'd failed to keep Nadia alive, and by allowing those girls to get inside the white van he'd failed them too.

He scowled, wondering why he'd resisted well-tuned instincts and not run to them when he'd first sensed the threat? Why had he listened to Nok instead? He cursed under his breath because he already knew the answer. His feelings for her had affected his judgement and put innocent lives at risk. He'd let two girls be taken by GAIT, the very bastards he was supposed to protect them from. He closed eyes and gave himself a mental uppercut.

*If they turn up dead it's on you...Bloody hell, Porter, what the fuck have you done?*

# TWENTY-FOUR

Porter scanned the endless rows of neglected warehouses lining the Chao Phraya river as Nok drove the BMW coupe towards Khlong Toei Pier's deep-water docks. He wanted to follow up on information provided by the Korean loan-shark boss, Park Heung-min, that vessels loaded at the terminal were transporting the abducted girls. He'd studied the huge area on Google Maps and realized the enormity of the task. Finding the exact dock utilized by the human-traffickers would be harder than finding genuine Nike sneakers at Bangkok's famous Chatuchak market. And although Heung-min could've lied and the traffickers might've moved to another location after being tipped-off, his avenues of investigation were extremely limited. Desperate times required equally desperate methods.

He'd worked with Fon until 3am searching for the girls taken from Nana Plaza then returned to the office at 8am to commence a new shift. Nok's eyes were blood-shot when she'd trudged into the office an hour after him and she hadn't stopped yawning since.

"You look knackered, sweet."

She yawned again. "I had my head in the toilet most of the night and couldn't sleep afterwards. I think it was food poisoning but I'm feeling better today."

She drove down a narrow lane, turned towards the river then parked alongside stacks of yellow and maroon colored cargo containers. She pointed towards a demountable building on the opposite side of the road and warehouses dotting the ridge beyond it. "That's the Customs office for these docks, where they should be filing the cargo manifests, records of searches conducted, shipping company data and so on. We'll start in there."

He nodded then checked his watch. 10.13am on Saturday the 29th at the Khlong Toei terminal would be a pivotal time, date and place for the Lost Angels team. They would either secure crucial evidence required to progress the investigation, or they would crash and burn at another dead-end.

An overwhelming sense of dread took hold as he stepped from the car. Fear formed a lump in his throat. The fear of failure, and of being too late, and of forever being haunted by the question…Were Lisa Baxter and others already on their way to China?

He followed Nok into the Customs office and accepted her invitation to sit at a circular table in the middle of the room. "Tell 'em we need a printout of all cargo that's gone to China in the past three months. On what ships and to which ports."

She smiled. "This is the Thailand Customs department we're dealing with. They're the same as most government bureaus here and still stuck in the 1980's…There are no digital records stored on a fancy database and we'll have to search the hardcopy files ourselves."

He made googly eyes. "Oh, joy."

She approached the counter and showed her official ID to the lone Customs officer, a stick-like man with a permanent scowl that said 'What the hell are you doing here?' After a brief conversation during which her tone grew more threatening and his scowl mellowed into a sheepish grin, he moved to filing cabinets in the back.

Five minutes later he returned with three document folders. She snatched them from him then joined Porter at the table.

They searched the records for two hours and found twenty-three incomplete cargo manifests of ships that had left the deep-water docks bound for China. Over a hundred shipping containers were unaccounted for, with no records showing which ships had transported them. When Nok quizzed the Customs officer about the discrepancies and asked why the 'Destination Port' column for each of the twenty-three entries was blank, he played dumb. And when she said she'd be seizing the three folders and several others, despite having no power to do so, he became aggressive and threatened to call security.

Porter pulled twenty-three pages they'd removed from the folders into a neat pile and handed them to her. "Please ask our corrupt little mate here to photocopy these records. We'll take 'em back to Helen to see what she can find."

Nok slammed the pages onto the counter and yelled at the Customs man. He picked them up and retreated behind a partition.

She answered her cellphone and squealed. She had a conversation in Thai then hurried to Porter.

"Great news," she said. "That was Som. Her and Bridget are safely back at home."

He returned her smile as guilt lifted from sagging shoulders. He listened as Nok relayed what Som had told her, that the guys handing out flyers were definitely with GAIT. Som thought they must've drugged her and Bridget, because they woke up in an abandoned building in Chinatown, tied to a post and unable to remember anything after getting into the van. A security guard had heard them calling out and freed them close to midday.

Porter scratched a stubbled jaw. "Strange...Were the girls assaulted in any way?"

"I was worried about that too but Som said no, they're both untouched and fine."

"That's beaut, but I don't get it...Why'd those blokes risk exposing themselves, only to let the girls go?"

"Maybe they lost their nerve after we chased them?"

"Yeah most likely. Which is a worry because it means they're spooked and will lay low for another couple of weeks. And we can't afford this investigation to stagnate for that long..."

Nok agreed, grabbed the photocopied pages from the counter and led him from the office.

They'd walked ten meters towards the BMW when the road in front of them exploded in a puff of dust. Fragments whizzed past Porter's ear.

"Get down," he shouted. He dropped to the hard surface and ignored his scorched palms. Another round pounded the road. Closer. He swiveled towards Nok. "Stay still!"

She flattened against concrete, her face a portrait of beautiful terror. "What's happening?"

"Someone's shooting at us."

She shrieked. "What? Where?"

Two more high-caliber rounds struck the ground behind them.

Porter realized the gunman was highly skilled and missing deliberately. "Stay down and hold tight. They aren't trying to kill us."

Silence for five minutes as they clung to the road.

He heard a shrill beeping noise sounding from near the BMW. He peered towards it and saw a portable radio had been placed on the hood. "Someone wants to chat...I'll get the radio. You run to the car, get inside and stay low. Alright?"

She frowned. "Are you sure they won't shoot us?"

He grinned, hoping to calm her with humor. "I'm so certain of it, I'll bet my left nut that they don't." He stood. "And I've really grown attached to my left nut over the years, it's my favourite."

She laughed before quickly covering her mouth as though she hadn't intended to. Fearful eyes locked onto his for a second. She jumped to feet and ran to the car.

He watched her slam the door shut. He plucked the radio from the hood then squeezed the button as he spoke into it. "Yeah?"

"My sniper won't miss you a second time, Porter," the man said with an unmistakable, guttural Russian accent. "Or perhaps he'll hunt someone else? Someone you're very fond of... Here, or in Sydney? Who knows?"

A direct threat against Jane and Amber? The bubbling volcano inside Porter erupted. "Don't you fucking mention my girls. You hear me? Or I'll find you and ri--."

"Leave Thailand. Immediately. Before you shame those you've no right to and get your loved ones killed."

Porter turned away from the river. He raised a hand to shield eyes from the sun then scanned the warehouses on the ridge. It's where he would've set up for such an ambush, hidden amongst shadow with the blinding sun at his back.

"Who is this?" He waited five seconds. "Too gutless to say? No worries, I've got a fair idea where you're hiding and will get answers soon enough."

The man chuckled. "As we say in Russia, Porter, you've got bigger balls than a black bear."

"Cheers, and I look forward to shoving yours down your throat."

"Your bravado is admirable but foolish… Attempt to leave this location within the next twenty minutes and my sniper will take great pleasure splattering your pretty girl's head throughout that sportscar. And we don't want that, do we?"

Porter glanced to Nok, who stared back. "Don't worry, we'll stay put."

"Excellent… Now, hold the radio out and away from your body, between thumb and forefinger."

"What?"

"Goodbye, Porter. Do it."

He did as the Russian instructed. Three seconds later a bullet pulverized the radio. It flew from his grip then smashed against the road. He got into the passenger seat and relayed the conversation to Nok.

Her hand trembled as she placed it on his forearm. "Thank goodness you're okay…Why did Russians send this message?"

"Dunno, but after those Russian blokes had a go at me in the airport I had our analyst in Sydney search for all known associates of the crooks Dragon Slayer's locked up. She found no links to the Russian government, their internal security forces, their intelligence agencies or the mafia… So I reckon this warning's about Lost Angels, about the Russian girls missing in Thailand."

"Maybe their government has something to hide too?"

"Yeah, and we need to find out what that is." He thought about the blond SUV driver who'd protected him from being run down outside the restaurant. Could he have been Russian? Likely, but why were they protecting and warning him at the same time? Why wouldn't the Russian government just kill him and be done with it? They couldn't be concerned about using their own men and a possible diplomatic backlash because life was cheap in Thailand and a local assassin could be hired for five hundred bucks. Nothing about the Russian involvement made sense.

Nok rocked forward to gaze into his eyes.

He thought she was about to kiss him.

She tapped his hand with hers then leaned back. "What did he say again, about shaming someone?"

He wanted her to kiss him but pushed the thought to the back of his mind. "He said, 'leave before you shame those you've no right to', or something like that." He remembered advice from Steve Williams regarding officials within the Thai government fearing the embarrassment the investigation might bring. "These Russian blokes could be working for your government too, Nok. Are they trying to scare us off so the truth stays hidden from the international media? To protect the façade that these abductions aren't really happening?"

She sighed. "It's often the Thai way... If not seen, it never happened."

"Not only here in Thailand, sweet. All over the world." He scoffed. "For too many in power, ignorance is bliss."

He recalled the second part of the Russian's warning, to leave before those he cared about were killed. He seethed with anger. The threat against his girls and Nok was obvious. Had his stubborn pride in persevering with the investigation no matter what placed them in harm's way? Were selfish motives, the endless need to mend his damaged soul, blinding him from the obvious?

He shook his head. No, they weren't. And self-doubt, and guilt, and all the bastards trying to scare him off could go fuck themselves. Because the missing girls were alone in a cruel and dangerous place and he was their only hope. He vowed to overcome the odds, find and take them home to their families. Dead or alive.

# TWENTY-FIVE

*Lisa Baxter's diary. Saturday 29 of September (maybe?)*

*I think it's Saturday. I know it's late in the afternoon because it's a few hours since the old lady brought my lunch and it's getting darker outside.*

*In my last entry I wrote about being frightened. And about the fighting and yelling. And I was worried the guy wouldn't come to give me my fix. Well I shouldn't have worried because everything has changed for the better now.*

*A new guy started coming to me yesterday. He came just after lunch. I didn't see him because I had the sack over my head but he smelt nice. And he spoke good English with a funny posh accent. He gave me more heroin than the other guy had been giving me. And he left a few different pills for me so I was grateful for that. He said he loves me and that I'm his and only his. He said the other guy had only been taking care of me until the time came when he was able to do it himself. And now he's here I'm so happy.*

*He came again today to take care of me. Before lunch this time. I don't know if it's different gear but the heroin chillaxed me more than ever. He waited a while after injecting me and then took the sack off my head.*

*Everything was a bit blurry but I think his dark brown hair is maybe a wig. He's skinny and he wears big sunglasses. Like the Aviator style they are. I think he's Asian maybe but hard to tell.*

*I wanted to pull the glasses off and see his face but my hands were tied to the bed posts and I couldn't. That's how I was on both days when we've had sex. Tied to the bed. But I didn't try to stop him. I feel that he's a good guy who really does love me. And if he gets angry he might not give me my fix. So I'll let him do whatever he wants if it keeps him happy.*

*We've only been together for two days but I already crave him as much as the heroin. The needle and his soft human touch are the only things that bring pleasure into my horrible world.*

*I can't wait until his next visit. The next shot. The next release from reality. Because I can definitely hear other girls in this place now. And I don't want to hear them so I put fingers in my ears. But they are so loud and crying in rooms all around me. And I hear strange men yelling in languages I don't understand. Really violent and scary sounding languages.*

*And I hear the sounds of girls being beaten. Then their screams of pain. They don't stop crying and I know they must be afraid. But I'm not afraid anymore. Because I know my man will protect me. And the needle is keeping me from going insane. I think.*

# TWENTY-SIX

Porter woke early on Sunday and wanted to work but Sawatri had insisted he take the day off. By 11am he was bored of watching Thai boxing repeats on TV and decided to head out and about. He took a taxi to the abandoned building in Chinatown where the GAIT members had left Som and Bridget. He went alone, needing time to himself and to ponder where his life was at.

A receptionist in the apartment block next to the abandoned building spoke perfect English. She summonsed the security guard who'd found the girls and interpreted while Porter asked him questions. The guard explained that Friday's nightshift crew hadn't reported seeing any suspicious persons or vehicles throughout the night or early Saturday morning. Porter thanked them both then dawdled to the street out front.

He took his phone from jeans' pocket and studied a map. Chinatown's main drag, Yaowarat road, was less than two kilometers away. He selected 'Best of U2' from his playlist, shoved in iPhone earplugs and set off towards it.

He thought about yesterday's events while he hummed along to a song, careful to dodge the dog shit and ankle-breaking crevices on the minefield of a pavement. Saturday's shift had begun with an apology to Helen, when he admitted he'd been wrong to assume she'd sent the email to Jane. She'd accepted the apology then helped analyze the Customs records they'd procured the day before.

He'd explained to Helen that in the past few months twenty-three ships with discrepancies on their cargo manifests had departed Khlong Toei Pier bound for China. He'd hoped tracking them would provide names of cities the girls had been transported to. But after spending most the afternoon making phone calls to Chinese Customs' liaison officers and searching every database and information source available to them, they still had no clue as to the destination port of those twenty-three ships nor the current whereabouts of numerous 'unaccounted for' shipping containers.

At 5pm Saturday they'd received information that another four Caucasian girls had disappeared from nightclubs in the Asoke district since Thursday. They suspected Tim and GAIT were responsible because the go-go dancer Som had spotted them in the vicinity of Asoke's Soi Cowboy earlier in the week. They'd left the office immediately to view surveillance footage and question multiple staff members from clubs where the girls were last seen. They identified no-one and learned nothing new.

Porter had finished work at 3am and struggled to sleep, frustrated with the search for Bangkok's 'little ghosts' and a population that never seemed to witness anything.

His mind joined him in the present when the haunting start of U2's 'With or without you' made him think of Jane. He grinned because she often sang the song in the shower or serenaded him with it on drunken karaoke nights. Bono hit a high-note and it sent a shiver through him. The lyrics echoed over and over. 'I can't live, with or without you…'

He loved Jane, no doubt. But for some reason he'd started doubting whether he loved her enough to spend the rest of his life with her. The alternate scenario was an equally disturbing thought…Could he live his entire life without her? And he was yet to tell her the secret from his past. The secret he'd promised to share before the wedding. He gulped, dreading the thought of it.

Nok's gorgeous smile pushed Jane's aside and the reason for his doubts became clear. But were his undeniable feelings for Nok about love, or lust? Were they because he was lonely and she was his only companion in the City of Angels? He wondered what she was doing on her day off. Should he invite her to meet him for lunch? He prepared to send her a message. Then a vision of Jane hovered again. She was crying, so he said sorry and banished Nok from thoughts.

He came to traffic lights, put the earplugs away then checked the map on his phone. If he continued straight on, he would reach Yaowarat road in less than five minutes. That route looked boring so he turned right down an alley, towards the shimmering temple dominating the horizon.

The alley led him along the temple compound's outer perimeter. He paused to study the intricate molded figures lining the top of ten-meter high walls. Bare-chested men wielded swords as they rode ginormous elephants and charged invading armies. He looked higher, to the main building made of shiny marble and admired its ornate wooden façade painted in shades of silver and yellow. He shielded eyes to marvel at the temple's highest point where a golden spire reached for the blazing sun.

He turned left and continued to appreciate the wondrous architecture as he strolled for a hundred meters alongside the compound. He spotted a bronzed plaque on the wall and moved closer to read it. The largest letters at the top were in Thai. And underneath them in English: *Wat Khongwihan, built 1789*. The temple still looked rather fine, he thought, for a joint that was two-hundred and thirty years old.

He continued along the alley in a daydream until a wall prevented him from going further. He spun on heels and saw he was still alone. He strode towards a street on his right, suddenly famished and hoping it would lead directly to Yaowarat road and its many restaurants he'd read about. When he reached the corner, movement at the far end of the alley caught his eye.

The man stopped walking and watched him. He wore dark sunglasses and the hood of a grey jacket over his head. Black jeans covered spindly legs and fell to black boots. Was he following him?

Porter quickened pace and peered to his left.

The hooded man ran towards him. What was the dark object gripped in his right hand? A pistol?

Porter cursed Sawatri for leaving him unharmed. He wasn't being followed. He was being hunted. Within a milli-second he weighed up survival options and chose 'flight' over 'fight'. He sprinted toward the sounds of busy traffic on the main road straight ahead.

He glanced back as he ran.

The hooded hitman turned the corner. He slowed to a walk and continued following.

Porter ran past an alleyway. Then another. He turned left into the third one and kept running. The alleyway doglegged to the left. He saw the temple's golden spire towering above him and realized his mistake. He'd doubled back on himself and ran into a dead end. A dead end bordered by barbed-wire topped walls that were too high to climb.

He swiveled, brushed sweat from eyes then scanned the urban environment.

The hitman came into view, now less than forty meters away. He hesitated at the intersection then strolled down the middle of the road.

Porter wondered why he made no attempt at concealment as he came towards him. Was he careless, over confident, or just downright cold-blooded and arrogant?

He spun right and saw another high wall blocking that exit route. A thick hedge by the wall was his only hope. He ran to it, hid the best he could, and waited.

The sound of heavy boots crunching on concrete got louder then stopped. He sensed the man was close and bent to peer through a gap in the hedge.

The hitman stood less than five meters away with his back turned. Porter thought he must have placed his gun in a jacket pocket because he couldn't see it. The man raised a cellphone to ear and had a conversation. A conversation in Thai?

Porter strained to hear. Did he recognize the man's voice? Bloody hell, where had he heard it before? Who was this bloke? He definitely wasn't a professional hitman because he'd made too many mistakes…Who was the bastard working for?

He stepped from the bush, fed up with hiding and needing answers. He ran at the hitman, drove a shoulder into his back and tackled him to the ground. Scorched concrete took chunks from unprotected elbows and ripped skin from palms.

He pushed himself forward as the hitman turned onto his back and tried to squirm from under him. His superior weight and strength made it easy to straddle his stomach then use his knees to pin the man's elbows to the road. He cocked his right arm and clenched a fist, ready to drive it into the would-be hitman's nose.

The man yelped. "No, please."

"Who the fuck are you?" Porter raised his fist higher and eyed the man's nose.

"No! No!" He squirmed. "Please, no my nose! Please?"

Porter recoiled at the sound of the high-pitched cry for mercy. He remembered where he'd heard the unique voice before.

He stared down at the man's chest, placed both hands on the bulky jacket and squeezed. Silicone tits!? He bent forward and ripped the hood and sunglasses away. "Kwang? Nok's ladyboy mate? What the fuck are you doing?"

Kwang tried to wriggle free but Porter kept her pinned. "I sorry...I not want you see me. But you walking very fast and I worry I lose you."

"You didn't want me to see you? For fucks sake you were standing in the middle of the road. And where's your gun?"

She snorted a laugh. "I no have gun. Only cellphone, silly...I forget my contact lens and not see very far."

Porter shook his head. That explained a lot. He jumped up then pulled her to her feet. "Now…Why'd you follow me?"

She brushed herself down and didn't reply.

He remembered she had a soft spot for him. "Come on, sweet, tell me why you've been following me." He smiled. "I'll take you for a nice lunch…"

"Really?"

He nodded.

"Okay…Nok ask me to do. So you safe when you walk in Chinatown."

His bemusement turned to rage. "Serious? I'm gunna frickin' strangle that girl..." He spoke quickly, forgetting Kwang could barely understand. "I thought you had a gun…I could've whacked you from behind and killed you."

She shrugged. "Okay…I sorry." She smiled and tried to jiggle her tits. "We go eat now?"

He grunted. "Nah, I lied. Now get out of my sight before I kick your skinny ass all over the street."

She flicked her head back as she glared. "I no like you anymore."

He watched her slink away then turned his thoughts to Nok. Was she trying to protect him? Or was she no different to all the others and worried about what he might find?

# TWENTY-SEVEN

Porter strode into the Interpol office at 7.50am on Monday, grunted a reply to greetings from Helen and Fon, then spotted Nok at a Xerox machine in the far corner and charged towards her. He grabbed her by the elbow and pulled her into the adjacent interview room. "I tried to reach you all yesterday afternoon and half the night. Why didn't you answer? What the hell are you up to?"

"I was visiting my mother and couldn't use a phone." She scowled and pushed his hand away. "What am I up to? I don't know what you're talking about."

"You had Kwang tail me around Chinatown...Or are you denying it?"

"Yes, I did ask her to follow you. For protection. After recent attempts on your life I'm worried."

"For my protection?" He scoffed as he laughed. "Kwang was bloody useless and it's lucky I didn't kill her...Nah, I'm not buying it. There's another reason you had me followed. You think I'm gunna do something rash and embarrass you. You don't trust me, do you?"

She broke eye contact to glance at the ceiling. A corner of her mouth twitched. "Of course I trust you, and there was no ulterior motive...I've got worked to do." She sauntered to her desk.

He had no doubt she'd lied. But why? What wasn't the 'little bird' telling him?

He left the interview room, walked past Jaru and ignored his snickering. He heard Helen and Fon whispering to each other from desks to his left. He sat, flicked the PC on, then nodded to acknowledge their stares. Nok occupied the desk in front of his and had re-positioned her chair to work with her back to him.

He'd been reading email correspondence for ten minutes when the desk-phone rang.

"Dan Porter," he answered.

"Hey stranger, it's Lyn."

He smiled, because they hadn't spoken for a few weeks and he missed her. "G'day, sweet, great to hear from you. Agent Lyn Foster, Interpol… It's got a good ring to it."

"Thanks. It's slowly growing on me."

"What were the odds of us both coming to work for this mob?"

"I know, especially after what happened with Carinya in Crooked River and the whole fiasco that followed. We loathed everything about Interpol."

"Yeah, but then again I loathed most of my time in the state cops too and stayed there for fifteen years." They both laughed. "Steve Williams told me you're in Los Angeles at the moment… Any luck with the missing students? Four Vietnamese-Australian girls, right?"

"Yep, and no, no luck. And as much as I wanted to catch up with you, you grumpy but lovable bastard, my assignment here's what I'm calling about…You okay to chat?"

He swiveled on the chair to look about the room. No-one sat too close or seemed to be paying undue attention to his conversation. "Yeah, go ahead."

"It's just past 6pm here and I'm finishing up a job I did with the LAPD anti-trafficking squad this afternoon. We executed a search warrant on a downtown massage parlor well known for its naughty 'extras'. So it's effectively a brothel and we received information about under-aged Asian girls working there." She sighed. "I was hoping to find our Aussie students."

"But you didn't? And everything was above board?"

"No sign of our students. And their operation's far from legit, which is where I'm hoping we can help each other...We removed five girls from the parlor and recovered their passports from a safe. It seems to be the usual scenario with girls held against their will until they've worked off their travel expenses and then some...Two of the girls are Filipino, of legal age and with proper work documents. But the other three are seventeen-year-old Thai girls who arrived in the US two weeks ago."

"Yeah? And they went there to do what?"

"The U.S. embassy in Bangkok issued them with student visas to attend a basic English course at a language school here in LA that offers employment opportunities afterwards."

"Except they never made it to the school. Right? And the poor buggers were forced into prostitution... By who? Who took their passports from 'em?"

"We had a Thai interpreter with us and she asked them several times. They likely have no idea or were too afraid to say. The massage parlor's owner is an older Cambodian-American woman. She's been locked up and isn't talking."

Porter thought of the African students who'd worked as street hookers along Sukhumvit. "Did someone sponsor their trip? Their visas?"

"Yep. And I'm hoping you, your analyst or any contacts in the US Embassy at your end can help. The organization that sponsored these girls is called...God's Angels in Thailand. Have you heard of them?"

Porter's eyebrows arched as he sucked a quick breath. "Too right I have. They call themselves GAIT for short and are supposed to be an NGO run by the Anglican Church."

"Interesting...The guys here made phone calls to local immigration and education departments. It's so strange, because no-one seems to have any information about them on record, yet they've still been able to secure student visas."

"I don't reckon you will find anything about GAIT, because we've had the same problem here. They're a phantom organization, this dodgy mob who miraculously get official applications approved and stamped without ever putting a name or address on 'em."

"Miraculously? You think there's corruption at play, don't you? I can hear the frustration in your voice."

"I've no doubt...It's on a massive level and makes me crook in the guts every time I think about it. Government officials from departments supposed to be looking out for these kids profit from their misery."

"Well, sorry, that was the bad news...Ready for some good stuff?"

He grinned. "Bloody oath, cos I need some. Hit me with it."

"Our interpreter's originally from Bangkok. Have you seen those amulets Thai Buddhists wear around their necks? Well, the girls all wore the same amulet and the interpreter recognized the temple that's portrayed on them. When she asked if that temple had sponsored their visas, they all denied it. She thinks they were lying to protect it, or I should say...To protect someone."

"We've got a temple in Bangkok that could be linked to GAIT?"

"Yep. Grab a pen…" She waited ten seconds then spelt the temple's name out for him.

He looked at the words written in his notebook and read them aloud. "Wat Khongwihan."

He sensed everyone in the office had spun towards him and realised he'd said the name too loud. He repeated the name under his breath and remembered where he'd seen it before. It was the massive temple he'd marveled at in Chinatown. He glanced left and saw Helen and Fon pretending to chat. Nok sat in front and had probably heard his entire conversation with Lyn. He peered to the right at Jaru, who made no attempt to disguise his eavesdropping. What was the sneaky bastard up to?

Lyn coughed. "You still there, Dan?"

Porter pictured the innocent faces of Lisa Baxter and the other missing girls. Were they being held in the Chinatown temple? "Yeah, sorry, was just thinking… Send me everything you have on the Thai girls."

"Will do…It could be that the temple's sponsorship involvement is legit and they're not involved with what's happening once the girls arrive in LA. But then again, why would a church backed NGO be tied up with a temple? Either way, any evidence you can find will be crucial."

"Agreed, and in the best-case scenario the temple's head-honchos are GAIT's bosses." Hope washed over him because he had faith in Lyn's information. "Don't worry, I'll get inside this temple. I'll search for our girls and any documents linked to the various places in LA you've mentioned."

"Well if anyone can pull this off it's the great Dan Porter…"

"Keep the compliments coming and you'll be able to scratch my head from over there." He chortled. "That all for now?"

"Yep, talk soon. And be safe, okay?"

"Always, sweet. Always…"

She ended the call.

He tapped the PC's keyboard with renewed vigor to submit a Google image search on Wat Khongwihan. Images appeared on the screen. He leaned forward and squinted. He nodded as he recognized the temple he'd seen in Chinatown. He studied more images and remembered how imposing the compound's outer walls had been and that multiple CCTV cameras had watched him from high above. The compound was too secure to breach. His entry would have to be a covert one.

He conducted a general query on the temple and clicked a search result that appeared as a 'related topic'. He read a recent editorial column from the Bangkok Post in which its author slammed the Thai judicial system. She said it continued to hamper efforts of police attached to the Counter Corruption Division (CCD) by refusing to issue search warrants that targeted certain prestigious temples and the Chief Abbot's who ran them.

He kept browsing and learned as much as he could about the temple and those associated with it. After two hours he found what he'd been looking for, printed the relevant page and formulated a plan in his mind. Problem was, it relied on help from a Thai agent and the only one he trusted to an extent was far from pleased with him.

He stood, tapped Nok on the shoulder and asked her to follow him into the empty meeting room.

He leaned against the table and grinned as she entered.

She looked through him. "What do you want?"

"I need your help. Please." He motioned for her to sit, closed the door then sat next to her.

She folded arms and huffed. "I'm busy. What's this about?"

He placed his open notebook on the table and pointed to the name of the temple. "What do you know about this joint?"

Her face screwed. "Wat Khongwihan in Chinatown…It's one of the most influential Buddhist temples in Thailand. Why you asking?"

He gave her a brief summary of what Lyn Foster had told him, that the temple might be linked to GAIT and human-trafficking syndicates in Thailand and the US.

She glared with cold eyes. "Don't be ridiculous…" Her face reddened as nostrils flared. "Why the fuck would its Chief Abbot and his followers associate themselves with a bunch of low-life criminals from a Christian NGO?"

"Because…" He paused for once to choose a more tactful reply, aware he'd already struck a raw nerve. "Because GAIT isn't a Christian NGO, and as we've suspected it's just a front for criminal activity on a much larger scale."

She shook her head at him. "These temples are sacred to so many people. They're not sinful places like your churches."

Porter chuckled. "My churches? Hey, you're preaching to the converted…But my dear old mum wouldn't agree with you and she's definitely no sinner."

"Whatever…But you're just dying to make a monk or anyone of faith one of your main suspects, aren't you? Because they threaten your beliefs as an atheist?"

He dismissed her accusation with a bemused grin. "Look, I've received solid info from a very reliable source and I will act on it by going inside that temple. You gunna help me or not?"

She sighed. "I'll help you apply for the search warrant, but such temples remain untouchable and the chances of getting one are next to none. And we'll have to tell Sawatri because he'll find out sooner or later."

"I've been reading about the CCD blokes and hurdles they've faced trying to investigate dodgy monks. If Thai coppers struggle to get search warrants, what hope have I got to convince a judge? Nah, applying for one's a waste of time…And as we've discussed before, it's best to keep Sawatri out of the loop on this one."

She frowned. "I told you he wasn't impressed when I questioned his directive not to go after the Arab dealers in Nana. And he's since warned me again not to disrespect him. He told me to report everything we do and that he'll dismiss me from Interpol if I disobey another order." Her exotic eyes mesmerized him. "Sorry Dan, but I won't risk my career on your hunch."

He met her stare. "That's the thing about following directions and the 'right' procedures. It all looks great on paper but has got us absolutely nowhere… The crooks we're after, the mongrels abducting and selling these young girls, they don't play by the rules, Nok. And to catch the bastards and stop 'em, we're gunna have to break a few rules too. And besides, Sawatri isn't here, he's on one of his junkets down south and won't know about this unless you tell him." He kept eyes locked until her icy resistance seemed to melt away. "I know you care about these girls and wanna save 'em as much as I do. And I know how to get into this temple and search for 'em. Covertly, with minimal risk."

She broke eye contact then punched his shoulder. "You know I hate you, right? Casting that spell on me with your sexy green eyes." She smiled. "Alright, damn it, tell me about this 'secret' way in of yours."

He unfolded the advertisement he'd printed and flattened it on the table. He pointed to the headline as he read it aloud. "**The Authentic Buddhist Temple Experience: Spend 3 days as a novice monk.** It's a program aimed at tourists," he told her.

She nodded as she read. "It's run by the Buddhism Council to raise funds for dhamma school projects."

"Yeah, and I've already confirmed that our Chinatown temple participates in it." He waited for her to stop reading, grinned and ruffled his fringe. "The part about having to shave my head's a bit of a worry..."

"It's the most absurd plan I've heard in over ten years of policing."

"I agree that it's crazier than trying to smuggle Euro made ecstasy into China using two-minute noodle packets, but it's my only way in."

She broke into laughter. "You're actually serious about this?"

"Bloody oath...There's a program starting on Wednesday and you're gunna act as my travel agent and get me on it. Fake name for you when making the booking and the name on my fake passport for me." He worried she might tell one of the others. "This stays between you and me. Yeah?"

Her facial expression became solemn as though deep in thought. "I want you to understand something…Only recently two Special Branch Detectives went into a temple undercover and were almost beaten to death when discovered…You being a non-Buddhist foreigner will make the intrusion a hundred times worse. If the monks learn you're not an innocent tourist but an under-cover cop who's breached their sacred inner sanctum under false pretense, they will kill you."

Porter nodded as jaw clenched. He didn't doubt it.

# TWENTY-EIGHT

Porter entered Wat Khongwihan in Chinatown with four other tourists at 6am on Wednesday. A novice monk was assigned to assist him during the three-day program. After a short registration process the monk led him away from the main temple building through well-kept gardens to one of five guestrooms bordering a paved courtyard. The room had limestone walls and a small window next to the door. A thin sleeping mat covered the tiled floor on one half of the room. A wooden desk and chair furnished the other side.

The monk shaved Porter's head. He gave him an orange robe to wear and handed him a book the size of a bible. He spoke his first words, in broken English. "Read this. It about what Lord Buddha say. Contemplate your being..."

Porter nodded and the monk left the room. He stood in the doorway and rubbed his shaved head as he watched him walk away. It felt rough and prickly and reminded him of the distant past and his previous life as a soldier. It was a time when the fear of death had made him 'contemplate his being' on a daily basis and he didn't need some kid explaining how to do it now.

He watched the novice monk greet two others who guarded an entrance to the main building then disappear inside it. The secure building was large enough to house a hundred rooms and he had no doubt it contained the temple's administration offices and the evidence he sought. But did it contain secret rooms? Were rooms deep within its golden walls being used to hold Lisa Baxter and the other missing girls? He desperately needed to search that main building. But how to get inside it?

Porter gazed at a flawless sky as the sun neared its zenith when the same monk came to collect him several hours later. He followed him into the main building and down a long corridor. He peered inside offices as he strolled past and saw monks shuffling papers behind desks.

The novice monk stopped outside the last office and performed a wai to someone inside it. He had a brief conversation in Thai then passed Porter and headed back down the corridor.

Porter stepped into the office and glanced about the large room. Its modern furnishings seemed to be as expensive as its ceramic floor tiles. A long window on the far wall gave a view of the courtyard beyond it. He noticed metal filing cabinets under the window and made a conscious effort to avert eyes from them.

"Please sit, Mr McKinnon," the rotund, middle-aged monk behind the bulky desk said fluently. "Mr Samuel McKinnon from Australia...Is that correct?"

Porter sensed doubt in the monk's voice. Had he already been detected as a fraud? On his first morning? Or was he being paranoid? He nodded. "Yep. That's me, sir."

The monk chuckled. "There's no need to call me 'sir'. I'm the Assistant Abbot here in Wat Khongwihan. My name is Ajarn Chalad, which means 'Wise Teacher'. You may call me Chalad."

"Thanks. And sorry, I'm not sure what my name means..."

Chalad studied him with kind eyes. "The shaved head suits you, Samuel, and your robe is also a good fit." He took a piece of paper from the desk and squinted at it. "Your registration form says that when you were searched on entry this morning, the registrar monk found only a watch in your possession. Did you not bring a cellphone with you?"

"Nah, I thought this experience would be more authentic without one."

"Very wise, because we forbid their use and teach our novices that they're nothing but a poisonous material possession."

Porter grinned on the inside. He'd spent most of the morning watching monks wander the temple's grounds through his window and all had buried their heads in a phone.

Chalad grabbed a ceramic pot and poured steaming liquid into a matching cup. He pushed the cup and saucer across the desk.

Porter raised the cup. The rich aroma of brewed tea leaves wafted to his nose.

"Try it," Chalad said. "It's the finest Jasmine tea in all of Thailand."

Porter sipped. Sweet earthiness soothed his throat.

"Lovely, isn't it?" Chalad waited for him to nod. "I must confess, Samuel, that I don't normally invite foreign visitors into my personal office. But I saw you're on holiday from Sydney and it's a city I'd like to know more about. If you don't mind?"

Porter placed the cup on the desk. "Sure, ask away."

"Well, is land close to the city-center expensive? Phra Medhikorn plans to build a sister-temple there to benefit cross-cultural dharma studies and we'd like to have some idea of the costs involved."

"Yeah, it's blood--." Porter remembered he was playing the part of a wide-eyed tourist interested in Thai Buddhism and cut himself short. "Yes, Sydney's very expensive. You would be better off looking for land in its outer suburbs...Who is Phra Medhikorn again?"

"Oh, please excuse me...Phra Medhikorn is my boss, the Chief Abbot of this temple and one of the most revered Buddhist monks in all of Thailand."

"Wow, amazing, you're lucky to learn from such a great man...I'd love to meet him. Is he here?"

"Unfortunately he's away on business at the moment and rarely graces us with his presence these days."

"Business?"

"Yes, meetings for various charities supported by the National Buddhism Office. And he performs special ceremonies for sponsors who in turn provide funds for the rather expensive maintenance of our temple."

Chalad pointed to a framed photo on the wall to his right, the first in a row of four. "That's him standing next to his private jet. He needs it to travel to the endless events he's asked to attend. You see, his wisdom is highly sought after in Thailand and much of Southeast Asia."

Porter gasped. "He must be rich if he can buy a jet?"

"No, it was a gift...Thailand's wealthy are a very superstitious lot. They make donations to the temple in the hope their generous deeds will protect them in this life and reward them in the next."

Porter nodded. "Ah, I've read about that. Good karma, right?"

"Yes, excellent, Samuel." Chalad's eyes sparkled as he stared. "Karma."

Porter glanced at the photos on the wall. All four seemed to portray the same man - Phra Medhikorn, the temple's head-honcho. "Do you mind if I take a closer look at the Abbot's photos?"

"Please…" Chalad waved a hand towards them. "Go ahead."

Porter stood, stepped closer to the wall and peered at the photo of Phra Medhikorn posing on a runway in front of a shiny jet plane. His brown face was covered in deep wrinkles and Porter guessed he was close to seventy. He seemed to be short in stature and his orange robe hung to the tarmac, loose on a skeletal frame. He wore a smug smile, a gold chain around his neck and a Rolex on his left wrist.

Porter shuffled to the next photo. The Chief Abbot posed on a street with a curved sign for 'Santa Monica Yacht Harbor' in the background. In the third photo he sat in the driver's seat of a Royal-blue Bentley with 'Phra 1' number plates. Porter scoffed under his breath. He knew exactly where the temple's 'donations for maintenance' were being spent.

He came to the last photo and studied it the longest. It appeared to be the Chief Abbott standing alongside a race car. But he wasn't dressed in his robe. He wore a collared-shirt with jeans and leather boots. Sunglasses hid his beady eyes and a blue cap covered his bald head. Two sexy blondes in bikinis, 'Budweiser' promotional girls, pecked his cheeks from both sides.

Porter pointed at the man. "Is this Phra Medhikorn? Was this picture taken in America too?"

Chalad came alongside him. "Yes, that's the dear old fellow at a NASCAR meet in California. About, oh, ten years ago now. We have a sister-temple near San Diego and he was invited as a guest of honor…He loves car racing and still attends meets at the International Circuit up at Buriram when his ailing health allows."

Porter leaned closer to the photo. "That's one beautiful looking motor vehicle he's posing with."

"Yes, it's a Chevy Lumina. His favourite." Chalad checked his watch. "I'm sorry but our chat must end here. I have a meeting…Can I help you with anything before I go?"

Porter nodded. "I love the architecture of these old buildings and would like to learn more about their history and construction… Am I free to explore the temple complex for a while?"

Chalad's black eyes narrowed before he smiled. "I sense you're a good man, Samuel, with pure intentions. We have nothing to hide from our friends and you may wander at will."

Porter did exactly that for the next two hours. He walked the corridors of every building within the complex he could gain access too. And areas he couldn't explore, he decided were too small to be holding thirty-odd girls in secret captivity. He saw and heard no evidence that the missing girls were, or ever had been, inside the compound.

He took mental notes as he strolled through gardens, of the location of security cameras, dog kennels, floodlights and watch-houses. He sat on a bench and studied two well-built guards. They wore similar orange robes to his, with ammunition belts secured around waists. He couldn't be certain from twenty meters away but curved magazines on the assault rifles slung over their shoulders looked like those of the Chinese made QBZ-95.

He watched the guards patrol the path that ran from the main building and past the five guestrooms to the compound's monstrous outer wall. He peered at his watch and timed how long it took them to dawdle from his room to the wall and back again. Five minutes.

Later that night he'd have five minutes to execute the second part of his operation inside the temple. Only five minutes to break into Chalad's office via the window overlooking the courtyard, search the filing cabinets and make it back to his room without being detected.

He ate a basic meal with the other tourists at 6pm, attended a chanted prayer session that finished at eight and was in his room by 9pm. He set the alarm on his watch, laid on the mat, and waited.

He awoke to the feel of vibrations against his wrist. He turned the watch's alarm off and confirmed the time. 2.30am. He moved to the window and saw he was in luck. Floodlights overlooking the gardens had been turned off. Thick cloud hid the moon and covered the path from his room to the main building in a veil of darkness. He listened and heard soft footsteps approaching. A torch's beam lit up the path outside his room. He pressed himself against the wall and watched the guards stroll past then towards the outer perimeter.

Porter started the stop-watch feature on his Tag Heuer. He opened the door, hoping its rusted hinges wouldn't squeak, and left the room. He scurried to the main building barefooted then grabbed the window sill and pulled himself up. He tested the window, smiled with relief to find it unlocked and pushed it open. He slid into Chalad's office and stood still, listening while he caught his breath. He activated the weak light on his watch and glanced at the timer. Four minutes. Three inside the office and one minute to get back to his room before the guards did.

He hurriedly searched the first filing cabinet and cursed. All the paperwork was in Thai. He moved to the second cabinet and flicked through receipts in the top drawer. Two words written in English across the front of a receipt caught his attention. 'For supplies'. He ripped the receipt from the drawer and shoved it under the robe and inside his boxer shorts. Then he froze, because a thin beam of light shone under the office door. From a light in the corridor? Were they coming for him?

He pushed all cabinet drawers slowly back into place and listened. He heard voices. Keys jangled. One slid into a lock and turned. A click. The office door creaked open.

Porter dropped to the floor and crawled under the desk. A second later the light came on.

# TWENTY-NINE

Porter raised bare feet from the floor and curled his body into the tightest ball he could. He held his breath, because whoever had entered the office only needed to glance under the desk to find him.

He heard feet shuffle over the floor. A deep cough. The man sniffed. And again, louder, as though sniffing at the air. A trickle of sweat ran down Porter's forehead and he noticed his own foul body odor. Could the man smell it too?

Feet shuffled again and the man seemed to be walking straight towards the desk. Then the sound faded and was drowned out by rustling plastic. A bag opening? Then rustling paper, falling into the rustling bag? A hollow sound echoed. Thin metal dropping onto tiles? A waste-bin being placed on the floor? By a cleaner? Porter grinned. Feet shuffled again, away from him, towards the door. The light was flicked off and the door pulled shut. Darkness.

Porter spun on the floor then knelt at the window. He saw the guards reach the courtyard outside the office, pause to shift rifle's onto opposite shoulders then start the loop back towards the outer wall. Should he keep searching the filing cabinets? Nah, he still had two more nights inside the temple and wouldn't push his luck.

Once the guards were out of sight he slid out the window. He stood on the tips of toes and pulled it closed. He swiveled, scanned the courtyard then returned to his room undetected. He fell onto the mat with his pulsating heart threatening to break through ribs. He felt the receipt in his boxer shorts rub against his thigh and considered using the light on his watch to better assess its worth. But he worried the guards might spot the glow coming from his room so decided to wait until daylight. He rolled onto his back and closed eyes.

It was only because he thought he was still dreaming that Porter didn't punch the monk holding the candle when he shook him awake.

The monk placed a strong hand over his mouth to muffle any sound. His dark eyes widened as he removed his hand and signaled for him to stay quiet.

Porter nodded to let him know he understood then sat up to accept the piece of paper the monk offered. He held it closer to the candle and read the handwritten message on it. 'Follow me before they kill you.'

The monk grunted, pointed to Porter's clothes beside the mat then gestured for him to remove the robe.

Porter had a thousand questions spinning out of control in his mind but knew it wasn't the time or place to ask them. He changed clothes and shoved the note and the receipt he'd taken from Chalad's office into jean's pocket. He rubbed sleep from sore eyes then checked his watch. 3.19am. He gave a thumbs up to the monk, who turned and quickly led the way.

Porter stepped from the room and frowned. Clouds had dispersed and silver moonlight flooded the courtyard and the gardens beyond. He kept low as he followed the monk along a path until they reached a padlocked wooden door at the bottom of the compound's outer wall.

The monk gestured for him to wait. He reached up the wall to search a crevice between crumbling bricks then pulled out a small object. He moved to the door then suddenly spun to look behind them.

Porter did the same and saw a guard-dog running towards him, seconds before its barking and ferocious growls broke the silence. Floodlights turned night into day. Excited men shouted from near the main building.

The monk panicked and fumbled the key as he tried to open the padlock. After five long seconds it clicked and fell to the ground. The monk pulled the iron latch up then across. He tugged at the wooden door and it swung inwards. He waved over his shoulder for Porter to follow then leapt though the opening.

Porter heard paws pounding on the path only a few meters behind him. He darted to the opening in the wall and had to stoop and shuffle sideways to get through it. He turned to see a huge Alsatian, its bloodthirsty red eyes sparkling under harsh lights. It growled and snapped jagged teeth at the calf of his trailing right leg. He winced but was able to shake his leg loose and push the dog away for long enough to reach back and pull the door shut behind him. He jumped away from the wall and into an alley.

He peered towards darkness at one end of the alley and remembered it led to a dead end. He saw lights flash, possibly from men searching with torches, but no sign of the monk who'd aided him. He spun to scan the other direction, desperate for an escape route, and saw angry monks with rifles running towards him. Nok's warning echoed through his mind - 'If they catch you they'll kill you.'

He sprinted for the darker end of the alley, hoping to hide. Lights flashed again, longer and stronger this time. Headlights? From a dark colored van? He ran towards the headlights until a black van skidded to a stop five meters from him.

Its side door slid open. A balaclava covered head appeared from inside. "Porter!" A male called out. "Here!"

The rattle from semi-automatic weapons echoed along the alleyway as the monks fired at him. He felt his body tense then shake in survival mode.

Wheels spun. The black van accelerated.

Porter swiveled to face it as it swerved. He waited for the exact split-second when the van came alongside then dived though the door opening. He tumbled over hard floor and crashed into the far-side interior panel. The door slammed shut. Sounds of gunfire faded. The van sped away from the Chinatown temple.

Porter composed himself and saw the man who'd called out had joined the driver on the front seat. The van swerved at high speed as he crawled forward so he grabbed the back of the seat to steady himself then knelt to study the men who'd help him escape. The driver's face was hidden by a balaclava and they both wore black combat fatigues. They ignored his questions and continued their conversation in Thai. At 3.46am the van stopped outside Porter's apartment building in Asoke and the driver told him to get out.

He watched the van drive off, not surprised to see it didn't bear registration plates. He took the elevator to the 27th floor and banged on Nok's door until she opened it and let him inside.

She wore fluffy, pink pajama bottoms. She doubled the front of her matching robe to conceal naked breasts. "Do you know what time it is? And why aren't you still inside the temple?" She slumped onto the armchair opposite his then smirked and giggled. "Nice haircut. You look like that famous bald guy."

"Kojak?"

"Who? No...Pitbull."

"Who?"

"You know, he's a singer."

"I look like a singing dog?"

"Oh, never mind, but the skinhead look suits you. It's kind of sexy."

"If you say so…" He grinned then passed her the handwritten note the monk had given him. "I reckon you know full well why I left the temple. You gave that message to the monk and told him to get me out of there, didn't you?"

She read the note aloud then met his stare. "No. I swear I know nothing about it."

He scoffed. "Come on, it's exactly like your handwriting with the same fancy loops and all that...And you're the only one who knew I'd gone into the temple undercover."

She shook her head.

He frowned, unsure why she wouldn't admit to helping him. "If not you...Who? A monk came to my room and unlocked a door to get me outside the walls. Then two blokes turned up just in a nick of time and brought me back here in a black van...Someone with enough clout found out I'd been compromised and got me out alive. Sawatri? But if you didn't tell him, how would he have known?"

She yawned. "He's still not back from down south and I've told him nothing... But someone inside the temple could've learned you were in danger and informed Sawatri of it. I guess we'll find out later today." She crossed arms and scowled. "And then I'll get the sack, with you having learned nothing from your little adventure."

"I wouldn't say that..." He stood to hand her the receipt he'd taken from Chalad's office. "It's the only paperwork I found with English written on it. See, 'for supplies'." He moved to lean on the back of her chair and studied the receipt over her shoulder. "What do you reckon they could be? The supplies? Some sort of code for selling our girls as sex-slaves?"

She shrugged. "Who knows?"

"Or drugs...More than a few monks inside that temple seemed to be off their heads and it could be how their leaders' control 'em."

"Possible, but doubtful..."

"And those," he pointed to squiggles he'd never seen before, "what are they?"

"Thai numbers," she told him. "This receipt is for fifty-million baht. Roughly one and a half million US dollars."

"Bloody hell, that's a lot of 'supplies'... Received from who? What's this other writing on the front say?"

"This whole document's confusing...I'm unsure if the Chinatown temple kept this receipt for goods they've purchased, or sold." She pointed to writing at the top of the receipt. "This here's the name of another temple and below is the name of its Chief Abbott...Phra Wadjitmedhi. I think he's the seller and the Chinatown temple bought from him. But again, I can't be certain of it."

"Is he the bloke leading GAIT? Is his temple holding and selling the girls? Is he a crook? Have you heard of him?"

She shot him a look of pity. "I know you must be tired but slow down. You're rambling and sound desperate... No, I don't know of him, but that means nothing as corrupt monks often change their religious names after falling foul of the law. And if you don't think the Chinatown temple's abducting and selling the foreign girls, then yes, the temple on this receipt is our only lead from here."

"You're right about me getting desperate, and it's because these girls become harder to find with each passing hour... After speaking to the second in charge and sniffing around, I know the blokes at the Chinatown temple are corrupt, but don't reckon they run GAIT." He noticed writing on the back of the receipt. "What's that say on the back?"

She flipped the paper, glanced at the writing then turned it back to the front. "It's nothing important..."

"Well we need to get an address for this other temple and search it. Our missing girls might just be the expensive 'supplies' referred to."

She nodded as she pressed her phone. Silence for a minute as she read from it.

He stretched his back. "What are you doing?"

"I just did a search. Give me a minute to book our plane."

"This temple isn't in Bangkok? Is its Abbot well-known?"

"No, and no… Now go and get some sleep. We're leaving from the private jet terminal at 10am."

"Destination?"

"The jewel of the south… Phuket."

# THIRTY

Porter sat next to Nok on the rear seat as the speedboat skimmed over a calm Andaman Sea towards the lone island on the horizon. He glanced at his watch. 11.45am, Thursday. He nodded, impressed it had taken them less than two hours to travel via private jet to the airport then reach their current location by speedboat. He peered to his left and studied Phuket island's most south-western point as they passed it.

Nok pointed straight ahead. "I checked the online maps this morning," she shouted to be heard above the sound of roaring engines and rushing wind. "That small island's called Koh Mayakun. It means 'Magic Island'. Can you see the golden Buddha statue in the middle, on top of the slight hill? That's where the temple is…"

Porter nodded and a sense of hope they would find the girls on the island made him shiver. He admired Nok out the corner of his eye. Her platinum-blonde hair, designer shades, the diamond-studded watch and thick gold bracelet, the tight-fitting t-shirt and jeans on a perfectly toned body… She looked more 'rock-star' than 'Interpol Agent', and he couldn't stop thinking about what her glistening lips would taste like.

She took a Glock pistol from her handbag and passed it to him. "It's a spare I keep in my apartment. I thought you might need it."

He pulled the pistol's slide back and saw it was loaded. He grinned. "And what, I haven't needed a weapon in this crazy joint before now?"

"I didn't care before now if you were killed or not…" She smiled. "But you've grown on me and I've decided it's fun to keep you around." She leaned forward to have a brief conversation with the Thai speedboat driver then turned to Porter. "He's going to drop us off on a small beach on the other side of the island. I told him to circle around and approach from the south so those trees behind the temple hide us from view."

He glanced ahead, to the island now less than five-hundred meters away. "It's more than just a tad stupid, you know."

"What is?"

"That we didn't tell anyone else on the Lost Angels crew exactly where we were coming today, worried about the wrong people finding out. Nor the local Phuket cops for the same reason…But we're trusting this speedboat driver not to sell us out and tip the temple's security blokes off. Why?"

"Don't worry, I trust Chai. He's my cousin, well, sort of…" She read Porter's dubious frown correctly. "And he doesn't have his phone. And I've told him to wait on the beach for us."

Ten minutes later they leapt from the boat and landed on the beach's shimmering white sand.

Nok pointed ahead to the right. "That stone path will take us to the temple's rear gate."

Porter saw a path leading from the beach into a dark-green mass of thick vines and palm-trees. He looked straight up, fifty meters he guessed, and shielded eyes as the midday sun's scorching rays reflected off the golden Buddha's head. "How do you know about this path? From the maps?"

"No." She panted as she secured her handbag to the rear and trudged over soft sand. She aimed her pistol to the front and stepped onto the path. "Chai told me about it."

She led the way as they followed the path away from the beach. They'd covered less than a hundred meters when she dropped into a squat and motioned for him to follow suit.

He duck-walked to stop alongside her.

"I can see a guard-tower on top of the rear wall," she whispered.

He peered to the tower, less than fifty meters ahead. "Yeah and it appears to be empty." He saw one side of a wooden gate and craned his neck for a better view. "And the gates next to it are…"

"Ajar, and wide enough to enter," she said. "But why would they be?"

He stood and aimed the Glock at the guard-tower then crept towards the temple's rear gates.

They reached them without incident and Porter peered through the gap towards what he assumed was the main temple. Its stone walls had been painted a radiant white and decorated with intricate teakwood carvings and patterns in all shades of orange and brown. A single wooden spire curved away from a yellow roof.

The terracotta-tiled courtyard leading to it was dirty and littered with dead leaves. Beyond the main temple several pagodas and other smaller buildings stood dull and neglected. The giant, golden Buddha statue rose up from the center of the compound to dominate its surroundings.

"The whole place looks deserted, as though no-one has been here for ages," Nok said.

"I agree but be careful all the same." He nodded as he slid between the gates. "Follow me. Eyes and ears."

They scurried across the courtyard towards the main temple's closed doors. Porter climbed four stairs then cautiously tried the door handle. Locked. He turned to frown at her.

"There'll be other entrances around the side," she told him. "Come this wa--."

"Stop! Stop or you is dead!" A male shouted in broken English from somewhere behind and above them. "Now!"

Porter froze mid-step then glanced at Nok. She returned a fearful stare.

The same male yelled in Thai for five seconds.

She dropped the Glock then raised hands. "Do the same," she told Porter. "They've got a heavy machine-gun aimed on us from the guard tower. They'll execute us both if you don't co-operate."

Porter nodded as he raised hands. His pistol clattered on the ground. He heard thudding footsteps behind him and looked over his shoulder. Two Asian men in camouflaged combat fatigues picked the Glock's up then retreated with them aimed at his head. He saw from the way they moved and handled the pistols that the men were well-trained, most likely ex-military mercenaries for hire. He looked back to the front as the temple's doors unlocked and swung open.

One of the men behind them shouted in Thai.

"Stay calm, Dan." Nok exhaled with a whoosh as she walked forward through the opening. "Just do as I do."

The doors slammed shut behind them and Porter heard Nok gasp. Her hand felt for his in the dark. He took a firm hold of it and let her lead him towards an orange glow at the far-end of the large room.

They stopped ten meters from the wall and stood before a shrine surrounded by flickering candles and smoking incense sticks. Soft light bounced off the smiling Buddha in the center, a golden figure that almost touched the high ceiling.

Porter's eyes adjusted and he noticed a person standing next to the shrine in a black, hooded cloak. The person stood with back to them.

"Welcome, foolish intruders, I am Phra Wadjitmedhi, Chief Abbot of the glorious Wat Mayakun," the cloaked monk said. "Come closer."

They shuffled forward.

Porter remembered that 'Wadjitmedhi' was the same name written on the receipt he'd found in the Chinatown temple. The receipt 'For Supplies'...Was this head monk the man who led GAIT? Had they finally found the bastard who'd abducted more than thirty foreign girls? Was he holding them captive somewhere inside the temple compound?

The hooded monk clapped three times. A switch clicked and florescent bulbs hanging from the ceiling lit up the room. Porter saw they were surrounded by five armed men who'd been lurking in dark corners.

"No doubt you're curious, Agent Porter?" the hooded monk said. "Curious who warned my men you were coming? About who has betrayed you?"

Porter glanced to Nok, who avoided eye contact.

She frowned at the monk. "I recognize your voice...From where? Who are you?"

The head monk slowly turned to face them. The hood fell back to reveal a bald, middle-aged Asian man with evil eyes. "Hello Nok, my dear little bird."

Nok gasped. "General Woracha? What?" She shook her head. "But...? Why?"

Woracha glared at her. "I am no longer Police General Woracha. Here in my religious sanctum you will show due respect and address me as Phra Wadjitmedhi."

Porter turned to her. "You know this bloke?"

"Of course she does, Agent Porter. We are partners in crime..." Woracha smiled fiendishly. "And that's why she's led you into this trap."

Porter scoffed. "Bullshit."

"Haven't you wondered how Nok lives so extravagantly on an Interpol agent's salary?"

Porter glanced at her diamond-studded watch then shrugged.

"Well, allow me to enlighten you, Agent Porter...You see, young Nok is nothing but a high-class whore who uses lovestruck men to pay her way through life. She had a ridiculously rich Singaporean sugar-daddy who put her through university. He bought her the designer clothes and all her expensive jewelry...And when she finished her studies she couldn't dump him and return to Thailand fast enough. The silly old fool died of a broken heart."

Porter shook his head, not wanting it to be true. "Nah, mate, I still don't believe you."

"Well, you should...By the time Nok's sugar-daddy money ran out she was well and truly addicted to the luxuries of wealth. But she couldn't continue that lifestyle with her lowly wages, so she joined my criminal enterprise and has since made millions dealing white gold to the rich and famous. Tens of millions of baht in profits have fed her greed."

Porter turned and forced her to meet his stare. "What 'criminal enterprise'? Tell me that aint true."

Her eyes watered. He saw pain in them. The pain of admitting to a devastating truth?

"Fuck me it's true, isn't it?" Porter said. "Dealing? White gold?" He thought of the abducted foreign girls. His heart dropped. "No? Tell me you're not selling the white girls…" His eyes pleaded with her.

A tear ran down her cheek. "No, not the girls, I would never…I've helped General Woracha sell Colombian cocaine. A lot of it. All throughout Thailand and in Malaysia and Indonesia as well."

Woracha laughed. "Yes, because she's a greedy whore who loves the money."

She kept her stare on Porter. "No, he's lying…My mother's very ill and I need the money to pay for the best doctors and full-time hospital care. I was struggling on my Interpol wage to buy the medication she needs. When her health deteriorated further I needed a lot more money just to keep her alive. Selling cocaine was the only way to get it."

"What a wonderful actress she is, Porter…Can't you see it? The fake tears? She and her friend Park Heung-Min are like obese children gorging themselves in a candy store, never knowing when enough is enough."

Porter recalled their meeting with Heung-min in the Babylon casino. "I suspected you and Heung-min knew each other and I was right, wasn't I? You've worked with that bastard all along?"

Tears streamed down her cheeks as she shook her head. "I'm sorry, I really am, but I had to do it for my mother."

"She's still lying, Porter." Woracha grunted. "My older brother's her boss and tells me others inside Interpol sus--.""

"What?" Nok glared at him. "Sawatri's your brother?"

"Half-brother. Same father but I use my mother's name…Don't pretend you didn't know."

"I had no idea."

"More lies, Porter. She's helped my brother impede your investigation from the start…And then when she fucked-up by taking you into Babylon casino, furious members of the elite gave her a choice to leave Thailand or betray you. That you'll die here on Magic Island after she's led you into this ambush says it all…"

"No, Dan, don't believe him." She stepped close and gripped Porter's biceps in trembling hands. "Please don't believe him."

He couldn't meet her gaze.

"She's betrayed you to save her own career, Porter. To feed her own greed... Men are nothing but pawns in her selfish game of chess and she's sacrificed you to the bishop."

Porter shook her hands away, unable to hide his disgust.

"Dan? Please? I love you and would never do this to you…He's lying, to tear us apart and make us weak…Can't you see that?"

"Enough!" Woracha demanded. He paused for five seconds as though in deep thought. "Porter, I must confess that our little bird is indeed telling the truth…She didn't betray you."

Porter frowned. Who else could've known or learned of their trip to Magic Island and given Woracha the heads-up? Jaru? Sawatri? Chai, the speedboat driver? Interpol's private-jet pilot?

"If it wasn't Nok, then who?" he asked Woracha.

"Ah, that's for me to know…And although she didn't betray you, she has betrayed her nation. She's made the mistake of putting her love for a stupid farang before her duty to Thailand." Woracha pulled a pistol from under his cloak. "And now she must pay the price…" He took aim and shot Nok in the head.

Porter's body tensed, rigid with grief. He wiped Nok's blood from the side of his face then knelt over her corpse and stared at the mangled mess where her left eye used to be. He spun towards Woracha. "You gutless mongrel." He stood, fuming and about to run at him. A rifle-butt slammed into the back of his skull before he could take a single step.

When Porter regained consciousness he lay on his back with rusted, iron shackles around his wrists and ankles. The shackles were connected to thick chains tied around a pole. A blurry pole in the middle of a cage. A cage in the center of a courtyard, shaded from the harsh sun beneath a wooden pergola's sloping roof.

His vision remained blurred as he stared towards the opposite corner. *Are they…?* He sat up and shuffled backwards until he leaned against the cage. Eyes focused and he blinked rapidly, trying to disprove what they saw. Fear heightened his other senses. He heard soft snoring and sniffed his nose at the foul odor wafting from the other side of the cage. The sounds and smells emitted by two adult, sleeping tigers.

Woracha appeared on his right and stepped towards the cage. "My beloved pet tigers have been sedated but are due to wake any moment," he whispered. "When they do they'll be famished, having not eaten meat for three days. And they'll be extremely pleased to find you in there with them…Because you, Agent Porter, are going to be their dinner."

# THIRTY-ONE

*My diary from hell by Lisa Baxter    about 4th of October    I think*

*I just finished my lunch and I think today is Thursday. But I'm not sure because I can't remember if I drew an X on the wall for yesterday. So it could be Wednesday. Wait. I will count the X's.*

*Okay there are 17 X's on the wall. I maybe missed some days and maybe some days when I was really wasted I put more than one X. So I guess I've been held prisoner in this place for almost three weeks now.*

*But at least I got moved to this bigger room yesterday. They put the cloth sack over my head when they did and they didn't carry me very far, so I guess I must still be in the same place. The room is twice as big as the one before but doesn't have a window. It has a bigger bed and nicer furniture and is fancy looking. It has nice pictures on all the walls and the paint is thick and the decorations look expensive. My mum would say it's classy.*

*And it's lucky this new bedroom has a nice big bed. Because me and my boyfriend made passionate love in it a couple of hours ago. And that makes me think he's a naughty boy. He got me this bigger room with the bigger bed so we could enjoy our lovemaking more.*

Today I so much wanted to pull away his sunglasses and wig. To see what he looks like. But again I couldn't because he always ties my hands to the bed posts.

He speaks good English but in a strange and posh accent so I'm not really sure if he's Asian or what. And today after he cum the first time he cried out and said something I couldn't understand. I don't know if it was some weird slang or from a language I've never heard before. And then after that when we were making love the second time he called me 'Claire'. And I got angry and asked him who Claire is. I asked if she's some other woman he's seeing. A mistress. And why won't he tell me his name. I said it's only fair that I know my boyfriend's name. Isn't it.

And then he got angry and slapped me. And then he kissed my bleeding mouth and said he was sorry. He said that I'm his Claire. His only Claire. I'm confused and don't know why he won't call me Lisa. But if it makes him happy and he keeps giving me my fix then I suppose he can call me whatever he likes.

I've been depressed since he left my room. I know he craves my body. And I crave him and his drugs. But does he only crave my body. Or does he really love me. Love me just for who I am. I hope he does. Because I love him. Anyhow he said he's coming back to see me again later tonight and that he has a surprise for me. I can't wait to see what it is.

I think it was thirty minutes ago but not sure because I'm kind of always going up and then coming down. Up *and down and around. About thirty minutes ago I heard the other girls crying again. And it makes me so sad. So sad that tomorrow I will ask my boyfriend to go see them. Maybe his magical drugs can take their pain away too.*

*I hope my mum and dad never have to read this. If you do please know that I love you both very much. I will always be your Lisa. I will always be your little girl.*

# THIRTY-TWO

Porter searched every inch of the cage that the chains shackled to his wrists and ankles allowed him to. It had been well made and he found no means of escape. He sighed as he slumped back down onto dirty tiles then checked his watch. 2.36pm. Almost an hour had passed since he'd come to and found himself locked in the cage with two hungry, sleeping tigers. And according to their demented owner, Police General Woracha aka Phra Wadjitmedhi, the massive cats would soon wake.

Porter saw movement. A tiger's hind leg shook. Then its whole body trembled. Was the tiger dreaming, in a deep sleep? Or was it restless and about to discover him? Was he minutes from being eaten alive?

He dropped chin to chest and closed eyes. A radiant vision of Jane appeared. He told her he loved her then kissed her and said goodbye. He did the same with Amber and his parents. And then an image of a fifth face appeared, fuzzy and obscure as though incomplete. The face of someone he loved more than any other but had forced himself over time not to think about.

The desire to hug each of his loved-ones a final time threatened to burn a hole in his heart. He opened eyes and sucked a deep breath to douse the flames. He wound the heavy chains around both clenched fists and forearms. He'd most likely suffer a violent death inside the cage but he wouldn't make it easy for the famished beasts and would go down fighting.

The closest tiger shook and Porter thought he heard a growl. He stared at it and listened. Another growl. Or was it? And then another growling sound became a deafening roar as the ground beneath him seemed to vibrate. The cage shook and chains rattled. In the far corner feline ears twitched as restless tigers stirred.

Porter smiled when he recognized the sound of whirring rotor blades. Twin engines screamed. From a Black Hawk helicopter? Then the unmistakable pounding echo of a heavy machine gun letting loose. He heard frantic cries and hurried footsteps to his right. He swiveled and saw Woracha's mercenaries running for cover with faces masked in panic and fear. One of them stopped to fire his rifle into the sky. Death rained from the helicopter and cut him in half.

The thunderous commotion woke the tigers. Striped tails slammed against dusty ground. The huge cats rolled onto chests and rested paws in front. Small-arms fire rattled close by. The tigers hissed and jumped to their feet as though startled. Heads rocked back as they sniffed the air. Fearful hissing became hungry growls. They turned to focus on Porter then snarled and started towards him.

Porter stood and braced himself with back against the cage. He held hands up in front of his eyes like a 19th century boxer, hoping the chains wrapped around them might repel the tigers' attack.

The magnificent beasts stopped a meter in front of him and sniffed his scent. They roared and shifted weight onto hind legs as though ready to pounce.

Porter thought he saw shock in the tigers' yellow eyes. A milli-second later their heads exploded and covered the cage's floor in bright blood and grey muck.

Weighty carcasses landed with a thud. He spun left to where the volley of bullets had come from and saw two men in black balaclavas and combat fatigues lowering their weapons. One of them ran to the cage and shot the padlock away from the gate. He entered the cage and fired at chains to set Porter free then led him from it.

Porter stepped out from under the pergola and watched a large transport helicopter touch down in the far-side of the compound. A Black Hawk hovered overhead then flew from view. Somewhere a man screamed as though surprised. Then another scream of agony, and another of fear. Weapons fire echoed all around. The transport helicopter's engine died and rotor blades squeaked to a halt.

One last scream before an eerie silence.

The man who'd freed Porter from the cage removed his balaclava and smiled.

Porter almost fell over. "Jaru? What the…?"

"Hello, Porter." Jaru pointed to the dead tigers. "A tough choice to make…Let you or those beautiful creatures live?" He grinned. Porter didn't. "I'm joking…It's terrible they were kept in this cage. I pray I've freed them from this cruel life and they'll be happily roaming jungles in their next one."

The man next to Jaru removed his balaclava. He was of similar age, height and build. He offered Porter his hand. "Agent Porter, I'm Senior Sergeant Chuchwaron, leader of the SWAT team attached to the CCD that's assisted Detective Seehakot and his unit in this raid."

Porter shook his hand then turned to Jaru. "Detective Seehakot? CCD? What's going on, mate?"

Jaru spoke to Sergeant Chuchwaron in Thai. The SWAT man nodded then walked away.

"My real name's Seehakot and I'm a detective attached to the Counter Corruption Division of the Royal Thai Police," Jaru told Porter once they were alone. "I've been investigating Police General Woracha and his brother for the past six months. Their cocaine distribution has brought them much wealth which they've laundered through this temple. I joined Sawatri's Interpol unit under-cover, hoping to gain more evidence and expose their connections to corrupt bosses higher up in the police and the National Buddhism Office."

Porter blew hot air through pursed lips. "I didn't see that coming...Woracha was here. Did you find him? And I can't wait to lock up his mongrel of a brother. Where's Sawatri now?"

"Sawatri's missing, presumedly on the run. And yes, we did find Woracha in the main temple building." Jaru broke eye contact and stared at the ground. "He was lying dead next to Nok. He must've shot himself."

Porter seethed. "Cowards, him and his brother both...How'd you know me and Nok were here?"

"We learned of Nok's involvement in Woracha's drug supply by mistake...I tried to form a close relationship with her in the Interpol office, as you know, hoping to cultivate her as an informant. But she was too smart for that, to let a stranger in...So we decided to let her keep working for Woracha and have tracked her whereabouts via her phone. Our CCD intell analyst didn't advise me until close to midday that Nok was here in Phuket. I guessed you'd discovered the links to this Magic Island temple and knew you'd be in danger. We called-out the SWAT guys and got here as fast as we could."

Porter grunted. "But too late for Nok...Bloody hell, it sounds like she got caught up in the wrong crowd and her hand was forced. I'm gutted mate, 'cos despite what she was up to, that girl didn't deserve to die here today."

"I know, Porter, I know…She told you about her sick mother?"

"Yeah. And is that legit, that she was selling coke to fund her mum's treatment?"

"Phone conversations we've recorded and checks on her family and financial records suggest that yes, while Nok's moral compass may have been broken, her reasons for needing all that extra cash were pure and for love…I know you two were close and I'm sorry for your loss. I was never a chance of dating her because she'd obviously fallen for you."

Grief kicked Porter hard in the nuts and he shook the vision of Nok's smiling face from his head. Then a cold shiver of guilt ran down his spine. The guilt of feeling relieved. Relieved that she was out of his life and would no longer tempt him.

"Jaru, were you fair dinkum jealous of me and Nok? Or was it all a part of your act?"

"As I said, I was trying to date and get closer to her…Jealousy's an easy emotion for a Thai man to portray and I wanted to see how Sawatri reacted to the conflict between us. I hoped he'd let his guard down and make a mistake. Hoped he would side with me against the 'cocky falang investigator' and reveal information he normally wouldn't."

Porter chuckled. "Well you had me convinced you hated my guts. And I was certain you'd spiked my drink in the nightclub."

"No, that wasn't me…But the part about me despising falang guys who mistreat Thai women was true, because I once had a girlfriend leave me for one. And yes, I do believe too many falang come here wanting to apply their western values to life in Thailand."

"And the racist comments about my missus?"

"I'm sorry, I got caught up in the heat of the moment and went too far there. I didn't mean what I said and I apologize."

Porter nodded.

Jaru met his stare. "Most of what I said and did was an act. Part of the illusion."

Hearing the word 'illusion' made Porter recall the team meeting on his first day. Fon had said words similar to, 'oriental illusions, where nothing and no-one are as they seem', and the phrase had been playing on his mind ever since. He realized he'd been an awestruck fool to trust Nok the way he had and needed to ask himself a pertinent question...Could he now trust Jaru?

He decided he had to and thumped him on the back with an open palm. "Cheers mate for turning up just in time. Those big cats were about to make a right mess of me."

"You're welcome, Porter. It wasn't the first time and I'm sure it won't be the last."

"Meaning?"

"That I've been protecting you from the start...Those were my CCD men who saved you from Russian assassins at the airport and have been following you almost every day since, not Dignitary Protection cops. And it was my informant who got you out of the Chinatown temple when you were about to be murdered, and my men who helped you escape in the van."

"The dead Russian contractors at the airport? Did you find out who they are? Who hired 'em?"

"No, we haven't been able to confirm their identities. But we suspect they worked for the Russian government, who also don't want you sniffing around in Thailand."

Porter nodded. "I thought the same, that it was related to Lost Angels." He smirked. "No wonder I've been paranoid and felt as though two surveillance teams watched my every move. They have been. One for me and one for Nok...How'd you know I was inside the temple and in danger?"

"I've managed to place informants in most of Bangkok's richest temples. My man in Wat Khongwihan overhead its assistant abbot speaking to others after dinner. Ajarn Chalad knew of your deceit and ordered armed men to deal with it."

"He'd been tipped off? By who? Only Nok knew I'd gone in there."

Jaru grinned. "You speak too loud on the phone while you're in the office. I too knew you planned to infiltrate the temple...Nok didn't have links to it so I don't think she gave you up."

"Yeah, I doubt that too."

"I heard you met with Ajarn Chalad. Maybe he made further enquiries that exposed you as a fraud?"

"Possibly... Listen, if you knew I was going inside why didn't you stop me?"

"I wanted to see what evidence the great Dan Porter could dig up. And now I'm curious, because my informant's been a failure. So, what exactly did you find there?"

Porter opened his mouth to explain when a loud, metallic bang distracted him. He looked past Jaru to where ten SWAT team members had formed two lines. One line of operatives threw assault rifles that clattered

254

onto a growing pile of weapons. The other line piled dead bodies.

Jaru called out to them in Thai then listened to the reply.

"We've killed twenty-three mercenaries, with two losses of our own," Jaru told Porter. "The recovered weapons - assault rifles, heavy machine guns and pistols - are military grade and the latest models... Sergeant Chuchwaron's currently leading a search of all remaining buildings. A third team's searching the rest of the island for places the girls might be hidden."

Porter nodded. "Ask these blokes where the weapons come from."

Jaru did then turned back to him. "They said they're all Chinese made. Why?"

"No reason..."

Jaru's cell phone rang and he answered it. He had a brief conversation in Thai. "That was Sergeant Chuchwaron," he told Porter. "The compound search is complete. They found no sign of the missing girls or of them ever being kept here. And they found no drugs, hidden money or other contraband. No sign of illegal activity whatsoever...He did locate a heap of files though, in what he thinks was Woracha's private office. He's left them there for us to go over."

Five minutes later they entered a large office in the temple's administration building. Porter saw a pile of files on the desk. He pulled a chair up to it and sat. Jaru did the same opposite.

Porter plucked a folder from the desk. "Let's have a sticky beak."

They searched through the files for thirty minutes and found nothing of note.

Jaru answered his cell phone and listened. He mumbled in Thai then ended the call.

"What's up?" Porter said. "You've got a face like a stunned mullet."

"Not good news…Our teams searched all over Magic Island, every square meter of it. The girls aren't here."

Porter had expected as much but the news still winded him. Was he too late? Again? Was it time to face the hard truth, that the abducted girls had already been sent from Thailand and would never be found?

"Let's keep searching these folders," he said, "you never know."

Jaru nodded. A few minutes later he slammed a fist onto the desk.

Porter stared at his beaming smile. "You got something?"

"Yes!" Jaru held up an A4-sized piece of paper. "This receipt's evidential gold. I've just flicked through this folder and it's full of them."

Porter hurried to stand behind him. He peered over his shoulder and read the words on the front of the receipt. "For supplies…"

Jaru pointed to various sections of the receipts as he flicked through them and explained what was written in Thai. "These are addresses for hundreds of temples all over Thailand. And each temple's Chief Abbot is listed as Woracha's customer." His voice rose as he pointed to Thai numbers in the bottom corner. "And these prices are incredible amounts. Transactions involving hundreds of millions of baht. These receipts tell us exactly who bought from Woracha and how much they paid him. It's the evidence I need to seize all money and assets owned in the 'Wat Mayakun' name."

Porter noticed scribbled writing on the back of a receipt. "Turn it over. What's that say?"

Jaru studied the squiggly lines. "I can't read it…It looks like a name's been crossed out."

"What do names on the back usually indicate in Thailand?"

"Hmm…" Jaru flicked multiple receipts over. All had the same illegible writing. "A name on the back of a receipt is usually a reference or reminder written by the seller about who, if anyone, supplied them with the original product. Before they then sold it on…"

Porter returned to his seat by the desk. "It's imperative we ascertain whose name's been crossed out multiple times."

"Correct. But we can't read it on any of them."

"You asked earlier if I'd found anything worthwhile in the Chinatown temple. I didn't get to answer…" Porter pulled a crumpled piece of paper from jean's pocket and laid it flat on the desk. "I believe this is a similar receipt issued by Woracha to the Chinatown temple, and also 'For Supplies'." He waited for Jaru to nod then turned the receipt over. "Does this writing on the back help us?"

Jaru leaned forward. "That's strange."

"Why? What does it say?"

"It says 'Park Heung-min', the Korean loan-shark boss." Jaru compared the name to several of those that'd been crossed out. "Corresponding letters of his name appear on certain parts that are legible. I'm confident it's his name that's been crossed out on all these receipts..."

"Which means Heung-min supplied product to Woracha, that he then sold on. But what's the product?"

257

"Cocaine, of course...The temples bought it from Woracha then sold it within their local districts for profit."

"You have proof of that?"

"I'm sure we can find some."

"Nah, the product Heung-min sold to Woracha, that these multiple receipts are written out for, isn't cocaine...Woracha had a plentiful supply coming in from South America that Nok distributed for him. Right?" Porter waited for his nod. "So why would he buy it from the Koreans?"

"You're probably correct...Phone conversations between Nok and Woracha revealed that Heung-min was helping her smuggle the coke in and out of Bangkok. But no, there's nothing to suggest he sold it..."

"And that's why when I asked her about this writing on the back of the receipt, she lied and said it meant nothing. Because if she'd told me Woracha's supplier was Park Heung-min, whether I knew what the product was or not, it would've jeopardized her whole operation."

"Yes, she feared the receipt might come back to bite her. And she couldn't take the risk."

Porter frowned. "If she knew Woracha was on Magic Island and there was a chance of these receipts being found today...Why'd she bring me here? She could've lied about the address on this receipt from the Chinatown temple and I'd never know."

"She could have, but she wasn't aware that Woracha ran this temple and was using it to launder money. She would've been more surprised than anyone to find him here. And a part of her was still a good cop, a person who cared about finding the girls and hoped they'd be saved." Jaru ran a finger over the crumpled paper. "And she was probably confused by this receipt, unsure who was selling and buying, because I certainly am."

"Yeah, she said as much this morning."

"She might've suspected Heung-min was selling coke on the side to pay his debts? That he supplied it to this Magic Island temple, who then sold it to Chinatown or vice versa? Who knows?"

"I'm happy to give her the benefit of doubt, but there's no cocaine here...So I'll ask you the same question I asked her. If the 'product' isn't cocaine, what is it? What does 'For Supplies' relate to? Some sort of code?"

"It could be a code for anything... Tobacco, ganja, alcohol, guns, stolen luxury cars, other drugs?"

"Abducted girls, bought and sold as sex-slaves?"

Jaru shrugged. "Nothing would surprise me where Woracha and Sawatri are concerned."

"With Woracha dead and Sawatri fuck knows where, the only common-denominator left in all of this is Heung-min. We need to find the bastard and I'll beat the info out of him if I have to."

"On return to Bangkok I'm executing a search warrant on Woracha's office at Yaowarat Police station. But I'll have Sergeant Chuchwaron and his SWAT team assist you with gaining entry to and securing the Babylon casino. And take Fon with you, because she'll be madder than a wounded buffalo once she hears about Nok."

Porter nodded. "And while she's holding a Glock to Heung-min's head I'm gunna demand truth from the little turd."

"Remember to ask if he knows Sawatri's whereabouts."

"Don't worry, I will. He's sabotaged this investigation from the start and has most likely cost innocent women their lives. I wanna find and lock up that mongrel Sawatri more than anyone does."

# THIRTY-THREE

Close to 7pm on Thursday, Porter and Fon followed Sergeant Chuchwaron's SWAT team into the casino beneath the Babylon Towers building on Ratchadaphisek road in Bangkok. Two security men standing by the casino's main entrance jumped as though surprised then offered no resistance when Chuchwaron's men charged from the stair-well. The SWAT police quickly searched and secured Babylon casino.

Sergeant Chuchwaron stopped in front of Porter. He nodded towards the Korean thug guarding the entrance to Park Heung-min's private apartment. "Need us to remove him?"

Porter glanced at the stocky thug in suit. He wasn't the same bloke he'd dealt with on his previous visit to the casino. "Nah, she'll be right. Unless he doesn't wanna play ball…Then you can have fun knocking the door in."

Chuchwaron grinned. "We've got your back. No-one enters or leaves until you say so." He retreated a few paces then barked orders to his men.

Porter approached the Korean guard. Fon came alongside. "I'm Dan Porter and I wanna speak to your boss."

"Boss not here."

"Bullshit. He's inside with no escape and my mates over there will obliterate his precious little door if he doesn't open up." Porter pointed to the portable radio in the thug's hand. "Tell him it's in his best interests to let me in. Tell him big, bad Americans with shiny badges will come huffing and puffing if he doesn't..."

The guard frowned then spoke into the radio. The crackled response was loud and abrupt. The guard turned and banged on the steel door three times. Ten seconds later the door opened. Porter and Fon were ushered inside. The heavy door slammed shut behind them.

A skinnier thug Porter hadn't seen before took over from the guard. He led them down a corridor and through the large open space with jacuzzi in the corner. He stopped outside an adjoining room and tapped on the doorframe.

A man yelled from inside, in a language Porter assumed to be Korean.

The thug stepped aside to let them into the massive bedroom then drew a pistol from his shoulder-holster and waited by the door.

Heung-min lay on his back on a king-sized bed in the middle of the room. He wore a white satin robe and had two half-naked Asian women clinging to him.

Fon shouted in Thai. The women covered their breasts with towels then ran from the bedroom.

Heung-min growled at Fon as he stared. "Who the fuck are you, girl dressed as a boy? And why'd you send my bitches away?"

Fon took a step towards the bed. "I'm the crazy Interpol agent with a gun who just found out my best-friend Nok was murdered...And right now I'm more pissed-off than sad and know you had something to do with it." Her voice shook as it got louder. "So unless you want to be forced-fed your own tiny balls, you'll answer Agent Porter's questions...Got it?"

"Nok's dead? That is sad, because she supplied me the best coke at the best price…Ah well, all good things must come to an end." Heung-min snickered as he shifted his stare to Porter. "I could say it's nice to see you again but that would be a lie…Your little friend's humorous hostilities aside," he nodded to Fon, "why should I tell you anything? And what's this nonsensical threat about Americans coming for me?"

"It's not a threat, mate, it's fact," Porter said. "You're wanted in the States on numerous drug-trafficking charges and face a minimum of thirty years in Uncle Sam's slammer…Don't wanna tell me anything? Then I'll just have to hand you over to my mates at the FBI waiting for you here in Bangkok. Tonight."

Heung-min's eyes widened as he sat upright with his back against the wall. Porter saw him gulp. "You're lying. You have nothing and no-one."

Porter took his cell phone from jean's pocket. He pressed the screen once to call a 'contact', then a second time to activate the phone's speaker.

The call connected and a male with a broad American accent said – 'You've reached Agent Caldwell of the FBI…Leave a message after the beep.'

Porter grinned at Heung-min. "G'day Caldwell, it's Dan Port--."

"Alright!" Heung-min shouted. "I'll talk…"

"Smart choice…" Porter ended the call and put his phone away. "Your name appears on multiple receipts issued by Police General Woracha in his corrupt role as Chief Abbot of Wat Mayakun in Phuket. I won't bother asking if you know who he is…The receipts are linked to his large-scale drug supply and money laundering operations. What have you been selling to him and his brother?"

"Nothing. I've no idea why he's written my name."

"Bullshit. Have you sold him the foreign girls and a heap of others? Girls your gang abducted from the Poipet border crossing just as Cambodian cops said they had?"

"That's ridiculous…"

"Is it? The receipts were issued to Woracha's customers in temples all over Thailand with the words 'For Supplies' written in bold letters across the front of 'em." Porter felt his face burning. He raised his voice. "I'm growing tired of these childish fucking games, mate. If the 'supplies' aren't cocaine or the abducted girls, what the fuck are they?"

Heung-min sighed. "Guns…I've been smuggling them into Bangkok and selling to Woracha. Most times when I transported cocaine via the river I'd bring a few crates of rifles in too."

"Did Nok know about the guns?"

"She might've suspected but had no idea I was supplying Woracha. If it didn't involve coke she had no interest in what I was getting up to."

Porter's mind returned to his time in the Chinatown temple. The novice monks had carried high-grade rifles. And Woracha's mercenaries for hire on Magic Island had been armed with the very same model. "Where do you get the guns from?"

Heung-min hesitated before answering. "Contacts in North Korea buy from the Chinese army then ship them to my men in Seoul."

"What model are they?"

"Chinese made QBZ-95 assault rifles."

"They use a short, rectangular magazine, don't they?"

"No. The magazine's long and curved."

Porter nodded, because Heung-min had named and described the exact weapon used by security operatives inside both temples. "Why didn't you distribute the guns throughout Thailand yourself? I've heard you used concrete trucks to move the cocaine…Why not the guns too?"

"I was after quick sales. Fast cash…I've got huge debts to repay and I'm behind on the exorbitant rent for this place. Not to mention the cost of retaining my men and paying for the copious amounts of coke me and my whores shove up our noses every day…And it's easier for Woracha to sell and transport the guns, with his connections to the police force and army. Selling coke to Thai yuppies in Chinatown and tourists in places like Pattaya and Phuket is one thing…Selling tens of thousands of rifles capable of slaughtering masses of cops and civilians, that's a different matter altogether…Especially for someone like me if I got caught."

"Fair enough…Tell me this then, assuming all receipts with your name relate to orders for assault rifles Woracha's fulfilled…Why was he selling 'em to temples? Why do they need so many guns?"

Heung-min shook his head.

"I'll answer that, Dan," Fon said. "While there may be hundreds of temples with corrupt head monks, there are many more led by honest and respectable ones. And modern temples have become expensive to maintain…"

Porter nodded. "Religion's become a business here, same as everywhere else in the world."

"True, and both honest and criminal Chief Abbot's alike rely on cash donations to keep their businesses

265

going. And corruption-busters like Jaru and others at the CCD put constant pressure on the government and the National Buddhism Office to ensure temples adhere to anti-money laundering regulations."

"I've read about that new legislation...They're making temples declare the sources of funds, right? Abbot's are now required to nominate the benefactors making donations."

"And rich Thais who regularly made large donations to their favourite temple have stopped doing it."

"Through fear they'll be named in subsequent corruption hearings?"

"Yes. It's detrimental for their reputations and bad karma...Chief Abbot's nationwide have adopted a common tactic to avoid declaring sources of income."

"Oldest trick in the book...They keep their money out of banks."

"Exactly."

Porter scoffed. "So they're no different to other scummy crooks then..."

Fon shrugged. "If a temple's money isn't in a bank, it therefore doesn't exist and no-one from the NBO or CCD can say otherwise...And the amounts involved are staggering. Even the smaller temples hide hundreds of millions of baht within their compounds."

"And they need armed men to protect that money." Porter grunted. "Which is why they've bought all these guns from Woracha."

"Yes. Chief Abbot's arm their monks to act as the temple's private security force. And they aren't worried about ill-gotten money being stolen because no-one would dare steal it. The guns are needed to keep honest cops out. To stop them from seizing cash and assets."

Heung-min chuckled. "Porter, you seem obsessed with Woracha but another man, equally sinister, buys twice as many rifles from me."

"What are talking about? Who?"

"Your friend from Phnom Penh. General Chea. He's armed his own private regiment of elite soldiers with my guns. Aren't you curious to know how and why?"

Porter smirked. "I can feel the phone vibrating in my pocket and it's probably Agent Caldwell from the FBI calling me back…Keep talking so I don't have to answer it."

"Ignore him. I'll tell you everything you need to know."

"Where's Sawatri hiding?"

"I have no idea. I only dealt with Nok and Woracha."

Porter considered Heung-min's smug face. He seemed keen to share but was he speaking the truth?
"Alright…Tell me what you know about General Chea. How's he making his money?"

Heung-min reached for a beer bottle on the bedside table. He drank from it then nestled it in his lap. "General Chea runs the Poipet border crossing and both Thai and Cambodian immigration officials are terrified of him. He and his elite squads control the movement of drugs, humans and stolen goods between Thailand and Cambodia. Everything passes through Poipet."

Porter recalled the meeting in Phnom Penh. Had General Chea shot the Cambodian gangster because he was about to name him as a major trafficker? And had Chea's men murdered the incorruptible Cambodian detective, Inspector Veasna? Because Chea feared he was too close to revealing the truth about him?

"That mongrel," Porter said to no-one in particular. "There was something about him I didn't like and this confirms it…" He considered Heung-min's motives and stared at him. "Are you nominating Chea to save your own bacon again?"

"No, it's the truth. He runs human-trafficking through Poipet so it's feasible he's abducted and sold your foreign girls to fund his private army… Isn't it?"

Porter agreed but wouldn't say so. "How's he involved in human-trafficking? What proof do you have?"

"I know because my men help him…Young Thai and Cambodian girls are forever racking up debts in the Poipet casinos. General Chea owns them, and when debt-ridden girls try to run and hide he hires my men to recover the money owed. But many of those girls don't have the money to pay him back."

Fon scoffed as though disgusted. "So your men return the girls to Chea, who then forces them to repay their gambling debts in kind?"

"Yes," Heung-min said. "They transport the girls overland to brothels in southern China owned by Chea and his fellow Generals…Most of them never come back."

"Mongrels…" Porter exhaled through gritted teeth. If Heung-min told the truth, his allegations made General Chea his main suspect for multiple abductions. "Why didn't you tell me this about Chea before? Why all the bullshit about a religious NGO and girls being shipped to China from the deep-water docks at Khlong Toei?"

"Back then I held all the cards…And why incriminate myself by admitting to large-scale weapons smuggling? Now circumstances have changed, and although Chea and I have been business partners of sorts, I owe the man no favors."

"I sense animosity…Why?"

"He told you my men abducted the foreign girls…That was a lie."

Porter nodded. "Which he told because…?"

"Because he wanted to deflect your attentions away from him and the Poipet border crossing. And because he wants control of the lucrative smuggling operation I've refused to give up…We all have our enemies, Agent Porter. And some, like yourself, are fortunate that powerful friends protect you from such enemies."

"Meaning?"

"Do you remember the young guy who was working for me during your previous visit? He had a scar on his cheek. The guy who shot the hooker in the jacuzzi…"

Porter nodded.

"He had a mad crush on Nok and was subsequently very jealous of you. In fact, and I must make it clear that I had no part in it, he hated you so much he tried to run you down outside a restaurant. But his attempt was thwarted by another vehicle blocking him. Men protecting you…"

Porter's jaw clenched. "That was him in the black pickup? How many times?"

"Yes, and I've no idea if he tried more than once. But I do know he was shot last night while eating his dinner inside it…Someone killed him because he was a threat to you. Someone's keeping you alive, Porter."

Porter pictured the driver of the SUV that'd prevented the black pickup truck from hitting him. The male driver had been blond and Caucasian, possibly working for the Russians and definitely not one of Jaru's men. As

Heung-min said, someone was keeping him alive. But who? And why?

"Let's assume I believe you, and Chea's been lying the whole time… If he's the bloke behind the abductions he's mostly likely leading GAIT. So where do we find him and the girls?"

Heung-min gave a fiendish grin. "I can tell you. But I want assurances first."

"Such as?"

"You keep you word and don't hand me over to the FBI. And you don't allow Thai cops to arrest me either, because after what I've told you about Woracha and his twisted brother," he glanced at Fon, "I won't last five minutes in a police cell…You'll let me walk from this casino and disappear. Do we have a deal?"

Porter nodded. "Where's General Chea keeping the girls?"

Heung-min grabbed his cell phone from a side table, pressed the screen a few times then tossed the phone to Porter. "Write that down…It's an address in the Ramkhamhaeng area, not far from here."

"Of what?"

"Chea's secure compound, the house where he stays in Bangkok and my men deliver his guns to. If he still has the foreign girls it's probably where he's holding them."

Porter's pulse quickened. Did he finally have a location for GAIT's headquarters? He wrote the address in his notebook then returned the phone.

Fon looked up at him. "Do we have what we came for?"

He nodded.

She drew her Glock from shoulder-holster and aimed it at Heung-min.

He raised hands and shuffled backwards on the bed. "What are you doing you crazy bitch?"

Fon kept her aim on Heung-min while she shouted over her shoulder at the Korean thug in the doorway. "Leave now and take your friend with you…"

The thug dropped his gun then ran away from the bedroom, towards the only exit.

Fon turned her hate-filled glare back to Heung-min. "I hold you responsible for Nok's death…If you hadn't smuggled drugs into Thailand for Woracha she'd never have got caught up in this whole mess… She was a beautiful, kind spirit and you destroyed her. You took her away from us."

Heung-min's mouth gaped open. His hands visibly trembled. "Porter! Tell this crazy tomboy to lower her gun…We made a deal. Porter!?"

Fon smirked. "Yes, you and Agent Porter made a deal but I sure as fuck didn't." The Glock boomed as she double-tapped Heung-min between the eyes. Blood and brain and bone splattered onto the wall behind him. His corpse crumpled into a heap.

Porter spun towards Sergeant Chuchwaron, who stood in the doorway with gun aimed at the bed. He assured him all was good then turned back to Fon. "What was that? You reckon I was really gunna let Heung-min leave? Just walk away after all he's done? No fucking way…"

She sighed. "Dan, shooting him dead was the only way to get justice for Nok. Thai police would've allowed him to flee back to Seoul because locking him up would be too embarrassing. And he was here illegally. Once he's disposed of he'll never be missed..." She punched his shoulder. "Besides, I've saved you a heap of time and paperwork with the FBI hand-over. Yes?"

He grinned down at her. "I reckon you're right."

"What now? Chea's house in Ramkhamhaeng?"

"Yeah..." He took his notebook from back pocket and read the address. "Sarge Chuch, are you and your boys up for one more rumble tonight?"

Sergeant Chuchwaron nodded.

"Good." Porter smiled at Fon. "Let's go and see just how secure Chea's compound is. And call me a stupid bloody optimist but I reckon our girls might just still be there."

# THIRTY-FOUR

Ninety minutes after leaving the Babylon casino, Porter, Fon and the CCD's SWAT team assembled behind an armored truck parked forty meters from the high walls of General Chea's compound in the Ramkhamhaeng suburb of Bangkok. They'd secured the immediate and surrounding areas, completed a brief risk-assessment and surveillance of the property, and formulated an assault plan. They'd cut power on the local grid to make darkness their ally and a half-moon illuminated the colossal two-story house in a mysterious silver light.

Porter pulled a ballistic vest over his head then secured its straps around his waist. He glanced at Fon as she did the same. "I'll go in with Sergeant Chuchwaron and the first team. It might be best you hang back for a bit and enter with the second one."

"Like hell." She glared at him then smiled. "I've waited my entire career for a job like this and I'll be by your side the whole way."

"Fair enough." He nodded to Sergeant Chuchwaron to let him know they were ready.

Chuchwaron barked orders in Thai.

Six SWAT operatives wearing black fatigues, night-vision goggles and full body-armor stepped from cover and ran forward. The first two knelt to fire canisters over the compound's barb-wired walls. The canisters landed in the courtyard and commenced veiling the area in thick smoke. The other four operatives continued straight ahead to the solid steel gate. They fitted explosives on both sides then signaled to Chuchwaron.

Chuchwaron led Porter and the first assault team forward and they lined up on the right side of the gate, shielded by the concrete wall. They waited with silenced, short-barreled submachine guns aimed in a safe-direction to the front. Fon stayed close behind Porter while the second assault team formed a tight line on the left side. Chuchwaron shouted in Thai. Seconds later an explosion blew the gate away and chunks of concrete flew in all directions.

Porter followed at the rear of Chuchwaron's team as they charged through the opening towards the house. He ran low as he peered through swirling smoke in the faint light, prepared to take evasive action if fired upon from large windows above. He slammed his shoulder against the house's front wall, surprised to have reached it without drama. He sucked humid air into lungs and slowed his breathing while listening for movement inside. The night remained quiet.

Chuchwaron turned to frown at him. "Something's up. The front door's open."

"Yeah, and if Chea's about we'd know it by now. But that doesn't mean our girls aren't here...Let's go, eh?"

Chuchwaron nodded then led the way. His SWAT team rushed inside the house and instinctively separated into pairs to search each room. Less than a minute later all teams had called out to indicate they'd safely cleared the entire ground floor.

Porter stood with Fon and Chuchwaron in the entry-foyer and swept his mini-Maglite torch over the empty floor space. "Strange, no furniture or any sign someone's been living here." He pointed to the staircase. "Upstairs?"

Sergeant Chuchwaron moved to the bottom of the stairs. He aimed his gun at the top and stepped slowly as he climbed.

Porter waited until several SWAT men had joined their team leader on the first floor then hurried up the stairs with his Glock gripped in both hands to the front. His jaw dropped as he leapt from the last stair and saw General Chea lying dead in a pool of blood in the middle of the room. The mangled heads and torsos of fifteen soldiers wearing the same olive-green uniform littered the floor around him to form a gruesome circle of death.

Porter trod carefully over slain soldiers. He dodged rivulets of bright blood and broken beer bottles. He knelt to examine an empty cartridge from a high-caliber weapon then rolled it between fingers. Warm. An empty beer bottle was still cool. He sniffed the air. The smell of fear lingered, as did smoke from discharged firearms. He guessed the assassins had left the compound less than ten minutes before the assault team arrived.

He rose as Sergeant Chuchwaron stopped in front of him.

"My men have cleared and secured the whole compound," Chuchwaron said. "I've just searched the security room. The hard-drives for their CCTV recordings have been taken and everything else in there destroyed. Filing cabinets in the office are empty."

Porter's heart raced. "Any sign of the girls?"

Chuchwaron shook his head.

Porter hissed through gritted teeth. "Fuck!" He inhaled deeply then blew steam at the ceiling.

Chuchwaron waited for him to stop cursing. "Who did this, Porter?"

"Someone who feared what Chea might tell us…Assassins known to him and his men. Possibly close allies…" Porter pointed to rows of shiny assault rifles attached to the far wall. "None of these Cambodian soldiers were armed when they died and there's no evidence of forced entry or a melee. The killers waited until these blokes were drunk and unprepared…Then they surrounded and massacred 'em."

"I agree they've been betrayed. And judging by the tight groupings of bullet-wounds on the dead the assassins are a highly professional unit. Special forces or an elite police squad."

"Or members of a well-trained private army?"

Chuchwaron nodded. He squeezed the radio handset attached to his shoulder epaulette and spoke into it. Ten seconds later the room was flooded with bright light as the electricity supply re-connected.

"Dan…" Fon said. "Come and check this out."

Porter turned to see her standing outside the second room in a row of five adjoining the main room. He stepped carefully past bodies and followed her into a narrow room storing three wooden crates. He'd seen similar crates many times before. They were six feet long, 3 feet wide and 2 feet deep. They usually contained military-grade weapons.

Fon placed a hand on the nearest crate. "These were all intact but I asked one of the SWAT guys to open one…" She removed a rifle from the crate and passed it to him.

Porter studied the weapon and its curved magazine. "A Chinese made QBZ-95 assault rifle…The same gun the security blokes in the temples were using. The same type as those attached to the wall outside. The exact gun Heung-min said he'd been dealing…"

She pointed to a white label stuck to the side of the crate. "My Korean's more than a bit rusty but I'm fairly certain I've translated this writing correctly…According to this label, these crates were shipped to Bangkok from a terminal in Seoul." She took a photo of the label. "I'll ask Helen to chase up the shipping company named on it and try to find out who sent them."

Porter nodded, because information on the label matched what Heung-min had said. And he'd been truthful about the location of Chea's compound and the type of guns he'd sold him. But had Heung-min been wrong to suggest that Chea led GAIT? He rubbed his jaw as he pondered the question. Chea had been murdered too easily and a criminal organization as sophisticated as GAIT would never leave its main man exposed the way he had been…He concluded that no, General Chea of the Royal Cambodian army had not been leading it.

"Agent Porter," Sergeant Chuchwaron said from the doorway. "Another of these small rooms contains a surprise."

Porter frowned. "What?"

"Follow me."

Chuchwaron led Porter and Fon to the last room in the row of five then left them alone.

Porter stopped abruptly and shook his head at the scene before him. Five men lay dead in the center of a long, narrow room. Four were on their backs. The other lay on his stomach with hair and face twisted underneath him and hidden from view.

Porter counted six bunk beds running along the left side wall. Three metal safes the size of a small bar-fridge occupied the right side. Their doors were ajar with keys still in locks.

He stepped closer to the men who'd died on their backs and saw they'd been shot in the chest at close range. The four were all Caucasian and he guessed they were between twenty-five and thirty years of age. They all wore the same uniform they'd worn while working Nana's seedy streets for GAIT - a white collared shirt, black trousers and a thin black tie.

Porter moved to the fifth man and rolled him over. He stared at the ghostly-white face framed by long, ginger hair. Tim Nazareth's haunting blue eyes stared back at him, smug and defiant and glazed in death. He noticed Tim had been shot in the stomach. He cringed, because the young man's death would've been slow and extremely painful. He saw his right index finger was covered in blood. Then he rolled him completely onto his back and studied marks of dried blood on the inside of his left forearm. Were the marks…Letters? Letters he'd written with his own blood as he lay dying? A message for the police who would find him, that he hadn't wanted assassins to see? Evidence?

Porter stared at the forearm, trying to make sense of illegible letters. A word formed and flashed to the front of his mind. 'CARLY'.

He was convinced Tim had left the message for him in particular to find. And he wanted him to speak to Carly. But why? What did she know that she hadn't already told?

A safe door squeaked as Fon yanked it fully open. She bent to peer inside. "Dan, I think the contents of these safes were swiped by our killers."

"Yeah? You reckon they were full of cash?"

She pulled an empty, A4 sized zip-lock bag from the safe and held it up in her left hand. She reached into the safe with her right hand then presented the small pill held in her palm. "I'd say the safes had stored these bags. Bags full of these…" She pushed her palm closer to him. "Ya-E. Ecstasy pills."

He took the pill from her and studied it closely. Bright yellow with a picture of Mickey Mouse pressed onto it. He recalled his conversation with Carly in Khaosan Road. She'd told him that while Tim volunteered at the Cambodian school he'd been popping unusually bright colored ecstasy pills stamped with cartoon characters and had offered them to her and Lisa Baxter.

"It's a bit weird, isn't it?" Fon said. "The killers took the pills with them yet left behind three crates of assault rifles worth a small fortune. Not to mention the twenty-odd guns still on the wall in the main room…Why?"

"I reckon they were in a hurry. Pills are much easier to move and transport than those heavy crates. And our crooks are probably well-stocked for weapons already."

"Or…?" She stroked an imaginary Adam's apple. "We're fairly certain this is GAIT's headquarters in Bangkok, right?"

"We've found the bloke who was most likely abducting the girls for 'em, Chea, and the blokes who sold drugs for 'em, Tim and co…So, yeah, I reckon it's safe to assume that."

"Is it possible the killers took the pills because they're a very rare label stamped by an exclusive dealer in the market, pills that could be traced back to GAIT? Or did these guys and Chea have their own supply business that GAIT's boss only recently learned about?"

Porter weighed up what she'd said because it made a lot of sense. Had Tim and his mates been killed because they were dealing ecstasy for Chea on the side? Were they selling a unique product to tourists and hookers in Asoke, an area GAIT didn't have permission to operate in? If so it was a possible motive for their elimination as their actions would've brought unwanted attention to GAIT's other criminal activities and placed all its members at risk.

Or had Tim and his fellow dealers been murdered for the same reason the naïve African students had been? Because they simply knew too much?

While both General Chea and Tim had performed important roles for GAIT, they would have been regarded as nothing but cannon fodder by its leader. But who was its leader? Porter couldn't shake Sawatri's face from his mind. It had to be him, didn't it? Who else was left?

His line of thought jumped all over the place…Sawatri had told him his mother was a British surgeon…Scottish? Had her ancestors been part of the formation of the Knights of Alba in Scotland during the mid-20th century? Was Sawatri the KA member Steve Williams feared had avoided taskforce Dragon Slayer's sweep through Southeast Asia? Had he ordered Lisa Baxter's abduction as revenge? Revenge against her step-father, Senator John Fitzgerald, the politician who'd help to dismantle the Knights of Alba's global network?

Fon cleared her throat and the noise jolted Porter and returned him to the present. "You okay, Dan? I think I lost you there for a few minutes."

He smirked. "Sorry sweet, I was just thinking that Sawatri's the bloke we need to find...I reckon he knows where our abducted girls are being held." He frowned. "Or where they've been sent to..."

"He could be hiding anywhere in the world by now. And we've no clue how to locate him."

"Ah, but maybe we do..." Porter pointed at Tim's forearm. "We have Carly."

# THIRTY-FIVE

Porter returned to his apartment at 2am Friday once he'd completed the necessary clean-up and paperwork regarding the raid on General Chea's compound. On waking at 6am he made coffee then stretched out on the sofa. For the next two hours he called Carly Newman's phone without luck.

At 8.15am she answered with a wary, "Hello?".

"Carly, it's Dan Porter, we met last week."

"Yep. Have you found Lisa?"

"Not yet... I'm sorry to tell you, but Tim from the Cambodian school is dead."

"Oh my God. Fuck! Now I'm really shitting myself even more... Are the same people after me too? Should I even be speaking to you on the phone?"

"It's okay, my line's secure...You don't seem surprised about Tim?"

"Because I'm not... He called yesterday afternoon, said he was scared and that his life was in danger. He told me a heap of insane info and asked me to pass it on to you."

"What info? Why didn't you contact me?"

A long pause. "I don't know."

"Bloody hell, Carly, if you'd told me this yesterday we could've saved him and his mates."

'I'm really sorry." Her voice quivered. "But cops at the Australian embassy said not to speak to anyone until they get me safely on a flight back home." She started to

282

cry then sniffled as though trying to compose herself. "Safely? What the fuck does that mean?"

"It's okay, sweet, I understand…He'd written your name before he died as a back-up plan in case you were too frightened to call me, and it's a good thing we found him first because the bad guys didn't see the message."

"Will these bad guys try to get me too?"

"No, but you've been smart to stay in hiding. You're safe, and me and those federal cops at the embassy will keep it that way. Now, what'd Tim want you to tell me?"

She sniffled then coughed as though clearing her throat. "Well, he said he couldn't go to you or any other cops because he needed to protect someone he loves. And he wanted to make it clear he had nothing to with Lisa's disappearance. Nothing to do with any of the missing girls. And after hearing his story I believe him…"

"Okay…Do you remember telling me Tim did a heap of ecstasy in Siem Reap? About the unusual pills he offered you and Lisa?" He waited for her reply in the affirmative. "Do you know why he had so many pills with him?"

"Sure, and I'll tell you exactly how Tim explained it to me…He said he joined that NGO, GAIT, God's angels or whatever they're called, honestly believing he'd be helping young Thai hookers get out of the sex-trade. But he ended up working as a drug mule and low-level dealer for some Cambodian army dude…He did say his name but sorry I've forgotten it."

Porter thought of General Chea. "No worries…Go on."

"Tim was originally from Los Angeles and had friends back there involved with making eccies. Like, a

283

lot of eccie pills and really good quality stuff…Tim mentioned it to the Cambodian army dude as a way of raising more funds for the NGO, so they could continue helping girls around Nana. Before Tim knew it the Cambodian dude negotiated with his friends in LA and set up a partnership."

"And Tim became part of that drug supply network?"

"Yep. He was travelling to Siem Reap every month to pick up a shipment of pills that'd been flown in from LA via Phnom Penh. He would volunteer at the school for a week to make it seem like his regular trips across the border were legit and then deliver the pills to his boss in Bangkok."

"Yeah, that's what I'd suspected…You're doing great to remember all this, sweet…Did Tim say how he got the pills into Thailand? If he was ever stopped?"

"He took them by bus through the Poipet border every time. He said he never got hassled by immigration cops or soldiers on either side of the crossing and never even had to show his passport or get a visa stamp. He said his boss paid them to turn a blind eye, same as when he was working for him in Bangkok. Tim had a fake passport and some charity-based work permit GAIT got for him. Local cops knew to leave him and the other GAIT guys alone."

"And free to deal their pills and other gear around Nana…Did Tim say anything about the students working for him?"

"Yep, he said the Cambodian dude gave him what he needed to offload and he'd then get Nigerian guys to sell it."

"Did he mention Arab drug dealers? Arab crooks of any kind?"

"No, sorry."

"Okay... Did he mention GAIT bringing African girls into Bangkok? About confiscating their passports and forcing 'em into prostitution?"

"Nope, he said nothing about hookers. And it's sad if that was being done to those girls but the same thing happened with Tim too."

"Meaning?"

"The Cambodian army dude took his real passport from him and wouldn't give it back."

"Yeah I know, because we recovered it and those of four other American blokes last night... Tim's real name was Timothy Jones. Have you seen that name come up anywhere? On Facebook etcetera?"

"Nope... But you know, Tim said he tried to leave GAIT and the drug business but his boss threatened to hand him over to police. And who wants to rot away in a cockroach infested Thai jail? He said that's why he ran or hid from you every time. He didn't want to go away for drug trafficking."

"You heard nothing to suggest he'd been involved in prostitution or the abductions? In any form?"

"Nope. If he did know anything about it, he didn't tell me. And yeah he was a criminal working for GAIT but I seriously doubt he would've helped them with that horrible part of their business...You might too once you know everything."

"Fair enough."

Porter realized he'd made a mistake early in the investigation. He'd given too much weight to information supplied by Nok's ladyboy informant, Kwang, who'd said Tim was pimping the African hookers on Sukhumvit road. Whilst he'd considered Tim the main suspect for Lisa Baxter's disappearance, he'd also started to doubt that his role within GAIT's overall criminal network was a major one. But Nok had eagerly steered the Lost Angels investigation towards Tim to make him the prime suspect for multiple abductions. He now knew she'd done it to protect Park Heung-min, worried his gun smuggling would eventually lead investigators to her cocaine trafficking. And that was something she couldn't allow to happen because her sick mother's life depended on the proceeds.

Had Nok ever really cared about the missing foreign girls? He would never know…

"Mr Porter? Porter?" Carly said urgently. "You still there? Mr Porter?"

Porter shook the vision of Nok's gorgeous smile from his head. "Sorry…Was thinking about what you just said… Um, did, did Tim say who GAIT's big boss was? Did he say who gave orders to the Cambodian army dude?"

"Nope."

"Did he mention anyone called Sawatri?"

"Sorry, he didn't."

"Okay, cheers, now bear with me…Back to Lisa…Are we correct in assuming Tim was on the same bus the day she disappeared?"

"Yep and he told me he was taking a suitcase of eccies to Bangkok."

"Right…Did he say why he didn't try to find Lisa when she didn't return from the casino?"

"That's the thing, he was worried because she'd been freaking out about some dude following her. She got off the bus 'cos she was busting for a wee."

"Who'd she think was following her?"

"The creepy headmaster. Mr Saysamone."

"Why didn't Tim tell the bus driver to stop, wait and look for her?"

"He did but the driver was copping heat from soldiers, like they wanted him to keep going...Tim told border cops Lisa was missing but they didn't want to listen. He took his suitcase off the bus and went to look for her. Security guards wouldn't let him into the casinos. He called her phone and got a message it'd been disconnected... She'd disappeared, just like that."

"What did he do when he couldn't find her"

"He said he took the next bus... He got off just north of Bangkok then took a taxi to that Ramkhamhong place or whatever."

"Why didn't he search longer? Harder? Why didn't he call the Oz embassy, or tourist police? Did he say?"

"Honestly, he did sound like crap when he told me all this yesterday. He said he'd felt very guilty since Lisa vanished."

"As he should've been...He could've done a lot more to help her."

"I know, but think about it from his point of view as a drug smuggler...He had a suitcase full of eccies and didn't want to bring attention to himself."

Porter grunted. He knew the criminal-mind well, and to a crook like Tim the excuse for not advising Australian authorities of Lisa's disappearance had probably seemed valid. But that didn't mean he had to like it.

He thought about the ecstasy trafficking route from LA to Siem Reap to Bangkok. Where was the link between it and those at the very top of GAIT's hierarchy? "Tell me again, so I know I've got this right… Tim and his mates dealt ecstasy in the Nana and Asoke areas, supposedly raising funds for legitimate charity work, in partnership with the Cambodian army bloke?"

"Yep, and Tim said that's how he met Parinda."

"Who's Parinda?"

"His ex-girlfriend, the reason he couldn't go directly to you with this info. He had to protect her and couldn't risk the wrong Thai cops finding out about her…Do you know what I mean?"

Porter pictured Sawatri. "Yeah, I do."

"Tim gave me an address for the Land Office building where Parinda works in the Bangkapi district. He said it's the office that covers the Ramkhamhong area. I'll text you it…He said you should speak to her, that you can trust her, and something about her office having info on the house he was living in…Stuff that might help your investigation."

Porter recalled his conversation with Jaru's CCD intelligence analyst earlier that morning. She'd told him her initial attempts to ascertain the legal owner of GAIT's compound in Ramkhamhaeng had been unsuccessful. "Parinda works for the Land Office? Interesting…"

At 10.35am, Porter and Fon strode into the Bangkapi District Land Office building. He stood back from the counter while she did the talking. They were shown to an interview room at the side and five minutes later Tim's ex-girlfriend Parinda joined them.

She gave Porter a shy smile then sat opposite at the table. She was attractive with long, light-brown hair. Her large breasts and sparkling blue irises looked fake. He guessed she was twenty-five or thereabouts.

Fon leaned forward and had a five-minute conversation with her in Thai.

Parinda wiped a tear from cheek when it ended.

Fon turned to Porter, said she'd explained to Parinda what had happened to Tim, how they'd found her, and how they hoped she could help. She told him Parinda had been a go-go dancer in Nana Plaza and Tim had supplied her and most of the dancers with ecstasy. They'd had a brief relationship and remained good friends after breaking up.

Parinda told Fon that unknown Cambodian men had visited her go-go bar eighteen months earlier and offered her big money to work in Los Angeles for a year. When she refused the offer, the men had threatened to hurt her family if she didn't go. She'd feared for their safety and asked Tim for help. He got her away from Nana Plaza, created a new identity for her and arranged the Land Office job.

Porter scratched a cheek. "Well, well, seems he wasn't a total bastard after all."

Parinda scowled at him then spoke to Fon.

"She didn't like you calling Tim a bastard," Fon told him. "She said he was her angel. She said millions of Thais live in Bangkok but it took a kind-hearted farang to save her from a miserable life."

"That's beaut…And I thought she couldn't understand English?" He smirked at Fon. "Does Parinda have any idea who these Cambodian blokes were?"

Fon asked the question, listened to Parinda's reply then faced him.

"Okay, this is interesting because she failed to mention it the first time…She says the men were Cambodian soldiers dressed in plain clothes. Dancers were regularly going missing from the plaza and rumor was that these men were responsible. Their boss was a big fat guy with a moustache."

Porter nodded. "General Chea. Makes sense…His soldiers were abducting sex-workers then forcing the girls to work in the US, no doubt to fund his private army and buy more guns from blokes like Park Heung-min." He recalled what Heung-min had said about Chea sending Thai girls overland to the north and that many never returned. His guts churned with hate. "And the bastard sent some of 'em into China too."

Fon's face screwed as she glared at the table. "Yes, the pii noi…The fucking prick."

"Can Parinda find what we need? Can she tell us who owns the house we raided last night?"

Fon spoke briefly then passed her a piece of paper with the address of GAIT's headquarters on it.

Parinda left the room and returned after ten minutes. She placed a manila folder and a laptop computer on the table.

Fon opened the folder and removed a single page. She laid it on the table in front of Porter and frowned as she pointed to Thai writing at the top. "This is a copy of the original title deed for the house in Ramkhamhaeng, what's called a 'chanote'…This one's very strange, because here in this row at the top the property's owner is usually listed."

"But this one's blank," Porter said. "Which means what?"

Fon spoke to Parinda then relayed her answer. "It means there's no record of who owns this land and the house on it. Not in this office or anywhere in Thailand. Not in hardcopy form or any digital records."

Porter scoffed. "Bloody hell, it's been the same throughout this entire investigation. All GAIT's assets are hidden and protected." He shook his head at Parinda. "Who's the corrupt bastard running this office then?"

"Dan, that's not fair." Fon reached across the table to squeeze Parinda's hand. "She's taking a significant risk to help us. She could lose more than her job if the wrong people learn of it."

He nodded. "You're right and I'm taking my frustration out on the wrong person." He made eye-contact with Parinda. "Sorry, sweet."

"Parinda says it's possible the property's owner is listed somewhere on this…" Fon slid a second piece of paper from the folder and laid it over the top of the title-deed. "It's a copy of the original land survey, from back when they sub-divided the district more than thirty years ago."

Porter peered at the diagram and tiny writing on the page. "Bloody hell, I reckon it's time I got glasses..."

Parinda stopped typing on the laptop. She spoke to Fon then pointed to three lines of writing in the bottom left corner of the survey page.

Fon squinted as she read. "Wait, this could be something…The address we're after is Lot 1474 on this diagram…And according to this info at the bottom, the owner of that particular lot is the same company who requested the land survey." Her voice rose, tone excited. "And the company is…Peking Duck Tours."

Porter rocked back in the seat. "What? Some Chinese mob? And who the hell owns them?"

Fon pulled her cell phone from breast pocket. "No idea…But I have a close friend working at the DBD, the Department of Business Development, and they handle all company transfers in Thailand. Hopefully she'll be able to tell us who owns this 'Peking Duck Tours'."

Fon spoke to her contact at the DBD for five minutes. She wrote on a notepad during the conversation. She ended the call and frowned at Porter. "The bad news…We don't know exactly who owns Peking Duck Tours because, surprise, surprise, they're listed as a subsidiary of GAIT."

He wiped a stiff hand across his forehead. "Fuck me, this never ends…Any good news?"

"Yes…" Fon pointed to her handwritten notes. "These addresses are of six properties listed as assets owned by Peking Duck Tours. My friend told me the asset type and its approximate market value… If the foreign girls are held in a GAIT-owned house, there's a very good chance it's one of these."

Porter sat upright. "I agree, and we'll have to choose carefully when placing our bet. After last night's raid they've no doubt started removing assets and incriminating evidence from all their properties."

"We'll hit a house tonight but only have the resources to hit one on this list…Which will it be?"

Porter asked Fon to state the location, property type and value of each property as he pointed to it on the page. He dismissed numbers one and two on the list.

"Where's this house, number three? And does that say it's worth one-hundred million baht? That's, bloody hell, five million in Aussie and more than three million US dollars…Where is it?"

Fon spoke to Parinda then plonked a finger onto the page. "Number three's in Laem Chabang, a coastal town and large sea-port about a ninety-minute drive south of Bangkok. Not far north of Pattaya. It has very large shipping terminals and multiple docks and piers."

Porter's eyebrows arched. "Shipping terminals? And what's the property type?"

"Um, it's listed as 'Private recreational', whatever that is…" She waved a hand towards Parinda. "You can see it there on the laptop. Parinda's found a satellite image."

Parinda pushed the laptop across the table.

Fon spun the screen to face Porter. "I'll zoom it in…There, perfect."

Porter scanned the image showing a seaside property of a few acres. The house in the middle appeared to be twice the size of that in Chea's compound. "This thick white line all around the property looks like a high wall…If so, helicopters will need to drop us inside." He pointed to the screen. "This appears to be a lawn area over here, with plenty of room for 'em to land…And what's this thinner line on the water, you reckon, where the property meets the ocean? And this blob next to it?"

Fon leaned towards the screen. "It's obscured and we can't zoom in anymore, but it looks like a private dock or jetty…And maybe the 'blob' is a large boat of some sort?"

He nodded. "A massive property with its own boat and jetty, close to a major shipping terminal."

He recalled what the Cambodian gangster in Phnom Penh had told him about abducted foreign girls being shipped from a large terminal 'south of Bangkok'. He shook his head, annoyed with himself. He'd allowed General Chea to divert attention from Laem Chabang port and make Heung-min a major suspect at the same time. Chea had successfully convinced him that the Khlong Toei terminal, 'in the south of Bangkok', was where he needed to focus attention. And it hadn't been difficult to do considering Nok wasn't present and he lacked knowledge of the geographical areas Chea referred to.

"Bloody hell, Fon, this is the joint and we need to hit it asap."

"It'll take a few hours to assemble Jaru's CCD guys and a couple of SWAT teams." She checked her watch. "By the time we fly to Laem Chabang it'll be late afternoon. And that's only if the search warrant gets issued quickly."

"Search warrant? Nah, stuff that, we can't afford to wait for some dithering judge. Besides, if we or Jaru's mob apply for a warrant every man and his dog will know about it, including our crooks…Nah, we keep this in-house and won't tell any CCD bosses or police chiefs about the pending raid."

"But we have to get a warrant, don't we? For legal and procedural reasons?"

"Listen, if we believe girls are in imminent danger inside the house that's more than enough reasonable cause to start kicking doors in. Yeah? And if flak comes our way regarding any illegal entry bullshit I'm more than happy to cop it…So let's make this the last time we speak of search warrants and doing things the 'right way'."

Fon nodded. "As I said before, we'll only get one chance...Are you confident this is the house?"

"As I can be..." He would never tell Fon that he'd started to doubt the girls were in Thailand or even alive. But he still harbored hope and over the years he'd found that a sense of it, no matter how small, was the ultimate motivation to keep going. "Someone's gone to much trouble to hide GAIT's ownership of this property...Is that someone Chief Superintendent Sawatri? And is this waterfront mansion, owned by some bullshit mob calling themselves Peking Duck Tours, where the mongrel's currently hiding?"

"It'll be too late to search the other houses if he's not."

"Yeah, spot on, so send a prayer to your Buddha that our girls are there in Laem Chabang. Because if they're not, I fear those lost angels might never be found."

# THIRTY-SIX

Porter glanced at his watch, 5.33pm, then towards the west where a crimson sun rapidly descended from a pink sky into a shimmering ocean. He travelled with Sergeant Chuchwaron and his SWAT team in the first of three Black Hawk helicopters. Fon travelled with another SWAT team in the second helicopter, while Jaru and seven CCD detectives flew in the third.

The Black Hawks hovered above the Laem Chabang compound then landed inside it. Three assault teams leapt from them and charged towards the mansion, each tasked with breaching it at separate points. The mansion was white and circular and wouldn't have looked out of place on the front cover of 'Town and Country' magazine.

Porter's assault team rushed the main entrance and swiftly dealt with armed resistance from three security guards. He jumped over their dead bodies and ran into the mansion's luxurious entry-foyer while Chuchwaron's SWAT team killed two more guards. He stood still, to concentrate on the various sounds all around him. He heard gunfire from multiple types of weapons, orders being yelled, doors being kicked in, shouts of surprise, anguished cries, the thudding and banging of violent confrontations, yelps of agony, and the groans of dying men. And then a much fainter noise. Coming from the end of the long corridor to his right? And then a louder noise. Of a frightened woman screaming?

Porter sprinted down the corridor towards the screams then slowed when he came to a closed door. He gripped his Glock in one hand and aimed it forward. With his left hand he turned the handle then pushed the door open.

He heard screaming as he stepped through the doorway and came to a junction of two marbled corridors. And then a louder, more piercing scream. Had it come from the corridor to his left or from the one leading straight? He hesitated, unsure which way to go.

A bald man entered the corridor thirty meters ahead. He wore a short-sleeved shirt, and trousers. He spun towards Porter, aimed a handgun and fired two shots.

Porter ducked then made himself a smaller target by standing side-on to his foe with back against the wall. He watched the man turn and run away from him. He chased him down the long corridor and quickly closed the gap between them. The bald man turned to fire two shots then darted through a doorway on the left.

Porter approached the doorway with caution, wary of an ambush. He slid along the wall sideways then peered around the corner into a dark room. Through the slightly ajar door on its far-side he saw a light on in the next room. Somewhere within that room a door slammed shut. Which way had the man gone?

He knew he'd lose him if he waited any longer to assess the risk. He side-stepped through the doorway then hurried through the darkened room towards the light beyond it. He reached for the door handle.

"Stop or I'll shoot you in the back!" A male shouted behind him. "Freeze, Porter. Freeze!"

Porter did. He raised hands as the light overhead was flicked on. Was the man's unusual accent familiar? From where?

"Drop your gun then kick it away," the man ordered. Porter did.

"Now keep your hands up and slowly turn around."

Porter faced the man holding the handgun on him. "Sawatri?" He chuckled. "I almost didn't recognize ya…Why'd you ditch the wig? Sorry mate but the bald look definitely doesn't suit that pig head of yours."

Sawatri gave a condescending smirk as he stepped closer. "Quite amazing indeed, Porter, how you're still at your sarcastic best, even now, this close to the end."

"Ah, as an old Sergeant of mine used to say…Why let death get in the way of a good laugh?"

"Intriguing…You're cornered with no hope of escape yet seem genuinely elated. Why?"

"Because I've finally got you, you bastard. I've finally found the leader of GAIT... And yeah, you'll probably kill me but you aint getting away from here."

Sawatri laughed facetiously. "Me? I'm leading GAIT?" He shook his head. "Don't be absurd."

"Then who?"

"You'll never know the truth, Porter…Because you didn't listen."

"Meaning?"

"I recall Fon telling you very early on that thing's here in Thailand are rarely as they seem…You didn't heed that advice, didn't learn from it, and therefore still don't understand."

"If you reckon so… Tell me then, what is 'the truth'? What's going on inside this mansion?"

Sawatri's eyes narrowed. "Alright I will, since you won't live long enough to share the knowledge with anyone else…You're inside the most luxurious and exclusive men's club in all of Southeast Asia."

"You mean it's nothing but a big, sleazy brothel. And you're a regular client?"

"Indeed…The club's luxury catamaran calls at my Samut Prakan villa in southern Bangkok then brings me directly to the front door. Well, to the private jetty out front, I should say…This club's an oasis, Porter, a sanctuary for mega-rich Asian gents who appreciate the rare, pure-white beauties of this world."

Porter grunted. "I reckon you meant to say it's a hidey-hole for other perverted psychos like you? For sick bastards with white girl fetishes?"

Sawatri snickered. "Indeed…And to be specific it's a fetish for 'young' white girls. White girls just like Lisa Baxter and the other foreign whores."

"They're all here?"

Sawatri nodded smugly. "And oh, how my friends and I have enjoyed them."

Porter snarled as jaw clenched. He eyed the gun aimed at his chest and resisted the urge to lunge for it. "You dirty mongrel…You've pretended to give a fuck about those girls while knowing all along what'd happened to 'em. And you've hampered our investigation from the start. Haven't ya?"

"Yes, indeed I have…And what did you expect, Porter? To come to Thailand looking to shame and embarrass us, and that we'd roll over and allow you to?"

"This has never been about shaming anyone, mate…It's about saving young, innocent girls from predators like you."

"We members of the elite wanted you dead from the minute you arrived. And the same as others, we've tried to kill you, but you're the luckiest farang on the planet and escape death as though protected or blessed."

"You said, 'we members of the elite'…You're one of that mob Nok warned me about?"

"Yes, I represent the cream of our society, those who couldn't allow you to disgrace this great nation. I am them, all rolled into one."

Portered sneered down at him. "What, a pathetic and corrupt little turd?"

Sawatri smiled. "Speaking of Nok…Did you enjoy watching her die after I had her ambushed then exposed in Phuket?"

"Nah, not one bit…But I did get a kick out of seeing your brother's blood and brains splattered all over the ground." Porter grinned as Sawatri's face flushed red. "You're the bloke who told Woracha we were coming…How'd you know?"

"My spies are everywhere."

"And they tipped you off today? That's why GAIT's boss isn't about?"

"I wouldn't still be here if I'd known, would I? And the 'boss' you refer to has friends much higher up the food chain than I could ever hope to…He would've been advised of your imminent arrival and you incompetent buffoons will never find him."

"We'll see…So you're close to the boss, yeah?" Porter waited for him to nod. "Tell me this then, why operate a human-trafficking syndicate under the guise of a dodgy NGO?"

"Because charities run by religious organizations are routinely left alone to fly under the radar." Sawatri

300

sniggered. "And don't you appreciate the irony of it? 'God's Angels in Thailand' was the perfect foil. And if they were ever arrested, why not let Christians be seen doing the devil's work?"

"Christians like Tim and the Nigerian students?"

"Precisely."

"Who slaughtered Chea and those young American blokes? And why?"

"I've no idea about the Americans but it's obvious Chea knew too much."

Porter nodded. "And you helped him and his goons commit multiple abductions? Helped him transport the girls to this brothel?"

"No, no, no...Wrong. Chea and his soldiers acted all on their own. They thrived on committing GAIT's dirtiest deeds."

"And the Nigerian students? The mass-murder in the Nana hostel?"

"Again, Chea and his men only..."

"So that Arab drug boss, Big O or whatever they call him, he had nothing to do with eliminating the African kids? He didn't see 'em as competition for his dealers and the Middle-Eastern hookers he had working along Sukhumvit?"

"No, Big O knows better than to meddle with GAIT's interests in the Nana area. Besides, he makes plenty of profit from criminal activities in the Arab sections of the city."

"Yeah, activities corrupt bastards like you and local police bosses turn a blind eye to...Who exactly are those police chiefs, the ones being paid off?"

Sawatri stepped into the middle of the room. "Your colleagues might find answers somewhere within this mansion…But you won't."

Porter swiveled to face him. "I reckon you drop the gun and show me those boxing skills of yours…Didn't you brag in the meal room one day about being your fancy school's middle-weight champion?" He stepped forward with eyes focused on the gun aimed at his forehead as it shook in Sawatri's hand. "Let's end this the old-fashioned way, mate. It's the gentlemanly thing to do…Right, old boy?"

Sawatri grinned fiendishly. "I may be a psychopath but I'm no fool." An evil eye closed as he took aim. "Goodbye, Porter. Until we meet again in hell."

# THIRTY-SEVEN

Porter was a milli-second from dropping to haunches and diving at Sawatri's legs when the door to the adjoining room swung open.

"Drop your weapon!" a high-pitched voice commanded. "Sawatri, drop it now!"

Sawatri gasped as he retreated a few paces. He kept the gun aimed at Porter and turned his head towards the open doorway. "Fon?" He frowned then spoke to her in Thai.

"Enough!" she said to interrupt him. "We'll converse in English because I want Dan to witness your pathetic excuses…Now, drop your weapon!"

"I will not." Sawatri shuffled forward with his gun levelled at Porter. "I hope you're a good shot, Fon. Because if you miss, Porter dies."

"I've longed for this moment. I won't miss."

"Ah, is this about you staying a poor rice farmer's daughter when all around you were growing rich? Listen to me, with Nok gone it's the perfect time for you to take over the cocaine business." He smiled at her. "Put down your gun, you'd be a fool to kill me. I'm the only one left who can give you the wealth you've always desired."

"Fuck you, Sawatri," she shouted. "Dan, I've known for some time about this vile man and his brother. I kept my mouth shut for Nok's sake but wish I hadn't."

Porter glanced at her and nodded.

"Ah, now I understand." Sawatri stepped closer to her. "This is about something else you've always desired. This is about Nok, isn't it?"

She snarled at him. Her whole body appeared to tremble.

"Oh Fon, I always suspected you were madly in love with her." Sawatri snickered. "But you're nothing but an ugly, fuck-up tom, and a beautiful woman like Nok was never going to love a camp little bit--."

The Glock pistol boomed as it recoiled in Fon's hand. She glared at her victim then turned and ran in the direction she'd come from.

Sawatri reeled from the bullet's impact. The gun slipped from his grasp. He clutched the wound in his chest in a futile attempt to stop gushing blood then staggered out of the room the same way Fon had left it.

Porter rushed to the corner to retrieve his Glock then ran after Sawatri. He heard women wailing as he entered a large, covered atrium. He saw four rooms on the far-side of it. CCD detectives blocked doorways of the first two rooms. SWAT team officers stood in the third doorway.

He peered at the fourth room.

Fon stood in its doorway.

Sawatri stumbled towards her, wheezing and gargling blood. He crashed against the marble-tiled floor and died a meter from her.

A woman inside the room screamed.

Fon looked down at Sawatri's corpse and smiled. She turned to enter the room.

Porter sprinted towards it, stepped over Sawatri then stopped abruptly in the doorway. He saw Fon sitting on the edge of a king-sized bed. He sucked a breath as he stared at the sickly-thin, blonde woman lying in the middle of it. She wore a pink satin robe. She cried with face down, rocking back and forth while she hugged a pillow.

He shifted his stare to Fon. "Is that…?"

She nodded. "Lisa Baxter…She's off her face on something, probably heroin judging by the needle marks and bruising on her forearms. She's in a bit of a mess but should be fine…I found her just before I started searching for you and heard Sawatri."

Porter slapped an open palm against his heaving chest. An overwhelming sense of relief and joy threatened to take his breath away. "You fucking beauty…And the others?"

"We've recovered thirty-eight foreign girls…That's the total number abducted, right?"

He nodded and stepped towards the bed. He wanted to hug Lisa and tell her everything would be okay, that she'd be home and safe with her family in no time.

Fon scowled as she pointed her gun at Lisa's head. "Don't come any closer, Dan…Do and I'll blow her pretty head off."

Porter froze. "Fon? What are you doing?"

"You led Nok to her death on that Phuket island. You took my precious girl away from me, the lover I'd searched my whole life for…" She glanced at Lisa. "It's only fair I take someone from you, someone precious that you too have searched for."

"A 'lover' you'd searched for?" Porter recoiled in disbelief. "Sawatri was right? You were in love with Nok?"

"From the moment I saw her gorgeous smile and heard her infectious laugh..."

"But didn't she only see you as a friend? You were like a younger sister to her."

"No, you're wrong," she snapped. "She'd repressed her true feelings for months and it was only a matter of time before we'd become a couple…Then you showed up and ruined everything. She fell in love with you, the handsome farang investigator with the envious reputation and forgot all about me."

He cursed himself for missing the obvious. "There I was thinking Jaru or Helen had acted against me…But it was you who spiked my drink in the nightclub…And you sent that bullshit email to Jane? And it was you who tipped off the Chinatown temple, wasn't it?"

"Of course, you idiot. I was controlled by jealousy at the time and couldn't care less about Lost Angels. I just wanted you dead and out of Nok's life. You're lucky I didn't kill you in your sleep…"

Porter's gut ached as it knotted, because the woman holding a gun to Lisa's head was delusional and dangerous. How to disarm her without endangering the hostage?

Fon grinned up at him. "I know what you're thinking and I'll save you the dilemma." She looked down at Lisa with the gun still aimed and stroked the back of her head. "Farewell, beautiful angel. You are no longer lost…"

Porter darted to his right then lunged towards Fon.

She sprang over Lisa and landed on the opposite side of the bed. She ran from the room then jumped Sawatri's corpse. She stopped in the middle of the atrium and turned to face Porter.

He watched from the doorway as she pressed the gun against her temple.

"I know Nok's waiting for me in the next life, Dan. But I miss her too much and must go to join her now."

She fired before he could call out. Blood and brain spewed from the gaping hole in her head like water from a geyser then splattered onto tiles. Her lifeless body dropped to the floor and quickly became a haunted island surrounded by a bright-red sea.

Porter shook his head as he turned back to Lisa.

Lisa sat upright on the bed, the look in her eyes vacant and her gaunt face full of fear. She screamed when he approached.

He hurried forward with hands patting the air, trying to calm her. "It's okay, Lisa, I'm a friend. I'm not gunna hurt you." He sat next to her on the bed.

The blue eyes he'd seen in Lisa's profile photos, the same that'd reminded him of a young Olivia Newton-John, stared back at him. He saw dark circles around them and crusty scabs on her face and lips. He cringed, disgusted by what they'd done to her. Disgusted by how they'd turned a healthy and independent young woman into a sick and needy junkie.

She squinted then wobbled her head as though trying to shake away a drug induced haze. "You're a cop? My friend?"

Porter nodded. "Yeah, and you're safe now, sweet. I promise."

He held her while she sobbed with head resting on his shoulder. He scanned the luxuriously finished bedroom and noticed three pictures on its wall. The first two showed golden temples amidst purple sunsets. There was an empty hook on the wall between the second and third pictures.

The third picture was a framed promotional poster from the 'Days of Thunder' movie starring Tom Cruise and Nicole Kidman. Cruise leaned against the hood of a green and yellow race car with a black '46' on its door. He wore a black racing suit with the sponsors name, 'Mello Yello', written in red and green on the front. He wore dark sunglasses and held a racing helmet by his side. His medium-length hair was dark-brown and thick. Kidman stood next to him with a hand on his shoulder. She wore a white t-shirt under a white, fitted jacket. She wore a black belt with a silver buckle, and blue jeans. Her strawberry-blonde hair was long and curly and framed a beautiful, sun-kissed face.

Lisa mumbled incoherently as she clung to Porter like a frightened child.

He noticed a dark-blue book on the bed and grabbed it with his free hand. He opened it and realized it was Lisa's diary, the one Carly had mentioned. He had skimmed over the last ten pages when Lisa raised her head, saw the diary and snatched it from him.

She wiped a tear from cheek then held the diary in two hands, tight against her chest. "This is mine. Secret. You can't take it from me."

"It's okay, sweet, you can keep it." He smiled then met her gaze. "Lisa, I know this is difficult but it's very important…The man you talk about in your diary, your lover." He pointed at Sawatri's corpse outside the door. "Was is that man? Is he the man who kept you here?"

She laughed. "No, that dead guy was just my lover's good friend. He came here to use the other girls and hide from you cops."

"Okay…" He looked into her dazed eyes with their dilated pupils, willing her to tell the truth. "When did you last see your boyfriend?"

"Today. About an hour ago, maybe…He gave me my fix and we were about to make love when he left suddenly."

"What's your boyfriend's name? How old is he?"

She frowned. "Um, I'm not sure but last night he asked me to start calling him 'Cole', so I did. He's the company's big boss and he's super rich. He's the guy who brought me and all the other girls here…But he told me I'm different from the others and he doesn't share me with anyone. I'm his 'Claire', his one and only love."

Porter assumed her delirious ramblings were a result of the opioids in her system. But had she also been brainwashed by her captives? He decided further attempts to ascertain her boyfriend's true identity were futile in her current state. His immediate concern was to find him.

"Where is he now? Still here in the house somewhere?"

She sighed. "He said he had to fly off in his little plane but will come back for me soon." Her head lolled as she giggled. "And then we're getting married and running away together…"

Porter swore because Sawatri had been spot on. Some corrupt bastard had warned GAIT's boss that Interpol and the CCD were coming and given him time to flee the mansion.

He recalled what Lisa said earlier. "Why'd he ask you to call him 'Cole'? And why are you his 'Claire'?"

Her mouth fell open while she gazed at him. "Don't you know anything?" She pointed to the framed movie poster on the wall. "Days of Thunder is his favourite movie. Tom Cruise plays 'Cole Trickle'. Nicole Kidman is 'Doctor Claire'. My god, haven't you seen it?"

Porter shook his head, because he hadn't.

She rolled away from him then got off the bed on the other side of the room. She seemed to float as she moved to a built-in wardrobe next to the bathroom. She slid its door open then sorted through expensive-looking clothes. She removed several items and placed them on the bed next to Porter.

He studied a dark-brown wig, Aviator sunglasses and a black helmet. He held the black racing suit at arm's length then compared it to the one worn by Tom Cruise in the poster. Exactly the same…

Lisa laid a white jacket, black belt and blue jeans next to the helmet. She pointed to the racing suit. "He brought these full costumes with him last night for the first time. He dressed-up like Cole. I wore my make-up and this outfit the same as Claire's, and then we had the most amazing sex."

He nodded, not wanting to hear what they'd done to her but needing to know. "Do you have a photo of your boyfriend?"

Her forehead crinkled and her eyes narrowed as she considered him. "Why? You said you're a cop…Are you going to chase him and hurt him?"

"Nah, I just wanna see what he looks like, so I can tell the other cops to leave him alone…"

"Okay…" She returned to the wardrobe then knelt to search a box at the bottom of it. She swiveled towards him with a framed picture clutched to bosom. "He gave me this last night. And then today he took it off the wall and told me to get rid of it."

"Why?"

"He didn't say…But I wanted to keep it so hid it down here instead."

He watched her stagger to her feet. She stumbled, carried the picture to the wall then visibly trembled as she stood before it. "I know he's much older than me but I don't care. He's so wise, and kind, and gentle." She placed the picture on the empty hook then glanced over her shoulder. "Cute and cuddly, isn't he?"

Porter moved alongside her. He squinted as he analysed the framed photo. After a minute he stepped back, buried his aching forehead in both hands, and cursed himself for being so stupid.

# THIRTY-EIGHT

Porter returned to Interpol's Bangkok office at one o'clock Saturday morning. It was 5am in Sydney but he called Steve Williams' private cell phone anyway.

"Sorry to wake you, mate," Porter said. "I've got great news that couldn't wait any longer…And much has gone down that I need to fill you in on."

Williams coughed. "No worries, my alarm was due to go off soon…Great news?"

"Last night we raided an exclusive brothel in a property south of Bangkok. We recovered all our victims, mate. Every missing girl Lost Angels had searched for…"

Williams whooped, his laughter loud and full of ecstatic relief. "That's fan-fucking-tastic, Port. I knew you'd get the job done…The girls are okay?"

"Mostly, except for minor injuries and bruising where they've been beaten. And the emotional scars they'll carry for the rest of their lives…"

"How'd you find them? What led you to the brothel?"

Porter spent fifteen minutes summarizing events of the past week. He told him about finding the receipt inside the Chinatown temple that'd led to Phuket, where evidence was discovered linking Superintendent Sawatri and his corrupt brother, Police General Woracha, to large-scale cocaine and firearms supply. He told him about Nok's involvement in drug trafficking and her tragic death, and how Jaru's CCD unit had arrived just in time to rescue him from hungry tigers. He recounted how

312

more receipts found in the Phuket temple had led him back to the Korean loan-shark boss, Park Heung-min, and then to the raid on General Chea's GAIT compound in Bangkok where he found that Chea and his men, and Tim Jones and four other Americans working for GAIT, had been slaughtered. He told him about the ecstasy pills located inside Chea's compound and that Carly Newman had provided information about Tim and his mates helping Chea smuggle the pills into Thailand from LA, and how Nigerian students brought to Bangkok by GAIT were forced to sell them.

He told Williams that he and Fon had spoken to Tim's ex-girlfriend, who confirmed suspicions General Chea's elite soldiers were abducting foreign girls on GAIT's behalf and sending Thai girls to work Chea's brothels in California. Another informant had provided a name for GAIT's subsidiary company, the listed owner of Chea's compound in Bangkok - Peking Duck Tours. A database search of all assets owned by the company had led them to the waterfront mansion in Laem Chabang.

Porter told Williams about Sawatri hiding in the brothel and described events leading up to Fon killing him and then herself. He described the terrible, drug affected state he'd found Lisa Baxter in and said he'd found her travel diary.

"Wow…" Williams said when Porter paused to catch his breath. "Great job, and good luck fitting all that into a two-page report… What's the story with the diary?"

"I've booked it up as evidence but haven't had a chance to read it all yet… In the parts I've read Lisa mentions this one guy who came to her room every day." Porter cringed at the thought. "It's bloody sad, Steve… They've been injecting her with so much H she's lost touch with reality, to the extent she describes this bloke who was raping her as being her boyfriend, her lover. She's become quickly addicted and sees them injecting her as a reward for compliance."

"Fucking scum."

"Yeah, so when I asked her about this 'lover' she told me he's the big boss, the owner of the mansion and the bloke responsible for keeping her and the other girls in the brothel."

"The guy leading GAIT?"

"Yeah... She pulled out a framed picture and hung it on the wall. I nearly fell over when I realized who the bloke in the photo was. And felt pretty bloody stupid too..."

"Why? For fuck's sake, Port, you're killing me...Who is it?"

"I'd seen the exact same photo before, of a short Asian bloke posing in front of a Chevy Lumina race car with a couple of promo girls kissing his cheeks...Lisa's 'lover', the bloke in the photos, is Phra Medhikorn, the Chief Abbot of Wat Khongwihan in Chinatown. Medhikorn's one of the most influential monks in Southeast Asia and the bloke who owns and runs GAIT's entire network and every criminal syndicate associated with it."

"Unbelievable... And you're certain?"

"Yeah, I am now... Just wish I'd spent more time inside that Chinatown temple. I probably would've found evidence of Medhikorn's involvement with the abductions and not dismissed him as a suspect... Stupid."

"From what you've said you had no choice but to get out when you did. They would've killed you."

"But what if I'd found the evidence incriminating him just a tad earlier?"

"Ah, 'what ifs'…They'll drive you mad if you let them."

"True."

"Don't be too hard on yourself. You rescued the girls within two days of leaving that temple. And that's the most important thing. Correct?"

"Yeah, but I still want Medhikorn."

"Me too. And I've gotta say he's a first for me – a crooked, rapist monk who's into motor racing."

"NASCAR racing to be exact," Porter said. "He seems obsessed with the 'Days of Thunder' movie. There was a poster for it in Lisa's bedroom and the sick bastard would dress up as Tom Cruise and make her dress up as Nicole Kidman's character."

"I loved that movie…Kidman played Doctor Claire and Lisa Baxter's her clone – Aussie, tall, strawberry-blonde and beautiful."

"Yeah and I don't reckon it's coincidence Chea and his men abducted foreign girls who all looked very similar…Medhikorn probably tasked 'em with finding the ultimate Kidman lookalike to fulfill his perverted fantasies. And when they found Lisa, his perfect girl, he lost interest in the others and put 'em to work in his exclusive brothel. Mate, they've been drugged and forced to service mega-rich Asian blokes with young white girl festishes."

"The girls themselves told you this?"

"Yeah, the few I was able to question who weren't as drug-affected as the rest…"

"Mega-rich Asian customers from where?"

"Credit card records retrieved show they were mostly Chinese, with smaller numbers of Japanese, Malaysian and South Korean…The brothel had a fleet of vans that'd collect businessmen from hotels in Pattaya and Bangkok. VIP clients like Sawatri, and others visiting the area on luxury cruise-ships, were brought directly to the brothel's private jetty via catamaran. According to paperwork found in its office the brothel's made close to a million US dollars in a month. Customers were paying incredible sums to spend time there."

"Where are the girls now? Safe and in good care I hope."

"Yeah, staff from most of the relevant embassies have been great. Except for the Russian Federal Security Service blokes, who were quick to snatch the Russian girls from us and have been a pain in the ass since."

"In what way?"

"I'll cover that at the end…Our Aussie girls are under guard in a secure hotel here in Bangkok and will be flown back to Oz later today. They'll spend a couple of days at a medical facility in Sydney when they arrive home. I've arranged for Lisa's friend Carly to be on the same flight…GAIT blokes operating the brothel were using elderly women to cook and clean, illegal immigrants from Myanmar held against their will who they'd beaten black and blue…We're sending those ladies home today too."

"Excellent stuff…Now, when you searched the brothel's office, I hope you also found documents that actually name Medhikorn as its owner? And you haven't said you've got him in custody…So, where is he?"

"That's the bad news…The bastard must've been tipped off just before we arrived because the others didn't have time to destroy evidence or hide the girls. Medhikorn's left Thailand via a private jet from U-Tapao airport near Pattaya. Him and his most trusted off-sider, a bloke called 'Ajarn Chalad'. Which reminds me, one of Jaru's CCD teams executed a search warrant on the Chinatown temple a couple of hours ago…All its offices were empty and they found novice monks throwing the last of its files into furnaces in the crematorium."

"That's what worries me, Port…Aside from you seeing the same photo of him in two different locations, and diary entries written by a drug affected Lisa Baxter, what evidence do we have that one-hundred-percent links Medhikorn to GAIT and all the rest of it?"

"This is where we got lucky…The search of the brothel's office uncovered registration papers for a private jet owned by Peking Duck Tours, the same jet Medhikorn left Thailand in…CCD blokes arrived at the airport too late to stop Medhikorn leaving, and while Aviation Authority officers did log the jet's exit from U-Tapao, they didn't record its intended destination or any details of the crew and two passengers on board."

Williams scoffed. "Paid off, no doubt…Please tell me the two passengers were subjected to proper immigration exit protocols at least."

"Yeah, they were…Medhikorn often travels under his religious name and a number of others he goes by, but yesterday made the mistake of using his original identification. The CCD detectives questioned immigration cops at U-Tapao's private jet terminal who reluctantly handed over a copy of Medhikorn's passport. From that they learned of his civilian name, his birth name. Something very few people in Thailand had known beforehand."

"And he'd used his birth name when registering ownership of GAIT's subsidiary companies such as this Peking Duck Tours?"

"Yeah, spot on…He's listed as director of multiple companies owned by GAIT and we found the whole paper trail in the office, information corrupt officials had deleted from various government bureaus' files. We have evidence linking Phra Medhikorn to GAIT and its role in human-trafficking, drug supply and money laundering syndicates throughout Southeast Asia."

"And GAIT's assets?"

"Jaru's onto it. He's applying to have 'em all seized."

"Good work…Now, the pessimist in me says Medhikorn only used his real name because he has no intention of returning to Thailand…Do we have any idea where he's gone?"

"As I said, the Thai Aviation Authority staff that Jaru's men interviewed are corrupt as… Medhikorn's jet flew north-east towards Laos and China and they reckon its flight path can't be tracked after it left Thai air space, which is a crock of shit… My gut feeling is he's flown to Beijing."

"Why?"

"Because that's where his Peking Duck Tours company is based and he'd be aware Interpol barely exists there after Dragon Slayer sent most of its staff to the slammer. And although we've already issued a red notice alert for him and his mate, he'd be confident we can't get to him in China."

"You said he's popular throughout Southeast Asia…Should we also be checking airports in Cambodia, Myanmar, Laos and Vietnam. Closer to home?"

"We have checked and will continue to do so…There's also a slight possibility he's stopped to refuel in China before flying across the Pacific to southern California."

"That's a long flight in a private jet. And why California?"

"His jet's a top of the range Gulfstream with a fuel capacity capable of making the distance…When I spoke to Ajarn Chalad, his assistant abbot in Chinatown, he mentioned they had a sister-temple near San Diego. It's a long shot but they could try to hide there."

Williams cleared his throat. "You said Chea was abducting Thai go-go dancers and forcing them to work in California…How do you know he owned those brothels?"

"From documents we found in the Laem Chabang brothel…I was gunna ask you to pass this info onto Lyn Foster, because there's no doubt it's linked to the underaged Thai girls she saved from that massage parlor in LA. One of GAIT's subsidiaries operates English Language School's throughout California. They sent the go-go dancers to the US on study visas but the girls ended up working in massage parlors owned by the same company. Paperwork recovered last night lists General Chea as that company's sole director."

"I think you're right about it all being related. And it seems Chea's biggest fuck-up was sending those three Thai girls to work in LA knowing of their links to the Chinatown temple."

"Spot on. And it's lucky he got lazy and too sloppy, 'cos if Lyn hadn't rescued those girls and seen their amulet's we might never have learned of Medhikorn's involvement."

"Lyn's already tried to subpoena all government records relating to any student visas sponsored by GAIT that've been issued by US embassies."

"Don't tell me…No luck?"

"No. She suspects corrupt officials in the Californian education and immigration departments who've aided and abetted human-trafficking between Thailand and LA, are the same who've thwarted her requests for information. I'll pass on what you've told me and hopefully she and the LAPD can locate all the girls Chea's sent over there."

"Fingers crossed, mate…We've dismantled an evil triangle of trade here in Southeast Asia where the currency's been human lives. We can't allow the same bastards to gain a similar hold in the US."

"Agreed. Speaking of General Chea…Who murdered him and his men?"

"Sawatri nominated Medhikorn, because Chea was a bit of a loose cannon who he worried would talk if arrested. I reckon that's fairly close to the mark."

"You mentioned Chea using the American boys to run his ecstasy supply on the side. And his supplier's based near Los Angeles? Email me what you have and I'll forward it to the relevant people at the DEA."

"Will do…And I've got details of the company who shipped guns to Park Heung-min from South Korea. I'll send them through for our unit in Seoul to follow up."

"Excellent…"

"Back to Chea…His entire network relied on control of the Poipet border crossing, and when Inspector Veasna in Phnom Penh threatened it, I reckon he had him killed…Thankfully his death wasn't completely in vain."

"How's that?"

"I spoke to a detective from his squad half an hour ago. They've arrested six corrupt politicians on human-trafficking and drug charges. The same Cambodian politicians Veasna had been investigating."

"Good news… It is fair to say Chea's ecstasy smuggling posed a risk to GAIT's operations and more reason for Medhikorn to have him bumped off?"

"Yeah, Chea was a greedy bastard. He probably had his eye on the top job and needed the extra funds to increase the size of his private army and challenge Medhikorn."

"Maybe unknown third parties decided he had to go? The corrupt officials in California we suspect have been helping him? Did they feel threatened because Lost Angels or Lyn Foster were too close, and was Chea the only player left in the game who could implicate them?"

"Possibly, and if that's the case we're seeking someone very high up in the US government. They'd have to be to order Chea's assassination on foreign soil."

"Exactly. Listen, you mentioned earlier that Russian security services were causing problems…How?"

"They wanted nothing to do with helping Lost Angels search for the missing Russian tourists. But now the girls have been found they're sticking their noses in where they aint wanted… Jaru tells me it's kicking off between them and the Royal Thai Police, with each organization blaming the other for a piss-poor response to the abductions."

Williams scoffed. "The Russians are fucking annoying. And it's pathetic they're only getting involved after you've done all the hard slog."

Porter chuckled. "Yeah, and I'll never know if it was their internal security blokes who tried to do me in at the airport." He thought about the Russian who'd threatened him at the Khlong Toei docks. Another enemy whose identity he'd never know?

"No, you probably won't, and it may be best to ignore the Russians from here on… How many days will you need to get everything squared away?"

"I reckon three at least."

"No, I can't let you stay in Bangkok that long. As you said, Thais and Russians are already squabbling and I don't want you getting caught up in their diplomatic shit-fight."

"Two days?"

"Okay. I'll get you booked on the Monday night flight to Sydney."

"No worries, I'll be glad to get back to Jane and Amber. I've got a lot of making up to do if there's gunna be a wedding." Porter sighed. "Listen, I've already had a few journos request interviews about Lost Angels and last night's raid. What's the official line?"

"I don't want you speaking to anyone… All governments involved in this fiasco will be crucified once the media exposes their cover-ups and we can't risk them making you their fall-guy… Give me something to quote now if you want and I'll include it in our media release."

"Alright…" Porter paused to think. "Write this down… Corruption's a poison that erodes the foundations of a just society, and Thailand still has much to do in the fight against it. But after working alongside dedicated police officers attached to the Counter Corruption Division, I'm confident the entire nation can win that fight."

Williams whistled, low-pitched. "That'll spark debate and most likely send unwanted attention your way… You sure it's what you want to say?"

"Yeah, and I'll stick by it and hope it creates chatter in a way the uncomfortable truth always should."

"Good for you...A bit of shameful controversy to push for positive changes, eh?"

"Spot on. And nothing affects dodgy politicians like shit hitting the fan…So let's hope this smelly pile of it splatters far and wide."

# THIRTY-NINE

Porter's flight touched down at Sydney International Airport shortly after 7am on Tuesday. Worry had kept him awake for the first hour of the trip because just prior to leaving Bangkok he'd phoned Jane and promised to finally share his most intimate secret. For the next eight hours the movie projector in his head had featured short films of his assignment in Thailand. Many of the events portrayed still haunted him yet were played over and over again. He'd begged his mind to stop the torture and let him sleep but it had mocked his exhaustion and cruelly persisted.

He exited the plane then trudged like the sleep-deprived zombie he was towards Passport Control. He winked at a mural of Sydney Harbor, glad to be home. The thought of Jane waiting to greet him with a multitude of questions made his stomach swirl and he pondered not revealing his secret. Maybe she'd forget or simply let it go?

No, he'd been a coward for too long and the time had come to honor his promise. Their wedding was only ten weeks away and if Jane was prepared to make a lifetime commitment she deserved to know the complete truth about his past. But how would she react to it? Would she see him in a whole new light and have second thoughts? He hoped not, because he loved her more than she'd ever know.

He passed swiftly through Immigration, placed the backpack he'd brought with him from Bangkok on a luggage trolley then zigzagged through the crowd towards baggage carousel number two. He left the trolley and stepped closer to the conveyor belt. He turned his phone on and after five seconds it vibrated.

He opened a photo sent by Senator Fitzgerald showing he and his wife sitting with Lisa Baxter on her hospital bed. He read the caption. 'Our little girl's home safely. Thanks and God bless you, Dan, from all of us.' He smiled at their joy. It made the tough times he'd endured throughout the Lost Angels investigation all the more worthwhile. He replied to a message from Jane. She and Amber waited for him in the Arrivals hall.

His suitcase appeared and he dragged it off the carousel. He hurried through Customs and had barely exited its enclosed walkway when Jane ran forward to greet him. He returned her longing kiss then pulled Amber into the huddle. The three of them laughed as they hugged each other tight.

They separated and Jane ran a hand over his head. "What's with da close shave?"

He grinned. "I'll explain later." He wiped a tear from her cheek. "Look at you all choked up. It's only been two weeks but you'd reckon I've been gone a year."

Amber groaned. "You haven't had to listen to her complaining every day. It's felt more like five years to me..."

Porter chuckled then pecked her on the forehead. "Cheers for looking after your mum, sweet."

Jane flashed her gorgeous smile. "That's enough you two." She looped an arm around his waist and directed him towards the exit while Amber pushed the trolley. "We'll get you home for bacon and eggs."

He stopped and pointed to a café at the side. "Let's sit and have a coffee together first. There's something I need to tell the both of you."

Jane clapped hands. "Oh goody, I've waited a long time for this."

He laughed as he led them to a table at the front of the café. He waited for Jane to sit then handed her his backpack. He swept a stray hair from the side of her face and bent to kiss her lips. "Love ya, babe, and thanks for being so patient. I'm ready to tell you what I've promised to."

She nodded. "I love you too. And it's great there'll no more secrets."

Amber took the suitcase from the trolley. She wheeled it to their table then sat next to Jane.

"What'll it be?" He yawned and stretched his back. "Same as usual?"

He waited for replies in the affirmative then strolled ten meters to the counter and ordered three hot lattes. His phone vibrated. He fished it from pocket and answered the 'unknown caller'.

"Hello, Agent Porter." The voice was male and without accent, distorted and robotic-sounding.

Porter frowned. He'd said it before. A caller disguising their voice was never a welcome one. "Who is this?"

"Let's just say that when so many others in Thailand wanted you dead, I was the man who kept you alive."

Porter glanced over to Jane and Amber. They held hands and smiled as they chatted. "Why would you do that?"

"Because I want to feel the elation of killing you myself, when and how I decide to. I deserve to take your life, not them."

"Who the fuck is this? And how'd you get my private number?"

"I'm the man you should fear more than any other, Agent Porter...Do you know why?"

Porter grunted. "No idea but I'm sure you're gunna enlighten me."

"You have shamed my family and I... And you took someone away who I loved dearly."

"Medhikorn? This is monk Medhikorn, isn't it? You depraved rapist bastard... Lisa Baxter wasn't yours to love and never will be."

The caller laughed. "Do you believe in karma, Agent Porter? I certainly do..."

"You're nothing but a sick mongrel who's gunna get caught. And I can't wait to see y--."

"Did you keep an eye on your belongings, Agent Porter? When using your phone at the baggage carousel, did you notice anyone acting suspicious near your backpack?"

"What?" Porter spun towards Jane and saw the backpack next to her feet under the table. "What the fuck are y--."

"Are you certain nothing was placed inside it while you weren't paying attention?"

"What?" Porter kept the phone against ear as he stumbled away from the counter. "Jane! Amber!"

They looked up at him from the table with faces frozen in puzzled frowns.

"Hurry, Agent Porter, before your girls go out with a...Bang!"

Porter dropped the phone and sprinted towards the table. "Get away from the backpack!"

Jane glanced down then stared at him as he crashed through tables and chairs. Her expression changed from surprise to fear in an instant. Her wide, brown eyes gleamed with tragic realization then twinkled with love as they said goodbye.

Time stood still. Porter ran forward as fast he could but went nowhere. He tried to shout another warning but no words came out.

A candescent flash blinded him. Searing heat scorched his face. The bomb's blast pounded ribs then threw him against a wall. Throbbing eardrums threatened to burst. Screams of agony echoed.

A sudden, surreal silence.

Porter slumped to the floor and descended into eternal darkness.

Dear reader,

We hope you've enjoyed 'Oriental Illusions' as much as we've enjoyed bringing the story to you.

Visit www.jameskeeganauthor.com to learn more about the author and 'The Cumal Files', book 1 in the Dan Porter series.

Thanks for your support, it's much appreciated.

SLEUTH HOUND BOOKS